Wrecked in Retribution Bay

Aussie Heroes: Retribution Bay

Claire Boston

BANTILLY
PUBLISHING

First published by Bantilly Publishing in 2023

Wrecked in Retribution Bay: Aussie Heroes: Retribution Bay

EPUB format: 9781922916075
Print: 9781922916082
Large Print: 9781922916099

Cover design by Mayhem Cover Creations
Edited by Ann Harth
Copyedited by Teena Raffa-Mulligan

About the Author

Claire Boston fell in love with romance and romantic suspense at eleven when she discovered her mother's stash of Nora Roberts novels. Like Nora, she writes series set around families or groups of friends with a guaranteed happy ending.

She loves travelling and learning about new cultures and interesting vocations which she then weaves into her writing.

When Claire's not at the computer typing her stories she can be found creating her own handmade journals, swinging on a sidecar, or in the garden attempting to grow something other than weeds.

Claire lives in Western Australia with her husband, who loves even her most annoying quirks and is currently learning how to knit.

You can find her complete book list on her website www.claireboston.com/books.You can connect with Claire through Facebook and Twitter, or join her reader group

http://www.claireboston.com/reader-group/

Also by Claire Boston

Romance
The Texan Quartet
What Goes on Tour
All that Sparkles
Under the Covers
Into the Fire

The Flanagan Sisters
Break the Rules
Change of Heart
Blaze a Trail
Place to Belong

Romantic Suspense
The Blackbridge Series
Nothing to Fear
Nothing to Gain
Nothing to Hide
Nothing to Lose
Shelter
Shield
Harbour
Protect

Aussie Heroes: Retribution Bay
Return to Retribution Bay
Trapped in Retribution Bay
Escape to Retribution Bay
Secrets in Retribution Bay
Beached in Retribution Bay
Adrift in Retribution Bay
Wrecked in Retribution Bay

Chapter 1

"You'll regret arresting me."

Sergeant Dot Campbell stared coolly at the short, tattooed man in handcuffs next to her. Kurt Webb's threats were nothing she hadn't heard before, though this man was further up the chain of the Stonefish crime syndicate than others she'd arrested. Maybe he had more sway, but right now she was too exhausted to care. Battling back her urge to collapse into the nearest seat, she turned to the officer in charge at the Carnarvon Police Station. "Do you need anything else from me?"

He shook his head. "We'll take it from here."

Dot nodded and walked outside, taking a deep breath of the warm afternoon air as she slid on her sunglasses. It did nothing to clear the heaviness in her eyes, or the fog from her brain.

What a day.

She tugged at her black hair, the fact that she could reminding her that she was overdue a haircut. It was no longer pixie short, more reminiscent of a messy yeti, and she couldn't remember the last time she'd had a day off. She sighed as she checked her messages. They'd found the two boys Kurt had kidnapped, doctors had assessed both and the boys were safe at home. No news on her friend, Senior Constable Nhiari Roe, though. She'd taken a suspect into custody and Lee had overpowered her and take her hostage. Guilt filled Dot. She should have been with Nhiari, should have never let her go off with only civilians as backup. It didn't matter that two of those civilians were ex-military.

Dot's friend Georgie swore Lee was on their side, but Dot wasn't convinced. Search and rescue were already mobilising to start the search of the ranges for Nhiari at first light tomorrow.

When would this end?

It had been six months of madness; sabotage, kidnapping, animal smuggling, poaching, and murder. What would be next? Frustration gnawed at her as she climbed into the police car. They had nothing but a name—Stonefish Enterprises. No one person to pin this on. Every time they got close, their lead was killed or disappeared. Stonefish was making a mockery of her and her town.

They hadn't even apprehended the schoolteacher, Miss Simpson, who had hidden the fact that the boys had been kidnapped.

Maybe Dot had been away from the city too long. She'd honed her skills razor sharp there. She had hated living in Perth, but it had made her a damned good cop.

Or at least she'd thought it had.

Dot drove to the petrol station, which was on her way out of town. The three-hour drive back to Retribution Bay would give her plenty of thinking time. Perhaps she'd come up with something she had missed.

After she paid for her fuel and a corn jack to keep the hunger at bay, she headed outside. Waiting in line behind her police car were two more cars; a small, white hatchback, and behind it, a large four-wheel drive. Dot made eye contact with the driver of the hatchback, her hand raised in apology for the delay, and met the startled, wide-eyes of Myra Simpson.

Dot smiled. Finally, something had gone right today.

She strode around to the driver's side window and waited for Myra to lower it. "Afternoon, Miss Simpson. Going somewhere?"

Myra swallowed audibly, her brown ponytail bobbing. "Ah, yeah. Just got news my mother is ill in hospital." She dabbed at her mascara-smeared eyes.

"I'm sorry to hear that. Which hospital?"

"Ah, Royal Perth."

"You're driving all the way to Perth tonight?"

She nodded.

"Surely it would be quicker if you waited for the early morning flight."

"I, ah, couldn't get a ticket."

Lie. When Dot had been to the airport yesterday to check on the supplies being flown in, someone had mentioned people had been cancelling their tickets to deal with the aftermath of the late season storm which had significantly damaged the town. "I need you to come to the station for questioning."

"What about?"

Dot raised an eyebrow and Myra's hands clenched the steering wheel, her gaze darting around, looking for an escape. Dot resisted reaching in and turning off the car. "We need to discuss what happened with your students, Jordan and Cody."

Myra slumped back in her seat. "All right." She seemed to have already forgotten about her sick mother.

The four-wheel drive behind them reversed, ready to move into the bay alongside, tired of waiting. Shit. "Pass me your keys."

Myra hadn't noticed the clear escape route behind her. She handed over the keys, and Dot exhaled as the cool metal hit her palm. "We'll take my car." She stood blocking the escape route behind them, but Myra could still choose to run for it. Not that there was anywhere to run to. Bush surrounded the petrol station and Myra wasn't dressed for a sprint, still wearing the skirt, blouse and small heels she'd worn to school that morning.

Dot's muscles tensed as Myra climbed out and walked to the police car. Dot opened the back door. "Hop in."

"Am I under arrest?"

"No." Not yet, but it was likely she'd be arrested for aiding and abetting.

When Myra was inside, Dot moved Myra's car to a parking spot. She called the Retribution Bay station, but as Constable Colin Lipscombe answered, she had misgivings about telling him she'd found Myra. "Colin, can you track down Myra Simpson's parents? They might be able to contact her."

"Will do."

"Run a check on her as well. I want to know anything you find."

"On it."

Dot hung up and stared at the phone, unease filling her. This case had her seeing conspiracies all over the place and she hated it. She tugged at her hair. Her colleagues would find out she'd caught Myra soon enough, but she wanted to see what information they revealed. For the past month, she'd wondered whether perhaps there was a leak in her station. They'd missed too many opportunities for it to be a coincidence.

She drove back to the Carnarvon police station, and it wasn't long before she was sitting in a plain, grey interview room with Myra, the plastic chair hard and uncomfortable. The young woman brushed wisps of her brown hair behind her ears and then clenched her hands together and sat straight, determination in her gaze as if she'd come up with a plan. "Why do you need to speak to me?"

Dot wanted to roll her eyes. This was how Myra wanted to play it? She pressed record on the recording machine and explained who was in the room and what was going to occur. "Two children from your class were kidnapped from school today. Why don't you tell me what happened?"

"I didn't kidnap them."

"No, but I need to know what happened at the school. When did you discover they were missing?" She clicked her pen, ready to take notes.

"After lunch, when they didn't come back to class."

"None of the children mentioned it to you?"

Myra shifted in her chair. "The children had been talking nonsense about buried treasure all morning."

Shit. One more headache she didn't need. "What were they saying?"

"Natasha claimed Jordan had found buried treasure and was showing off a fake gold coin."

Dot had had misgivings when she'd heard the children had seen the treasure. "Did you see the coin?"

"I confiscated it."

Interesting. "And where is the coin now?"

Myra's gaze shifted to the wall. "At the school."

"Where exactly? I'll get one of my officers to collect it for evidence."

Her eyes flared briefly. "I think I left it in my desk drawer. In all the excitement, I don't recall."

Dot jotted a note to get Colin to check. She'd bet the coin was somewhere in Myra Simpson's car.

"None of the children told you Jordan and Cody had been taken from the school?"

Myra blinked at the change of topic. "No."

"Not even Lara Stokes?"

She glanced at Dot as if trying to figure out what she knew. "Lara has a fanciful imagination."

That was a non-answer. "So she did mention it to

you?"

"She might have."

Dot flicked back a few pages in her notebook. "Lara says the moment the boys were taken, she ran to tell you, but you wouldn't believe her."

"The children had been pretending to be pirates all morning. I thought it was part of their games."

"Does Lara normally lie about things?"

Myra ran her hands down her top, flattening out any wrinkles. "She is a wonderful storyteller."

Dot smiled. "Does she lie?"

Myra pressed her lips together and Dot tried another tack. "How long have you known Kurt Webb?"

"A few weeks." It took a split second for Myra to realise what she'd done. Her mouth dropped open and her skin paled.

Caught you. Satisfaction filled Dot. "Tell me about your relationship."

"That's none of your business."

"It is my business when he kidnaps two boys, and it appears you helped him. That makes you an accessory, Miss Simpson, which, if convicted, would see you going to gaol for ten years."

Myra hesitated for a moment before she whispered, "He has a right to see his son."

Her voice carried very little conviction. Interesting. "What did he tell you?"

Myra stared at the table, running her fingers along a scratch in the vinyl. "Gretchen took Jordan away years ago and he only just tracked them down." Her gaze was fixed on the table.

The woman would never win an Oscar. "What did he threaten you with?"

Her fearful gaze darted to Dot's face. "What?"

"You don't strike me as the type of person who would put her students in danger, and you don't appear to be a woman in love. Am I wrong?"

Myra shook her head and picked at her cuticles.

"I can't help you if you don't tell me."

"You said I'm going to gaol." She glanced up, her eyes full of tears.

"We may be able to avoid it, but I need you to be honest with me." Dot layered sympathy into her tone, though right now she just wanted answers, so she could get home. There was so much paperwork she still had to do.

Myra stared at Dot for a long moment. "What do you need to know?"

"How did you meet Kurt?"

"It was at the brewery a few weeks ago. He tried to chat me up."

"Did it work?"

She shook her head. "There was something kind of intense about him. It creeped me out."

"What did he do then?"

"He said he knew… something about me, and if I didn't do as he asked, he'd make sure everyone knew."

Dot filed that away to ask about later. "What did he ask you to do?"

"Initially, he wanted to know about Lara Stokes, what she said in class, if she talked about her family. It didn't seem like a big deal."

"How often did you have to report to him?"

"Daily, but there wasn't much to say."

Dot nodded with encouragement. "Then what happened?"

"Last week he added Jordan to the list, as well as Cody and Mischa—Jordan's and Lara's best friends."

"Did he say why?"

"I didn't ask. It wasn't an issue until I heard Jordan whispering about treasure to Mischa."

"You told Kurt?"

"Yeah, but I didn't think it was true until he got demanding. Wanted me to talk about shipwrecks in the area during class and report on what they said."

Dot held her pen over the notepad. "When was this?"

"Tuesday. Then there was the storm on Wednesday and school didn't go back until today."

"What happened today?"

"Jordan brought the coin to school. I rang Kurt at recess. I thought the information about the coin would be enough to make him go away. I didn't think he would take the boys." She leaned forward, eyes wide, pleading for Dot to understand.

"What did Kurt say?"

"That whatever happened, I shouldn't call the police, or he would tell everyone."

Dot raised an eyebrow.

"I was scared. I didn't know what to do."

"Then what happened?"

"I returned to class. At the beginning of lunch Lara came to me and said Jordan and Cody had been taken by a man that fit Kurt's description."

Dot waited for Myra to continue.

She was silent for a long moment and then she said, "I told her not to tell lies."

"But you believed her?"

Myra hesitated and then nodded, her shoulders hunching.

Dot's grip tightened on the pen but she kept her tone light. "And then?"

"She got upset. Wanted to find another teacher to speak to, but I wouldn't let her. Kurt would have ruined my life if I had. When the bell rang, I told the principal the boys hadn't returned."

"So you gave Kurt a thirty-minute head-start."

"Yes."

"What was Kurt blackmailing you with?" What could

be so bad that she would risk the lives of two ten-year-old boys?

"I'd rather not say."

"Without the full details, I can't do you a deal." Dot let that sit with her a moment before she asked, "After telling the principal, what did you do?"

"The principal asked me to ring Gretchen and ask her if Jordan was with her."

"What did she say?" Dot knew what had happened from speaking with Gretchen earlier, but it would be interesting to see what Myra disclosed.

"She told me to call the police and asked to speak to Lara." Myra shrugged. "I didn't want to put Lara on, but Gretchen insisted."

Dot waited for her to continue.

"Lara told her everything, then she handed the phone back."

"What did Gretchen say to you?"

"She said Kurt was coming down the street. She gave me his licence plate number and told me to call the police."

"And did you?"

She shook her head.

"Sorry, can you speak your answer so the machine can record it?"

"No."

"So even after two explicit pleas for help, you did nothing?" This woman was a piece of work. "Tell me what Kurt had on you."

"No."

"Without any justification for your actions, no judge will be lenient with you. You wilfully endangered two children and then hindered their rescue. That's accessory to kidnapping, hampering a police investigation, child endangerment. You'll be lucky if ten years is all you get."

Tears streamed down Myra's face, but Dot wouldn't

let it sway her from getting the answers she needed. She leaned back, crossed her arms, and waited.

The clock ticked relentlessly. Myra sobbed and sniffed, and still Dot waited.

Dot's phone buzzed. *Can't track down parents. Myra has little background information.*

Interesting. "Your mother isn't in hospital, is she?"

Myra shook her head.

"Where were you planning to go?"

"I don't know. I panicked. After school, I packed some stuff and left."

"What were you scared of?"

"Being exposed. Being arrested. Being killed."

"Was your life threatened?"

"Kurt said bad things happened to people who crossed him."

They weren't getting anywhere. "When did you move to Retribution Bay?"

"January before the school term started."

"Where did you work before?"

Myra flinched. "Ah…I took some time off last year and travelled."

"Where?"

"Europe."

Dot stood. "I'll be back in a minute." It would give Myra time to stew, and Dot's police senses were tingling. Whatever Kurt had over Myra had happened last year. The officer at the desk looked up. "You finished?"

Dot shook her head. "There'll be one more in the lock up tonight, but I need to ensure Kurt Webb doesn't see her."

The man nodded. "We can arrange that. What else do you need?"

"A computer. I need to search for a couple of things."

"This way. Some of the guys have gone home."

Dot started by calling Colin. "What have you found

on Myra?"

"She's got no social media presence and the only mention of her online is on the school website."

Very few people weren't on social media. "Keep looking." She searched for *teacher scandal* and then added *Australia* when the results were too broad. Far too many results still, but she opened a dozen windows to see what they were about. She closed any relating to men or incidents over five years ago. The last link contained the headline, *Graduate teacher fired for sleeping with student*. The photo of the female teacher had been taken from a social media site and Dot nearly closed it, but something in the woman's eyes grabbed her. She enlarged it and visualised the woman with brown hair instead of blonde, a smaller nose, higher cheekbones, and larger breasts. It could be Myra Simpson. Stonefish had the resources to change a person's identity.

Dot typed the teacher's name into the police database and discovered she had skipped bail and hadn't been seen for almost twelve months. She printed the photo and then returned to the interview room. Myra straightened her spine but didn't look at Dot.

"Do you have anything you want to add to your statement?" Dot asked.

"No."

Dot compared the photo with the woman in front of her. Same hairline and skin tone, same jaw and lips, same eyes. When they fingerprinted her, they would get confirmation, but Dot was already convinced. "You must love teaching."

Myra frowned. "I do. It's my life's work."

"Why come back to Australia then? Why not work overseas?"

"My family is all here."

Not a strong enough motivation. She'd know the police would watch her parents, waiting for her to contact them. "Stonefish ordered you here, didn't they?"

She jerked at the name. "How—" She stared at Dot.

"Courtney, you need to tell me everything you know about Stonefish."

Myra gasped at the use of her real name and then buried her head in her arms and cried.

***

It was almost nine o'clock before Dot left the Carnarvon police station. She'd considered spending the night in Carnarvon, but she wanted to be on hand when the search for Nhiari started tomorrow. It was pitch black after leaving the town's outskirts and she put her high beams on to give herself more field of vision. The last thing she needed was to hit a kangaroo.

Fatigue pummelled her, and all she wanted to do was pull over at the next rest stop, but she kept going. She had to process the information Myra/Courtney had given her after she'd realised Dot knew everything.

She wound down the window and let the cool air flow over her face.

Courtney had had an affair with a year twelve student. When it had been exposed, the boy's parents had been out for blood and Courtney had gone to a friend who could help her. In a matter of days, she had a fake passport and had travelled to Thailand to get plastic surgery.

When questioned about what she had to promise in return, Courtney said Stonefish had told her they liked helping people in need. She'd been too desperate to question it further.

So Courtney had changed her appearance, adopted the name of Myra Simpson and spent a year abroad while Stonefish had cemented her identity back in Australia. She kept swearing she'd done nothing wrong, that the relationship had been consensual, and she shouldn't be punished for it.

Others Dot had come across who had been ensnared by Stonefish had been trapped trying to protect loved ones; Courtney was in it for self-gain. Much like Mark had been.

Dot ignored the dual stabs of guilt and grief at the thought of her brother. In the two months since his death, she still couldn't shake the idea that she should have known, should have made more of an effort to find out what he was up to. Should have supported him better.

She exhaled and focused back on the road, slowing as eyes glowed on the side. The kangaroo watched her drive past but didn't move.

Stonefish had arranged Myra's job in Retribution Bay. She'd been told she needed to keep a low profile before she moved back to a city to resume her life. A punishment in her eyes. Then Kurt had started his demands, and she'd realised how trapped she was.

She wouldn't be teaching again any time soon.

Dot sighed. Stonefish had contacts everywhere; Parks and Wildlife, the school, all over Australia and Singapore. How had they stayed under the radar for so long? The organised crime division had taken all the information Dot fed them but didn't have people to spare to go to Retribution Bay. They were building a case with her data.

She turned the air-conditioning to high, hoping the air would help to refresh her.

Almost everything centred on Retribution Bay. Even if Stonefish were an international organisation, they had to have people based in town. She'd arrested Declan, the manager of Parks and Wildlife, over a month ago, but he refused to cooperate. His fear for his family was very real, and though Dot had offered to get them protection, Declan was unconvinced it would be enough.

Stonefish definitely had contacts in the police. She

had known that for a few months, but she hadn't known how widespread it was.

When she got home, she'd go through her mind map of those involved again, try to spot a connection somewhere. It had eluded her and Nhiari so far, despite the number of hours they'd spent on it.

Movement to the side caused Dot to slam on the brakes as half a dozen goats ran across the road. She narrowly missed the last one and took a moment for her heart rate to settle before she accelerated again. The feral nuisances had caused many an accident. Thankfully she hadn't added to their tally tonight.

Pushing aside Stonefish for the moment, she concentrated on the road ahead, scanning the sides for movement, or glowing eyes. The number of dead carcasses on the side of the road attested to how dangerous this stretch could be, especially at night when the animals searched for food.

She passed the turn off to Retribution Ridge, her friends' sheep station, and exhaled. Not too long now.

Just up ahead, her headlights illuminated a minivan on the side of the road. She slowed as a person moved onto the road, waving their hands.

What now?

Dot assessed the situation as she pulled to a stop behind the van. A couple of twenty-something males were sitting on the dirt outside the car, one who looked to have Indian heritage and the other south-east Asian, and at least one other person was inside. She checked her gun was in place and radioed dispatch. "A minivan appears to be in trouble about sixty ks south of Retribution Bay. Getting out now to check the situation."

"Roger."

She kept her headlights on as she stepped out of the car. They looked like a group of uni students on a road trip, but why they'd be heading to Retribution Bay at the end of the season when the weather really heated up was beyond her. The male who had waved her down jogged over. His T-shirt had an image of Columbus on it, and his skinny jeans, canvas shoes and shaggy hair reminded her of her first years in Perth when she was that age. Freedom, independence, first love. Her gut clenched, but she forced a smile. "Run into some trouble?"

"Hit a 'roo. Destroyed the front of the van. We thought we'd be stuck out here all night. There's no reception."

She walked over to examine the car. Sure enough, the van had been caved in, and the bonnet had lifted, showing significant damage. "Anyone injured?"

"No, we're fine. Our lecturer is walking to town to get help. He thought he might get phone reception closer to town."

Not for at least another fifty kilometres, but he might catch the attention of a pack of dingoes who roamed the area. A sole person in the middle of the night was enticing. "When did he leave?"

"About an hour ago."

Shit. "How many of you are there?"

"Four."

They'd fit in her car, but the lecturer wouldn't, unless he sat in the prisoner section of the paddy wagon. "All right. Lock up the van and I'll take you into town. We can get a tow truck out to get the van in the morning."

The man shook his head. "Our lecturer told us not to leave it. It's got valuable equipment in it. We're researchers, come to do work on the new wreck discovered in the gulf."

Maritime archaeologists just like Oliver, the man who'd broken her heart. The thought made Dot's thin thread of patience even weaker, and she held onto it with both hands. "It's almost midnight. You're in the middle

of nowhere. No one has come along in the past hour—
"

"He said he'd sack us if we left it," the man interrupted.

The lecturer sounded like an idiot, probably one of the musty, old academics who were brilliant but lacked an ounce of common sense. Hopefully she wouldn't have to deal with him, but she felt sorry for her friend, Sam, who had been contracted to take the researchers to the wreck site on his boat.

But thinking of Sam gave her an idea.

She radioed dispatch. "Can you contact John and ask if he can tow a Kia Carnival into town? Also contact Sam Hackett and tell him to bring his tour bus to pick these guys up. They're in town to dive the new wreck. If Sam complains, tell him he owes me."

She doubted Sam would complain. He was a decent guy. She turned to the student. "What's your name?"

"Tom."

"Where did the kangaroo go?"

The man raised his eyebrows and gestured to the bush on the other side of the road. "That way."

"Gather your friends and see if you can find it, but don't approach it if you do."

"Why?"

"Because it's probably injured. Kangaroos can bound away from an accident, only to collapse later. And if the kangaroo is female and carrying a joey, then the joey will die as well."

"Oh."

She walked over to the police car and took out a road lantern, placing it on the bonnet of the van. "Use your phone torches and don't lose sight of the lantern. I don't want to have to send a search party for you. Stay in teams of two. I'll go pick up your lecturer."

Two other men and a woman joined Tom on the

road. "Isn't it dangerous out there?" asked the man who had a moustache like from a bad seventies porno film.

"Stamping your feet will scare away any snakes but watch where you tread. If the kangaroo is hurt, it won't have made it more than a hundred metres. If you find it, don't approach it. I'll deal with it when I return."

She hoped if they found it, it was already dead. She didn't want to put a bullet in it.

With reluctant agreement, the students spread out.

As Dot got back into her car, her radio squawked. "Tow truck and Sam are on their way."

"Copy." She closed her eyes and took a deep breath. Another two hours and she should be able to crawl into bed, as long as nothing else went wrong. She accelerated away, keeping her speed low as she scanned the road for the lecturer. In an hour, he couldn't have gone more than about five kilometres, unless he ran marathons in his spare time. All of Oliver's university lecturers had been old and mentally sharp, but rather flabby in places.

She sighed. The discovery of the new shipwreck had uncovered a million memories she'd done her best to bury forever.

Ahead, a figure appeared in her light beams. Not old, grey and chubby. No, the man who turned as she slowed had strawberry blond hair, a fit swimmer's build, and a smile that had once made her feel as if she was the most important person in the world.

The Fates were really messing with her today.

Of all the thousands of empty hectares of land in the country, he had to walk into hers.

Oliver Anderson.

Chapter 2

Oliver checked the battery on his phone. The torch app used more than he'd like and only a sliver of moon lit the sky. Could he risk turning it off? He shivered, wishing he'd grabbed his jacket out of the van before he'd left, but the adrenalin from the crash had warmed him. He'd forgotten how cold it could get at night.

And he'd been desperate to get help. The kangaroo had appeared out of nowhere, two bounds and it was right in front of the car and, though Oliver had jammed on the brakes, it was no use. His windscreen was a spiderweb of cracks and the bonnet was destroyed.

He was relieved the glass had held and the 'roo hadn't entered the car.

Then he might not be walking here.

He exhaled. At least his students were fine, and the equipment was undamaged. It would be just his luck if the first expedition he was in charge of was a failure because of a kangaroo.

Maybe he should have refused to come, but the lure of the ocean and running into Dot Campbell again was too much to resist. He'd never quite been able to forget her despite his efforts.

He rubbed his arms, trying to warm them. It was darker, colder and a longer walk into town than he'd anticipated. Surely it couldn't be far before the mobile signal kicked in. Then he'd call for help and return to his students.

The grumble of a car engine behind Oliver lifted his spirits, and he glanced behind at the headlights heading his way. Finally.

A couple of dingoes howled, and his gaze moved to the dark bush. He hadn't heard of dingoes attacking people on the side of the road, but he was an easy target.

The headlights lit the road ahead, and he waited for the car to stop before he turned, shielding his eyes against the glare of the light. His heart stuttered. A police car.

What were the chances it was her?

The passenger side window lowered and he stepped over. "Thank you so much, Office…" Oliver's eyes widened and his breath left him. It *was* her. "Dot." Her dark hair was short now, and it was messy, as if she'd been tugging on it the way she did when she was stressed over something. Her petite frame seemed small in the large car, but she sat straight as she stared at him.

"Get in, Mr Anderson and keep your mouth shut."

What was her problem? He'd thought after all these years he'd get polite disinterest, or maybe surprise and a sharing of warm memories, but not anger.

She'd been the one to break up with him.

"Get in, or I'll leave you behind," Dot ordered.

Oliver blinked. The petite, dark-haired beauty who had captured his heart over a decade ago had developed a steel backbone. He slid into the passenger side, doing up his seatbelt as Dot did a U-turn and headed back the way she came.

"We need to get to town. There was a crash—"

"I know. Tow truck and transport are on their way to

pick up your van and students."

Of course. She would have driven past and seen them. He studied the woman next to him in the dim light of the car. Her hands clenched the steering wheel and she stared ahead, silently shouting, *Don't talk to me.*

A faint scent of lemon myrtle filled the car, and he inhaled the memories. Getting ready for the day side by side in the cramped bathroom at Dot's apartment. The tube of lemon myrtle moisturiser on the bench. Dot's insistence on using it, and his insistence on helping her spread it on her body. The laughter and more which came with it.

He hardened and pushed away the memory.

That was ten years ago. From the glimpse he'd caught of her as he'd got into the car, dark bags hung under Dot's eyes, suggesting she hadn't slept in a while and had been under a lot of stress. What could a police officer in a sleepy tourist town have to be stressed about? He'd never understood why she'd wanted to return here rather than advance her career in the city. He opened his mouth to speak as they arrived back at the crash scene. "It's good to see—"

Dot braked and got out of the car without a word, slamming the door behind her.

"—you." Oliver frowned. What was she so angry about? Perhaps it was better she'd left him and broken his heart if this was who she'd become.

He climbed out and moved over to his students, who were talking to Dot.

"It's over there." Tom pointed into the bush.

"Thanks." Dot returned to the police car, taking gloves and a shiny survival blanket out of a first aid kit. Then she took the lantern that was on the bonnet of the minivan and strode into the dark.

"What's going on?" Oliver asked.

"The kangaroo we hit is over there," Rajesh

responded, stroking his moustache. "She's checking if it has a joey."

Andrew shivered and rubbed his arms. "It's gross and freezing. Can I get back in the car?"

Oliver nodded. He hadn't wanted to bring Andrew, because he was a first-year student who didn't seem to enjoy maritime archaeology, but his father was funding the trip, so Oliver hadn't had a choice. Andrew had complained the whole twelve-hour drive.

"I'll see if she needs help." Suzyn strode towards the light.

He should be the one helping, but before he walked more than a couple of metres, Dot was handing Suzyn a bundle wrapped in the silver blanket. Together, they walked back to the road. Dot pressed the radio on her shoulder. "I've got a joey. Can you call Donna and tell her I'll bring it by?"

"Roger. What's your ETA?"

Dot ran a hand through her hair. "Probably another two hours."

She looked exhausted now Oliver could see her properly in the lantern's light. He knew nothing about police rosters, but surely she shouldn't still be working this late at night.

"You should all get back into the van where it's warmer," Dot said to the students. "It will be another half an hour before people arrive to help. Get some rest."

"Are you leaving us?" Tom asked.

"No. I'll stay until help arrives." She checked the joey in Suzyn's arms. "Keep him rugged up and close to your body. He's still quite young, so he shouldn't move around too much."

"What about his mum?" Suzyn asked. "Can we save her?"

Dot's face darkened. She shook her head. "She's too injured. The best I can do is put her out of her pain."

Oliver's eyes widened. The Dot he knew had once saved a spider from a swimming pool, despite her dislike of the creatures. "You'll kill it?" His tone came out harsh and incredulous.

She turned to him, expression hard. "It's the most humane thing to do." To the others, she repeated, "You should get into the van."

His students followed her instruction, but Oliver couldn't move. He watched Dot stride back into the dark. After a brief silence, a shot cracked through the air.

Oliver jumped. She'd actually killed it.

Definitely no longer the sweet Dot he had known.

He stood where he was, arms wrapped around him to keep the cold at bay, waiting for Dot to return.

She didn't.

He moved towards the bush, letting his eyes adjust to the lack of light. He could just make out the shape of Dot standing there. "Dot?"

No response.

He moved closer. His steps crunched over grasses, and he was about ten metres away when Dot called, "Go away, Oliver."

The strength in her voice almost fooled him, if not for the slight waver at the end. It was rarely present. Dot had always kept up the facade of being strong and capable around others—he'd called it her police mask—but underneath all of that she was emotionally vulnerable. Her family had done a number on her.

He took several more steps towards her.

"Stop." The waver was almost gone now.

"I know how hard you must have found that, Dot."

She whirled at his words. "You don't know anything," she hissed. "You have no idea who I am, or who I've become." She strode further into the bush.

Oliver rocked back at her words. This was reminiscent of the Dot he'd first met, the one with a wall a mile wide in front of her so she couldn't be hurt. He'd spent time burrowing under it to get to the real woman underneath; the sweet, giving person with a wicked sense of humour and a penchant for bright colours and loud music.

What had made her revert to this woman?

Or were his memories twisted by age and sentimentality?

He debated going after her, but she was likely to keep walking. She'd come back in her own time.

With a sigh, he headed back to the van and his students.

Suzyn was cradling the joey and one look showed it was sleeping. Poor little thing. Andrew played on his phone, while Rajesh and Tom chatted about the upcoming footy draft. Not much of a research team yet, but hopefully over the week, they'd meld and work well together.

Suzyn glanced in the direction Dot had gone. "Is she all right?"

"She will be."

"It was rough to have to kill the 'roo," Tom added.

Oliver nodded.

"We should have flown up and then none of this would have happened." Andrew didn't even look up as he muttered his complaint.

Oliver bit his tongue. Though Andrew's father was funding the expedition, it was Oliver's decision where to spend the funds. Driving up and hiring a house rather than flying and staying in a motel meant they could stay longer if required, and Oliver could pay his students for some of their work.

But now they'd be stuck without a car for the foreseeable future. Would there be a mechanic in town able to fix the damage? Maybe they could walk from the house to the boat each day, but he'd have to make sure they could secure the equipment at night.

Too many issues and they hadn't started the dive yet.

Headlights illuminated the road ahead of them, and Oliver turned away so they didn't blind him. A small tour bus slowed and then did a U-turn behind them.

This must be their ride. The name on the bus was that of the boat he had hired and the tall, blond man who got out of the driver's seat was the captain Oliver had met on a video call.

Oliver smiled and strode over. "Sam, this wasn't how I envisioned us meeting in person." He shook the broad-shouldered man's hand. "Sorry for getting you out of bed."

Sam smiled back. "No problem. I'm always happy to help Dot." He glanced behind Oliver. "Where is she?"

The rush of jealousy made Oliver frown, and he nodded towards the bush. "She had to shoot the kangaroo we hit. She's over there."

Concern crossed Sam's face. "Here." He handed Oliver the keys to the bus. "Load your gear into the back and we'll have you in Retribution Bay in no time." Without waiting for an answer, he strode into the bush.

Did Sam not know Dot well enough to realise she wouldn't want to be disturbed right now?

Or was he the person she *would* want to see?

The envy in his gut was unexpected, and not something Oliver needed right now.

He returned to the van. "All right, gang. Let's get this stuff moved."

By the time they finished moving all their things from the van to the bus, the tow truck had arrived, and Sam had returned with Dot. She went straight to the police car and wiped her face, and then checked the mirror.

She'd definitely been crying.

Oliver felt a tug deep in his gut, but he didn't move

to speak with her. Instead he headed for the tow truck driver.

"Thanks for coming out so late."

The man nodded. "Better to remove the car from the road in case someone doesn't see it."

"Do you get this kind of damage often?"

"Yep. Probably take a while to get parts up to fix it, though."

Not what he wanted to hear.

"You got your bus licence?" Sam asked.

"Yeah." He'd got it at university because they'd regularly done class outings and he saw the value of being able to move a large team at once.

"You can borrow the bus then," Sam said. "It will just be sitting there during the off-season."

Relief filled him. "How much per week?"

Sam laughed. "Nothing, mate. Just pay for petrol and keep it clean. You'll be on the boat most days anyway, and it will save me having to pick you up."

"Thanks. I really appreciate it." He was used to people thinking he had a decent budget because of the shipwreck reality television show he'd been on.

The tow truck driver yawned. "Let's get this beast on the truck."

Sam moved the bus out of the way, and before long the van was on the back of the tow truck. Oliver grabbed the tow truck driver's phone number and address, and then waved as he drove off. Sam waited patiently, chatting to Tom and Rajesh, and Dot was with Suzyn, dealing with the joey. Dot glanced at him and then straightened and walked over. "Suzyn has agreed to hold the joey on the journey to town. She can come with me, and we'll stop by the wildlife carer on the way. Where are you staying?"

"A house on Lansdell Street." He couldn't remember the number.

"Lindsay's place?"

He nodded. He was surprised Lindsay hadn't told her. Dot had been close to her when he'd visited Retribution Bay all those years ago.

"All right. We shouldn't be more than ten minutes after you." She gestured to Suzyn to join her.

Oliver watched her go, ignoring the urge to follow. Their relationship was long over. But he still had questions as to why it had ended and only Dot could answer them.

But he didn't need to know today. He had plenty of time while he was here.

Oliver climbed into the bus and smiled at Sam. "Let's go."

Chapter 3

Oliver yawned and did his best to keep quiet as he moved around the share house. It had been after one by the time they'd arrived in Retribution Bay, but that hadn't stopped him from waking at first light. He wandered into the kitchen and spotted the coffee machine on the bench, with a jar of coffee pods next to it. The plastic pods weren't the best for the environment, but right now, they would do in a pinch. He'd see if there was somewhere in town where he could buy reusable capsules. He switched it on and checked the fridge.

Bless Lindsay. She'd delivered the groceries he'd ordered and had put them away. The fridge contained milk, butter and various vegetables, and the non-perishables were in the cupboards. He was a little surprised Lindsay hadn't been more antagonistic towards him, considering Dot's attitude. She had been a surrogate mother to Dot and he thought if Dot disliked him, Lindsay would too. But perhaps she hadn't remembered him. He'd have to buy her flowers to show his appreciation.

Maybe he should buy Dot some as well. She'd been partial to bright, cheerful gerberas when they'd been dating.

Had she stayed up to do paperwork after she'd got back last night, or finally got the sleep she so obviously needed?

He headed outside onto the patio, which contained a small wooden outdoor table with half a dozen chairs around it. He settled in and glanced around the pretty courtyard garden that featured native grevilleas and wattles. Water wise and low maintenance. Smart.

He yawned again and sipped his coffee as the wind rustled the bushes. Today was all about preparation. His students were under instructions to go through their notes and come up with a plan of action for tomorrow. Then they were to orientate themselves with the town. Conditions were still dismal after the storm a couple of days ago, and visibility was low. No point in them all going out to the site.

He wanted to do the first dive by himself, without the students peppering him with questions or being disappointed by the murky water. Perhaps it was selfish, but there was something special about the first dive, and he didn't want to be in teacher mode for it.

He flicked through his emails, noting one from a publisher expressing an interest in him writing a memoir about his shipwreck experiences.

He leaned back and frowned. It wasn't something he'd ever considered, but he had enough journals that he could probably cobble something together. And the work at the museum hadn't given him the satisfaction he'd hoped it would. He missed being part of his team more than he'd expected. Perhaps writing a book would help.

Oliver checked his watch and then worked out how long it would take him to walk to the marina. All the gear was still on the bus which Sam had locked up for the night, with the promise to bring it with him this morning.

Easy-going.

Oliver appreciated that. He'd worked with other boat skippers who thought they were doing Oliver a favour allowing him to even be on the boat. Oliver needed someone who could take instructions and offer feedback on the site conditions.

If last night was any indication, Sam should be easy to work with.

His thoughts drifted to Dot.

Capable, efficient, smart. Gone was the warmth and vulnerability he remembered, and the sweetness which appeared when he'd least expected it.

She had shown her softer side with the joey, so maybe it was still in there somewhere.

He wasn't sure what he'd expected. They'd both changed in a decade.

His finger slipped through the emerald ring he kept on a chain around his neck. His good luck charm, the one piece he'd been allowed to keep from that first expedition. The colour had reminded him of Dot's favourite fluffy jumper. He'd spent many an hour snuggling her on the couch while she wore that jumper. Good times.

He sighed. He'd never regret taking the role which launched his career as a maritime archaeologist, but he regretted the end of their relationship. He'd thought they could make long distance work for the time he was away, but Dot stopped answering his calls and texts, totally ghosting him. This was Oliver's chance to find out why. He'd thought they loved each other.

His relationships since then had been sporadic because of the nature of his work, but he wanted to settle down. Which meant he needed to excise the ghost of Dot. See who she had become so he could stop comparing every woman to her.

Put her into the past where she belonged.

The discovery of a new shipwreck in Retribution Bay had come at the perfect time. He'd been about to apply for a grant to catalogue the wreck when a shipping magnate named Lucas Fitton had called the museum, saying he was happy to pay for the expedition as long as his son was part of it.

Oliver sipped his coffee, grimacing. He hated having conditions attached to the funds, but it was part of the process. And at least Andrew was studying maritime archaeology.

The expedition meant Oliver could get back to diving and move on from Dot at the same time.

He hadn't expected to miss the diving so much.

The expeditions had become a circus with the reality TV crew following them, and during his last expedition he'd never had the chance to relax without a camera on him. They didn't give him the opportunity to do the research or take his time. It was all about the story they needed for the episode.

He'd thought lecturing and working at the museum would allow him to do what he loved.

But he hadn't dived an unknown wreck in over twelve months, and he missed the thrill of the discovery.

He exhaled and rubbed his chest. And then there was Dot.

It had been good to see her, and not only because she'd rescued them. Now the shock of the first meeting was over, he felt… *different* being so close to her. Calmer, or more settled, as if he'd found something that had been missing for a long time.

Odd, considering she'd barely been civil to him.

Ten years since they'd seen each other and yet he still felt something for her. His goal had been to see her, and put the past behind him, but maybe he needed to reconsider, wait until he had time to get to know her again before he made a decision.

Sure, he might have done a bit of social media stalking to check if she was married or in a relationship, but that was normal.

When he was finished today, he'd go to the station and thank Dot again for rescuing them. They could chat and he could figure out whether the something he'd felt had been a product of fatigue and the relief of being rescued.

His phone rang and he smothered a groan at the caller ID. "Good morning, Lucas." Less than seven hours since they'd arrived and he was already on the phone. This didn't bode well for the trip.

"Oliver. I heard you had some difficulty last night."

It surprised him that Andrew had already told his father, but perhaps Andrew had complained to him. "Nothing to worry about. Everyone is safe, and the equipment is undamaged. We've got transport for our stay while the car is being fixed." He made a mental note to call the mechanic later today.

"Good. What are your plans for the day?"

Oliver finished his coffee and went inside. "I'm going out to the wreck to do some reconnaissance. Visibility is still low from the storm, so I don't think it will be the best day for a full dive." He rinsed his dishes with the phone held between his shoulder and ear. "The students are going over the notes and revising our plan to account for the changes in weather."

"Should you be wasting a day?"

Oliver scowled as he grabbed his backpack and headed out. "I don't feel as if it's a waste. If the ocean settles, we can go out this afternoon, and the students are tired after the incident last night."

Lucas hummed his displeasure.

Oliver rolled his eyes and reminded himself that Lucas was enabling this expedition. "The advantage of this wreck is it's less than an hour away by boat. It gives us flexibility that we don't have on dives where we need to stay on the boat."

"Call me this evening with an update." Lucas hung up.

He scowled as he tucked his phone in his pocket. Lucas wasn't going to be a silent benefactor on this dive, but Oliver could deal with him.

With an exhale, Oliver glanced around. It had been almost a decade since Dot had brought him to Retribution Bay to meet her family.

Piles of green waste, debris from the storm, lined the streets. Tarps covered a few roofs, and most of the leaves were missing from plants in gardens, but aside from that, the town had fared all right and was much as he remembered. He hoped the storm surge had left the wreck undamaged.

In the centre of town, he stopped at a cafe for a toasted bacon and egg sandwich. The woman behind the counter narrowed her eyes, squinting at him. "Do I know you?"

Oliver had no desire to be recognised today. "No, I don't think we've met." He stood to the side while he waited for his food to be made.

She stared at him for a minute longer before turning her attention to the next customer. Then she beamed. "Jenifer! Is it true two boys were kidnapped from school yesterday?"

The woman frowned. "I can't tell you that, Tammy."

Tammy pouted. "Come on, Jen. What about the rumours of treasure? Did Jordan really bring a golden doubloon to school?"

Oliver's ears pricked.

"I didn't see it, but the children believed it. It was probably just one of those chocolates shaped like a coin."

Tammy shook her head. "I heard Myra Simpson confiscated it and has disappeared. Even the news was reporting it this morning. What's going on?"

Oliver took out his phone and searched the local news sites. Sure enough, the headline read, *Buried Treasure Found in Retribution Bay*. The article mentioned the rumours and questioned whether the discovery had anything to do with the new shipwreck which had been found in the gulf.

Shit. The last thing he needed was people flocking to the town and interfering with his wreck. He needed to get moving. His sandwich was sizzling in the sandwich press. He approached the counter where Tammy was still trying to get the information out of Jenifer, who must be a teacher at the school. "Excuse me, Tammy. Is my sandwich ready?"

Tammy jumped and spun around. "Oh, yes. Sorry!" She quickly wrapped it. Meanwhile, the teacher reached over, grabbed her coffee that Tammy had been holding hostage and hurried out.

Tammy's shoulders slumped when she noticed she'd lost her target, but managed a smile when she handed Oliver his sandwich. She paused, not letting it go. "Wait. I know where I've seen you. You're on that show about shipwrecks."

Damn. He tugged at the sandwich and she let go. "Nice to meet you."

"Are you here to dive on the new wreck?"

The rumours would spread either way. "I am, but I'm working for the museum now. Have a nice day." He hurried out of the cafe.

Oliver couldn't do anything about being a recognisable face. The show wasn't mega popular but had its die-hard fans.

He debated ringing his department head for more information, but the man would call as soon as he heard the news. He wouldn't be happy, but neither was Oliver. Treasure hunters were the bane of his existence. They cared nothing for the history of a wreck, or things like provenance, and were just out to make their fortune. He strode to the marina, his appetite gone.

The *Oceanid* was in its pen and Sam and another man were on board. Oliver waved to get Sam's attention and Sam met him at the gate. "Morning. We've moved the gear onto the boat, but left you to decide where you want it," he said.

"Have you heard the rumours about treasure?"

Sam blinked and his expression shuttered. "Yeah. What did you hear?"

Oliver noted Sam's immediate tension, as if ready for defence. Not good. "Something about kids being kidnapped and treasure being found."

Sam's mouth set in a hard line. "Who's been talking?"

No denial of it, which was interesting. "Tammy at the cafe."

Sam swore. "Just what we need."

"It's on the news. People are going to flock to town." Oliver followed Sam on board, the urge strong to order him to hurry. He needed to think this through, not simply panic and react. He sipped his coffee. "You don't seem tired."

"Years in the military means I'm used to lack of sleep." Sam gestured to the other man. "This is my cabin boy, Arthur."

The 'cabin boy' was solid and, though not as tall as Sam, was taller than Oliver and in his late twenties or early thirties. Arthur rolled his eyes and held out his hand. "Ignore him. He thinks he's funny. Call me Sherlock."

Oliver grinned at their teasing. "Nice to meet you." He'd bet Sherlock was military as well, not just from the way he'd assessed Oliver, but also from his prosthetic leg. Lindsay had told him about Sam's new crew member when he'd rung her about the groceries. They might be useful in scaring away would-be treasure hunters. "We need to get out to the wreck. If enough people believe the rumours of treasure, it will be crawling with divers in days." Maybe he should wake his students.

Sherlock turned to Sam.

"Word has spread," Sam explained. "Let's get the equipment tied down before we go anywhere."

Oliver let out a breath. He was right. They couldn't afford for it to be damaged. The deck was wide and flat, giving a great space for the equipment. A couple of tables were fixed in place and they could mount some of the smaller gear on them. Bench seats ran along both sides where they could attach the scuba tanks, and the air compressor he'd hired to refill the tanks was already on the deck at the back.

"Does it pass?" Sam asked.

"It's perfect." Oliver pointed to a couple of machines. "Those need to be mounted on the tables."

They got to work.

"Are your students coming?" Sherlock asked.

Oliver shook his head. "They're sleeping. I don't expect they'll rise before midday." At Sherlock's incredulous look he added, "I'm worried the storm might have done some damage and the visibility won't be great. They're more useful to me going over their notes than being on the boat, disappointed."

The man nodded and went to untie the boat while Sam started the engine. Soon they were motoring out of the marina and south towards the wreck.

Oliver inhaled the salty air. Blue skies, and a bit of chop to the water, but combined with the low hum of the engine, it released the tension in his shoulders. He'd spent so much of the past year surrounded by people: regular classes at university, and then his work at the Shipwrecks Museum. He hadn't had time to be on the ocean. Some of the stress melted away.

It was like coming home.

"You're welcome to join us on the top deck," Sherlock said.

Oliver turned and smiled. "Thanks. I'll sort a few things out here first."

He took his time preparing his dive gear and then going through his notes, appreciating the time alone. No crew stood next to him, pointing a camera and microphone in his face. He didn't have to think about his facial expressions or what he was wearing. It was just him, by himself.

He smiled.

When he was satisfied he was ready for the dive, he climbed the ladder to the top deck. As he did, Sam asked, "How are Gretchen and Jordan this morning?"

Sherlock smiled. "Good. Gretchen's taking Jordan over to Cody's place to talk about everything."

"No nightmares?"

"None."

What were they talking about? Maybe his question was written on his face, because when Sherlock spotted him, he said, "Those rumours about the kidnapping were true. My partner's child was taken from school by his father yesterday."

Not all divorces were amicable. "He's all right now?"

Sherlock nodded. "The kid's resilient." The wonder in his voice was clear. "We're both keeping an eye on him, but he seems to have got through the ordeal without any problems. Gretchen's going to arrange a visit with a psychologist when he's next in town just to be sure."

"Where's the father now?"

"In gaol." Satisfaction laced his tone. "Dot took him to Carnarvon last night."

"She was coming back when she ran across you," Sam added.

No wonder she'd looked so tired. "Lucky for us."

Oliver pursed his lips as he sat on the bench seat across from Sherlock. "So if the kidnapping rumours are true, what about the treasure?"

Sam laughed. "Have you ever lived in a small town?"

Oliver shook his head.

"You'll learn pretty quickly how rumours can expand. A kidnapping isn't exciting enough, it's got to be kidnapping *and* treasure."

Sherlock nodded. "People love to associate shipwrecks with treasure."

One thing he'd learnt over his time working on numerous shipwrecks was, people only told you what they wanted you to know. In this case, both had avoided answering the actual question. Unfortunately, they were also right. The moment news of a new shipwreck was announced, people thought of pirates and doubloons. He changed the subject. "Do either of you dive?"

Sam nodded. "I've been diving for years."

"I'm planning to get my ticket this year," Sherlock answered. "There's too much opportunity up here to dive."

"You know we've got the two shipwrecks here?" Sam asked. "The *Retribution* is at the other end of the island to the new one."

Oliver nodded. "I'm hoping to have time to assess both of them. It's been a while since anyone from the museum has been out to look at the *Retribution*."

They were approaching the base of the gulf and multiple islands dotted to the east of them, but it was the long, low island that caught Oliver's attention. "That's where we're going?"

"Yeah."

He squinted. Something was scattered along the shoreline. Perhaps debris from the storm. "Do you have binoculars?"

Sherlock handed them to him, and he adjusted the

focus as he scanned the shore. A plastic barrel and lumps of rubbish. His shoulders tensed. "Looks like the storm washed up some litter." He handed the binoculars back. It was like this all around the world. People thought it was fine to dump rubbish into the ocean and it would magically disappear. Unfortunately he knew all too well that wasn't the case. He'd swum through fields of litter to get to some of the wrecks he'd worked on.

"I'll take a look," Sam said. "I promised Penelope I'd check the islands while I was down here." He turned to Oliver. "My partner is with Parks and Wildlife, and she hasn't visited all the islands since the storm."

So he wasn't involved with Dot. Oliver couldn't ignore the wash of relief through him. "I'm going to get ready."

He went down to the bottom deck and by the time he'd changed into his wetsuit and suited up, they were at the dive site. They anchored nearby, and Sam checked Oliver's gear. "I'm going to take the tender over to the island and clean up, but Sherlock will stay on the boat to be your watch. We've got radios to communicate with each other."

"Thanks." Oliver grabbed his waterproof camera from the table and headed for the marlin board at the back. A shimmer of excitement settled over him. The first dive on a new wreck was always special. It was the unknown—how much would be recognisable? What fascinating items might he find? He slipped on his fins. "See you in a few." He placed the regulator in his mouth and stepped off the boat.

Cool, refreshing water. He smiled around the mouthpiece and gave Sherlock the 'all good' signal before descending. It wasn't more than ten to fifteen metres deep and visibility was a little murky, with sediment from the storm yet to settle. He checked his watch and swam towards the coordinates he'd been given for the wreck.

The sand sloped upwards, getting shallower. He scanned the bottom, trying to see the lumps of coral as shapes and just after he checked his watch again, he spotted the anchor. Not much more than a T-shape on the bottom, blending into the surrounding coral. He was impressed the woman who'd found the wreck had even realised what it was.

He snapped a couple of photos and then dived closer to examine it. It was the right size for the anchors used by the Dutch East Indies company, but there was no reason for one of their ships to enter the gulf. Before coming here, Oliver had reread the report the museum had commissioned back in 2014 to help find and identify Dutch East Indies ships off the Western Australian coast. He wanted to familiarise himself with their cargo and dimensions, but of the known ships, all were suspected to have gone down further south or west of here.

He continued swimming, slowly examining sections of coral, and his heart rate increased as he spotted something long and cylindrical. A cannon. It had to be. He moved closer to examine it. Encrusted in marine life, but definitely a cannon. It might even be stamped with the name of the ship, which would make identifying it much easier. There! Definitely a clump of cannon balls which had settled on the bottom close to one another when the ship had broken apart.

Though he longed to pick things up, he held back, instead photographing what he found. When he came back with his students, he'd get one of them to video the find. Hopefully tomorrow the sediment would have settled and they would get some decent footage.

He spread out, following the wreck plume to see if he could spot any other remnants. He'd set up a grid pattern tomorrow so they could search thoroughly, but he was aware he had limited time, so he wanted to focus on identifying the ship and cataloguing as much as he could.

When he surfaced, he was close to the island. He caught Sherlock's attention and waved as he inflated his BCD vest. Sam was still on the island, taking photos of the rubbish, with the rubber tender pulled up on the shore. It would save him from swimming back.

Oliver pried off his fins and walked over to the tender, putting his gear inside. Then he spotted what Sam was taking pictures of. Sealed plastic bags full of white powder. Drugs.

He frowned as he joined Sam. "Is that what I think it is?"

Sam nodded. "I think it came from the barrel." He pointed to a blue plastic barrel which had been ripped apart and now lay further up the beach. "Dot's on her way."

Oliver stiffened at Dot's name. He wasn't ready to see her like this, in his wetsuit, doing the job that had come between them.

The hum of a boat engine reached him, and he turned as a police boat came up alongside the *Oceanid*. No chance to get changed.

"Did you see any barrels down there?" Sam asked.

Oliver shook his head. "Nothing but coral and shipwreck."

Sam smiled. "You found it all right? Any distinguishing features?"

"There might be a mark on the cannon or anchor which will give us the information we need."

Sherlock boarded the police boat and Dot steered it towards the island.

The sun heated Oliver's wetsuit, but he didn't pull it off. He had the burn-in-an-instant skin of an on-the-redder-shade of strawberry blond and he hadn't put sun cream on his torso. Better to be uncomfortably warm for an hour, than burnt to a crisp and painful for days.

Still, the sensible decision didn't stop him from feeling foolish. He held the police boat in place as Dot cut the engine and Sherlock handed him the anchor. By the time he'd dragged the anchor up the shore, both had disembarked. Dot wore her blue uniform, including a hat, and strode across the sand towards Sam with a scowl on her face.

He hadn't seen her smile yet. She'd never been one of those effervescent, bubbly girls who smiled at everything, but her default expression had always been more open and friendly than it was now. Oliver joined them in time to hear Dot murmur, "I don't have time for more of this shit."

Sam touched her shoulder. "Maybe this time they've made a mistake."

Who were they talking about?

"Have you touched anything?" Dot demanded, shrugging his hand off.

"No. Just took a couple of photos."

She nodded as if satisfied. "I'll take it from here. You can go."

Oliver frowned. "Shouldn't you have a second officer with you?" Surely she wouldn't be left alone out here. If whoever had left the drugs discovered they'd been found, they might come back for them. A single female police officer might not be a deterrent, especially when there was no one around.

Dot turned to him. "My usual partner is unavailable—" Was that a flicker of concern? "—and my other officers are busy in town."

He shook his head.

"I can work by myself," she snapped.

She misunderstood him.

"Sure you can," Sam said easily. "But we're not leaving you out here alone. We'll hang around until you're done."

Dot glared at him. "You're a pain in my arse, Sam Hackett."

"But you still love me." He grinned and blew her a kiss.

She rolled her eyes and stalked back to the police boat. Oliver watched her go.

"Don't mind Dot," Sam said. "She's got a lot on her plate at the moment. She's not usually this abrupt."

"I know." Oliver pulled at the collar of his wetsuit, hoping to let a bit of air in.

"How?" The question was quick, insistent.

Oliver frowned. "What?"

"How do you know Dot?" Sam studied him, eyes narrowed, gaze probing.

Shit. He rubbed the back of his head. "We dated back when I was at university and she was at the police academy."

Sherlock moved closer and Sam's eyebrows rose. "Was it serious?"

They might as well have him tied to a chair in a dark room with a heat lamp spotlighting him for their intensity. He shrugged, glanced over to make sure Dot was out of hearing range. She was getting equipment from the boat. "We had plans to move in together."

"What happened?" Sherlock asked.

"I got an opportunity to work on the expedition of a lifetime and I took it."

"Long-distance relationships can be hard," Sam said.

Oliver nodded, though that wasn't the problem. Dot hadn't been willing to try. "I'm not sure she wants to acknowledge it, so don't say anything to her."

They both nodded, but he wasn't convinced they would keep their mouths shut.

Dot carried a camera and a case over to the first packet of drugs. She placed the case down and took photos, moving up the beach, documenting everything.

Sam and Sherlock followed her, keeping a respectful distance, but both constantly scanned the surroundings as if expecting someone to burst out of the bushes and attack.

Oliver jogged to catch up. "Do you think someone is around?"

Sam turned to him. "What makes you ask?"

"You're both like bodyguards, keeping a watchful eye. Do people camp on the island?"

"Not usually," Sam replied. "There's been some odd stuff occurring in town lately, and we've learnt to be careful."

Oliver tensed. "Is Dot in danger?"

"She's a cop," Sherlock said. "Some level of danger comes with the job."

That didn't answer his question. Dot had done some street duty in Perth, but he hadn't considered it dangerous, as no one carried guns. She'd never expressed a desire to go into any of the more dangerous areas like organised crime or the tactical response group. When he'd heard she'd moved back to Retribution Bay, he figured drunk and lost tourists were the most she had to worry about. Definitely not drug smuggling. "Should we search the island?"

"Dot will when she's finished documenting this." Sam swatted a fly buzzing around. "Do you want to do another dive?"

The wreck. He'd forgotten all about it. He should spend his time working, not worrying about the woman who'd left him. "Yeah."

"Sherlock, take him back to the boat. Get his tank refilled. There's food as well."

Sherlock nodded, unperturbed about being ordered around. "Let's go."

Dot was still focused on the drugs that had washed

up and wasn't paying any attention to him. Oliver debated saying something to her. No, better not to disturb her.

But it was with reluctance that he followed Sherlock back to the tender.

Chapter 4

Dot's shoulders relaxed the moment the tender engine growled to life. Oliver was gone. She exhaled and mentally shook herself to focus on the drugs in front of her. Their voices had carried to her and as much as she'd tried to block them out, she couldn't. Oliver's voice still had a warm timbre that sank deep into her soul, making her feel cared for and important.

It was ridiculous. Their relationship had ended a decade ago. It shouldn't affect her. The only reason it had was because she hadn't been prepared to see him.

The excuse soothed her even as part of her acknowledged it was a lie.

Oliver had been studying maritime archaeology at university when she'd met him at a party in Perth. She'd been at the police academy and determined not to let any guy get in her way. Not after Brandon Stokes had broken her heart.

Not that she'd ever let him know.

But Oliver had been persistently charming, had genuinely seemed to care for her, and she'd been so pathetically desperate for love that she'd let him sway her plans. She'd agreed to stay in Perth and start her police career there instead of heading home to Retribution Bay.

What a mistake.

She shook away the memory and took the last photo

before bagging the drugs. In the distance, the tender arrived at the *Oceanid* with only two people on board.

"Have you heard anything from Nhiari?" Sam asked.

Of course he hadn't left with the others. That was too much to ask for, but if she was honest, she'd grown used to having him around. "Not yet."

The search and rescue party had gone out this morning. Dot had been planning to join them when Sam had called about the drugs. "She's not answering her radio." Dot hoped Georgie was right and Lee, the man who had kidnapped Nhiari, was on their side. If it was true, Nhiari would be safe. If not, she might already be dead.

She squeezed her eyes closed and pushed the thought out of her head. She couldn't think like that. Her best friend was strong and capable. She would survive this.

Though, as her brother discovered, it only took one bullet to end a life.

The grief lurking constantly below the surface threatened to appear, and she forced it away. Clearing her throat, she said, "I'll bag this and then do a pass around the other islands to check if there's anymore."

"Oliver didn't see any signs underwater."

She flinched at his name.

Sam fell in step beside her. "So, there's history between you two."

Dot flashed him her back-off laser glare, but it bounced off.

"You haven't seen each other in how long—ten years?"

Her chest tightened, and she swallowed the urge to tell him to mind his own business. That would only make him more persistent. "About that."

"Quite a coincidence he should turn up now."

Dot narrowed her eyes. "What are you suggesting?"

"Stonefish brought Kurt to town to get information

out of Gretchen. They could have arranged for Oliver to come for the same reason."

She should have thought of that. Foolish. The tiny sliver of hope that Oliver had come to town because of her vanished. She hadn't thought herself an easy target, but it appeared she could be manipulated just like everyone else. With their contacts, Stonefish could have had a hand in who led the expedition. "Noted."

"Was it a bad break up?" Sam asked.

"That's none of your business."

"No, but I'm watching out for you."

Her radio crackled and a female voice came over. "Dot fifteen."

Dot's heart lurched. Nhiari was alive and using their secret code. She pressed her button. "Dot eleven." Then she switched to channel thirteen.

"Heading to the waterhole at sunset."

Dot exhaled. She was safe. "Want me to join you?"

"No, I need to be alone."

Odd. "You coming back tonight?"

"No."

"I'll check the lighthouse is working." Dot waited, but no response came. "Damn it."

"What was that about?" Sam asked.

She wiped away the sweat trickling down the back of her neck as hope filled her for the first time. "Nhiari's safe, and she wants me to call off the search."

Sam frowned. "How do you figure that?"

"It's a code we set up at the academy." Could she fully trust Sam? Waterhole meant Nhiari was safe. It was her happy place. Sunset meant she was to the west of where she had been. Dot had asked her if she needed rescuing and Nhiari's request to be alone meant to call off the search.

But the only reason to use the code was because she didn't trust who was listening. Was she worried about

Stonefish, or one of their officers?

It also meant she was working with Lee. But to what end?

"Could Lee have forced her to use it?"

Dot shook her head. "No, only we know what it means."

"What are you going to do now?"

"If I call off the search too soon, Stonefish will be suspicious. I'll keep them searching to the east of the ranges today." She switched back to the main channel on her radio.

"Dot, do you read?"

Dispatch.

"Yeah, what do you need?"

"What was the call about?"

They hadn't recognised Nhiari's voice. "Nothing, just testing something. I'm almost done here. Be back by midday."

"Copy."

Sam raised his eyebrows. "You didn't tell them Nhiari was safe."

"If she'd wanted them to know, she would have told them herself." Dot continued to bag the evidence. "I trust she knows what she's doing." But it didn't mean she would avoid the west of the ranges. In fact, she might head to the lighthouse this evening. It was her happy place and she could do with some time alone. If Nhiari was in the area, she'd make herself known.

Over by Sam's boat, Oliver was climbing back into the tender with Sherlock. His black wetsuit clung to his skin, proving he hadn't lost any of the muscle from his youth. If anything, he'd bulked out a bit, which made the suit fit him even better.

Not that she cared.

He'd be diving for at least forty minutes, so hopefully she would be gone before he surfaced.

Avoiding him wasn't the mature thing to do, but he was an extra stress she didn't need right now. She dusted the barrel for fingerprints and grinned. "Hallelujah." Finally a potential break. Four clear prints on the lip of the lid where someone had grabbed it to pick it up. Carefully she recorded them and then handed Sam a pair of gloves. "Help me put the barrel in the boat."

She showed him where to grab it to avoid smudging the fingerprints, and they carried it to the police boat.

"What's the likelihood of a match?"

"If they belong to whoever sold the barrel, it will be slim, but it might be from the culprits. If they match, we'll finally have a suspect." Though suspects had an annoying habit of disappearing or dying.

When she had collected all the evidence, she scanned the island. It wasn't overly wide, but took about half an hour to circumnavigate. The middle was full of shrubs and trees. A great place to hide.

"You want to do a loop?" Sam asked.

She nodded. Though she didn't want to put him in danger, she also knew he would follow no matter what she said. "Let's go."

The trees all grew slightly angled towards the southeast from years of sea breezes blowing them that way. Between them were wide enough patches of sand so they didn't have to force their way through. No footprints, but that wasn't surprising considering the severity of the storm which had passed through a few days ago.

"There should be a cave somewhere along here," Sam said.

Dot glanced at him. "Brandon tell you that?"

He blinked. "Yes."

Bullshit. He had a pretty good poker face, but her question had caught him off guard. "What aren't you telling me, Hackett?"

He hesitated, wincing slightly, and then sighed.

"Brandon's ancestor, Lilian Stokes, was shipwrecked here on the *Retribution* in the 1870s. We recently found her journal, which led us to the treasure. Her journal mentions a cave."

He had to be kidding. She placed her hands on her hips. "You didn't think the journal might be relevant to my investigation?"

He didn't answer.

Frustration welled in her and with it came anger. "I'm fed up of you all drip feeding me information as you think I need it. What else haven't you told me?"

His gaze was steady on hers. "Maybe we should do dinner at the Ridge."

Great. That meant there was a whole heap of information they'd neglected to tell her. "I should haul you all to the station."

"But you won't." Sam smiled at her. "The information had to be kept quiet until we found the treasure."

"I wouldn't have told anyone."

"We didn't want you to feel conflicted. I'll call Brandon when I get back and arrange dinner for tomorrow night." He pointed behind her. "There's the cave."

Dot clenched her teeth and turned. The cave was little more than an overhang which protected anything underneath from the elements—including footprints.

She jerked Sam back when he went to move inside. "It's not smooth." She pointed at the divots in the sand. "Someone has been here recently." The sand was too dry and soft to hold a proper print, but it still told a story.

"We believe Stonefish has been using a drone to spy on the Stokes," Sam said. "This would be a good place to set up. They could have a boat on the far side of the island, which no one would spot if the Stokes came to the beach."

Dot moved into the cave, pulling out her torch for better illumination. Had they left any rubbish behind?

She did a first pass, checking the sand and then running her beam over the limestone rock, searching for any holes where rubbish could be tucked.

Bingo.

She slipped on a glove and placed the end of a cigarette butt into an evidence bag.

"Nice find," Sam said.

She couldn't get her hopes up.

When they got back to the police boat, Oliver and Sherlock were on the deck of the *Oceanid*. "I'll drop you there," Dot said.

"You heading back now?"

"I want to loop past the other islands on the way."

Sam glanced at his boat and then back at her.

"I'm fine on my own. I want to make sure no other drugs have washed up."

"Good idea, especially since Oliver thinks this place will be heaving with treasure hunters any day."

Dot groaned. "I want to throttle Jordan for spreading the rumour."

Sam nodded. "He's just a kid. I couldn't have kept it a secret when I was ten."

That was beside the point. Her resources were already significantly overstretched. Oliver grabbed the rope Sam tossed him as they neared. He'd pulled the wetsuit down to his waist, giving her a nice view of his muscled chest. She remembered the thrill of running her hands over his skin, feeling his sharp intake of breath and rapid heartbeat that quickly led to other things.

Her face hot, she looked away as Sam climbed on board, but when Oliver didn't throw the rope back, she had to meet his gaze. His eyes were bluer than she remembered, more like a baby's blanket than a stormy ocean. Her heart twinged, and she hardened it. "I need the rope back."

He nodded and threw it onto the deck.

Dot accelerated away, ignoring her rapid heartbeat. She had been over him for years. His arrival in town reeked of Stonefish manipulation. She had to remember that.

She headed towards the first island, keeping an eye out for debris, and also on the depth. It could be tricky to navigate the coral around here, especially with the varying tides, and she didn't want to add her own boat to the list of shipwrecks in the area. At least the drugs would be enough to get the organised crime division up here. They couldn't ignore millions of dollars' worth of drugs washing ashore. The only problem was, she wanted to be the one to make the arrest. Stonefish had killed her brother.

Pushing aside her grief, she focused on the task at hand. It had been some time since she'd been in this area of the gulf on the water. She'd been to the shore, where the monument to the *Retribution* was, and it had been only a couple of kilometres away where she'd discovered her brother shot through the head.

Damn it. The memory flashed into her mind. Mark lying on his back, flies buzzing around him, a perfect hole in his forehead, and a mess at the back of his skull.

Her stomach heaved and she shoved the memory away. It was one more reason why she had to stop Stonefish.

She should have made more of an effort to be a better sister. Her parents hadn't cared for them, but she and Mark could have been a family.

She'd hoped becoming a police officer would stop him from his petty crime activities. She thought it had. But he'd just hidden it from her.

It was too late now.

Now she had to search for evidence. She'd been

meaning to explore the area more thoroughly, but something always cropped up that stopped her. Stonefish had to have some kind of haven here. They'd got planes in the air quickly after her brother was killed, but there'd been no sign of the dinghy the murderer had escaped in. He had to have hidden it somewhere.

Dot decreased her speed, splitting her attention between watching the water and scanning the shore of the nearby island. It would be more effective to go ashore, but Sam was right. It wasn't safe to go alone, especially not with Nhiari away. Her other three officers were capable, but on her suspect list.

She hoped she was being paranoid, suspecting everyone, but her gut and circumstances were hard to ignore.

Her radio squawked. "You on your way back, Sergeant Campbell?" Colin called.

"Almost. What's happening?"

"Got word from the airport. The plane that just landed is full of treasure hunters. There have been a few arguments at the hire cars, with everyone wanting one. Do we need to set up a checkpoint into town?"

She swore. Checkpoints worked at the height of the season when accommodation was booked out, but there were plenty of rooms available now. Perhaps they could stop people and tell them treasure hunting wouldn't be tolerated. "Yeah. Can you get Martin to help you?"

"He said to contact you. He got called out to the boat ramp."

"What about Pierre?"

"He's settling a dispute about a dog."

Damn it. "I'll be there as soon as I can." But it wouldn't be in time to catch those coming into town and telling them they were wasting their time. Even announcing they'd found the whole chest of treasure wouldn't help because it would just encourage people further. They would be sure there was more to be found.

Dot examined the two remaining islands she hadn't circled. Tomorrow.

With that thought in her mind, she gunned the engine towards town.

***

It was dark before Dot finished at the roadblock. They might have missed all the people who had flown in, but what seemed like every single person within driving distance of Retribution Bay had arrived. Most swore they had booked days ahead, and the announcement of treasure had nothing to do with why they were coming to town, but they were lying. It was going to be a nightmare. She could hardly forbid the boat hire companies from renting their boats. It was extra revenue for them during the low season.

She called Sam and gave him the heads up. They would have to monitor the site. Maybe they could mark out the no-go zone with buoys, although it would pinpoint exactly where the wreck was.

Too tired to brainstorm solutions today, she climbed into the car and her stomach growled. She hadn't eaten since breakfast and her fridge was empty.

With a sigh, she pulled into the shopping centre car park and went into the supermarket. Lindsay was behind the cash register as she often was at this time of the day. A fixture in the town with her now greying blonde hair, and a few more wrinkles on her face than when Dot had worked here as a teenager. She still wore a blue polo shirt with the store logo in the left-hand corner, and a single pearl necklace. The only gift from a lover over thirty years ago who could not marry her due to family obligations. He'd broken her heart again when he'd turned up at the beginning of the year, vowing to leave his wife for her, but she hadn't heard from him since.

A lesson Dot should learn from in relation to Oliver.

"Dot Campbell, you look dead on your feet." Lindsay smiled at the customer she was serving. "I'll be right back." She pulled a plastic chair over and patted it. "Sit down for a minute."

Dot's feet took her towards the chair before she pulled herself up. "If I sit, I won't get up."

Lindsay grinned. "You can sleep here if you need to."

Dot smiled for the first time today. "Thanks. I'll be back in a minute." With a little more energy, she trudged to the frozen food section and perused the options of ready-made microwave meals. Using the step ladder which was always around because Lindsay was as vertically challenged as Dot, she grabbed a couple of Indian curries and went via the milk section to get two litres before returning to the front. The customer was gone and Lindsay had flicked the sign to closed. At the front of the counter were a couple of buckets full of flower bouquets, the colours enough to make her smile. Dot debated buying one. No, she wouldn't be home much to enjoy them and it would remind her how lonely she was.

Lindsay tutted as she rang up Dot's purchases. "You're not taking care of yourself." She took two of Dot's favourite chocolate bars from the nearby shelf and tucked them into Dot's bag.

"Lindsay, you don't need to do that."

"Nonsense. Someone needs to look after you. You haven't stopped working since you started with me as a fresh-faced fourteen-year-old."

"I could say the same about you." Lindsay had been her lifeline then, giving her as many shifts as she wanted. Working with Lindsay, who always seemed happy to see her, had been preferable to the disinterest her parents showed her.

"It's not really work. I pay myself to listen to gossip

all day and ring up a few groceries."

Dot straightened. Lindsay knew everything going on in town. "What gossip have you heard today?"

Lindsay waggled her finger at Dot. "Don't you use your sergeant tone on me. If you want gossip, you're going to have to have dinner with me. I put a meal in the slow cooker this morning, and it will be ready by now. Go home, have a shower, and I'll be around in thirty with food."

The temptation was too strong. Lindsay's slow-cooked meals were heaven. Dot slung her bag of groceries over her shoulder and then squeezed Lindsay's hand. "All right. Thank you."

She waited while Lindsay put the day's earnings away and locked up, and then drove home. The police station was dark, and the others were already home.

Except Nhiari.

Damn, she hadn't gone to the lighthouse. It was too late now with Lindsay coming over. Tomorrow. Dot sighed and unlocked the door. She needed a break. It had been years since her last holiday. She frowned. When had she last gone away?

Maybe three years ago when she'd visited a friend in Karratha. They'd gone to the police academy together, and she and Nhiari had decided to get away. Except Ryan's wife had been a jealous woman, and hadn't liked him spending any time with them, so they'd gone camping in Karijini instead.

Ryan had since left his wife and taken his son to Blackbridge and was working with his best friend, Lincoln, at the station there.

He'd mentioned something about coming to Retribution Bay before Christmas. She'd have to find where she'd written the dates. It must be fairly soon.

She dumped her keys on the table and continued through to the bathroom to shower. The bright pink of the towels perked her up and made her smile as she turned on the taps. The water hit her, warm and refreshing, and she tilted her head backwards to let it run over her face. Lindsay was right. She needed a break. But that was impossible until she stopped Stonefish.

The fingerprints and cigarette butt were packaged ready for shipping to Carnarvon and the organised crime division would be here tomorrow. There was a measure of relief to be getting extra help.

Perhaps so many years in the country had dulled her skills. She'd been stuck in Perth for years, and she'd hated the anonymity of it all. Not being able to connect with people, not knowing who they were. It didn't matter how hard she worked, or the extra responsibilities she had, she'd kept coming back to wanting that face-to-face contact, wanting to know about those people she helped.

When she'd left Retribution Bay, she'd considered finding another small town to work in, but Nhiari always said the land and its people got stuck under your skin, it was in their blood, and she was right. The moment Dot had returned, she'd felt at home. Connection. Community.

She turned the water off, the accompanying thunk speaking of an old house with old pipes. By the time she'd dressed and poured a couple of glasses of wine, she was ready to eat. She flicked on her favourite playlist, the rock tunes helping to push away today's stress.

The knock on the door made her smile. This was what she needed. A night with the woman who'd been more like a mother to her than her own. She swung open the door. "I'm starving—"

Oliver.

He gave a half smile from behind the bunch of brightly coloured flowers he held. "Sorry, I'm not sure if these are edible." His dimple deepened and her gut clenched as she remembered kissing that spot.

Her smile faded. "What are you doing here?"

Oliver held out the flowers and she took them automatically. It was a collection of gerberas with a single red rose in the middle. He'd been to Lindsay's supermarket today. Which meant Lindsay knew he was in town, and she had said nothing. Perhaps that was the real reason behind her invitation to dinner. Or maybe she hadn't recognised him.

"I wanted to say thank you for rescuing us yesterday."

She scowled. "I wouldn't leave you stranded."

"I still appreciate it." He brushed his sun-bleached strawberry-blond hair back. "Did you find anything else this afternoon?"

Dot stiffened. Was he fishing for information? "That's not your concern." She had to get rid of him before Lindsay arrived. "Thank you for the flowers." She started to close the door as another car pulled up out front. Damn it.

Lindsay got out with a wave and then reached into the back seat for a large pot. As she came over, she grinned. "Oliver, nice to see you again."

"Likewise, Lindsay."

The betrayal was sharp. So she had known he was here. Dot had to stop this before Lindsay invited him for dinner. "He was just leaving." She shepherded Lindsay inside. "I'll see you around." She closed the door before either of them said anything else.

"That was rude," Lindsay said. "The man brought you flowers."

Dot said nothing as she dumped the bouquet on the bench. "You knew he was in town."

She nodded. "I would have called, but he said he'd already seen you." Lindsay set the crock pot on the sink while Dot got plates out.

"You rented your place to him," Dot said, her muscles tense. "You could have warned me days ago."

Lindsay held up a hand. "The university booked it. I didn't make the connection until he walked into the supermarket."

Oliver wasn't a common name, but Lindsay had only spent a short amount of time with him. He probably hadn't seeped into her thoughts and memories like he had with Dot.

Besides, Lindsay was a hopeless romantic, always looking for a happily ever after.

"How are you feeling about it, hon?" Lindsay found a vase and filled it with water.

Dot wanted to tell her not to bother, that she would throw them in the bin as soon as Lindsay left, but it would just make her ask more questions. "I'm fine. Why wouldn't I be?" She cringed at her rookie mistake. Never ask Lindsay a rhetorical question.

"Because he was the love of your life, and he shattered your heart into a million pieces when he flew away without a backwards glance."

"I'm surprised you let him buy anything from your store."

"When he said they were for you, I thought maybe he'd seen the error in his ways."

"Linds, it was years ago. If he had actually missed me, he would have been back a lot sooner."

Lindsay smiled that knowing smile some mothers had. The one which read far too much into the words than what she meant. She dished up the curry and carried the bowls to the table. "He said you never responded to his calls."

Shit. She hadn't even considered the fact Oliver might run into Lindsay, hadn't thought they would remember each other since she'd only brought him home once for a short week-long visit. "He left me."

"For a temporary job."

Dot shoved the curry into her mouth. She wasn't

defending her decision. He had betrayed her, hadn't even discussed it with her. He proved she wasn't important enough to him. She didn't inspire loyalty or dedication. Even Nhiari had returned home when she'd got the chance. "This is good curry."

"You can keep the leftovers, so you have more than one decent meal this week."

"I'm going out to the Ridge for dinner tomorrow." She sipped her wine. "Tell me about the rumours you've been hearing about treasure."

Lindsay raised her eyebrows, acknowledging the change in topic, before saying, "*Everyone's* talking about it. There wasn't a single person who came in today who didn't ask me what I knew."

Just perfect. Dot didn't have to just worry about tourist treasure hunters, she'd have to be concerned about the whole town as well. "And what do you know?"

"Less than you, I'm sure." Lindsay took a bite of her food. "Jordan showed up at school on Friday with a gold doubloon, which was then stolen from him and shown around the school. At lunch, he was kidnapped and was later found safe, but Nhiari was taken as a substitute."

It was close enough to the truth. "Where do people think the treasure came from?"

"That shipwreck Oliver is investigating. People believe Georgie Stokes found the treasure when she found the wreck."

Dot cursed inwardly. They had tried to keep Georgie's involvement quiet. "Why do people think Georgie found the wreck?"

"Because Tony loaned Georgie his boat a couple of days before the discovery was announced and Georgie had been in the area. She'd told him she was doing Parks and Wildlife business, but if that had been the case, she would have taken their boat."

Sometimes intelligent people were the bane of Dot's

existence. "Why keep searching if they think the treasure has already been found?"

"People are always looking for a get rich quick scheme. The romance and fantasy of it all is too much of a temptation."

"You'd be doing me a huge favour if you told people to stay away. Oliver and his team don't need people swarming the shipwreck, and I don't have the staff to guard it day and night."

"You don't believe anything is there?"

"If there is, it's government property. It's illegal to take anything off a shipwreck in Australian waters." She sighed at her briskness and softened her tone. "But no, I don't think there's anything there."

"Where did the doubloon come from then?" Lindsay asked.

"There's no proof there ever was a doubloon. Myra said she confiscated it, but it's disappeared. It was probably some old bit of metal that had been painted gold."

Lindsay looked sceptical, but she said, "I'll advise people to stay away."

"Thanks, Linds, I appreciate it."

"Anything for you, you know that." She stood and cleared the dishes. "Any news on Nhiari?"

"No." Dot ignored the guilt of lying to Lindsay. "But she'll be all right. She can hold her own."

"I hope so. That Lee seemed like such a nice guy when he came into the supermarket."

Dot murmured in agreement and then frowned. "Who mentioned Lee to you?"

Lindsay tilted her head, thinking. "Holly mentioned him when she came to get ice cream today."

That made sense. Holly's son, Cody, had been kidnapped and held by Lee.

"It's been a hard few months, hasn't it?" Lindsay said.

"Who would have thought Retribution Bay to be a hot spot for animal smuggling and poaching?"

Though Dot trusted Lindsay, there were things she couldn't tell her. Dot took her time before answering. "It's been surprising." Someone in town had to be involved. They'd caught one person, but he wasn't talking about who he'd been working with. She was tempted to ask Lindsay if she'd heard rumours about that as well, but she didn't want her friend involved. Stonefish could target Lindsay if she started asking questions. "What have you been up to?"

"Work keeps me pretty busy. There was talk about starting a swimming club and someone asked me to play bridge with them."

Dot glanced at her. "Who?"

Lindsay busied herself washing the dishes. "Mitchell."

"From Parks and Wildlife?" Mitchell was several years younger than Lindsay.

Red tinged Lindsay's cheeks. "Yes. He needed a partner, and he heard I like cards."

Dot grinned. It wasn't often Lindsay avoided her gaze. "He's nice." And he'd been cleared from any involvement in the poaching.

"Yes, he is."

"You deserve to be happy." And Dot was pleased Lindsay was moving on from her mysterious lover. It had been almost a year since he'd promised to be back as soon as he'd left his wife.

"Thank you, hon." She patted Dot's arm. "So do you. Don't dismiss Oliver out of hand. He might have his own reasons."

Dot pulled away and put the kettle on. She'd had her heart broken twice now. She would not make it a third time.

"Have you seen your parents recently?" Lindsay asked as she got out the mugs.

"Not since last month." Lindsay was great at finding topics Dot didn't want to talk about.

"Are they still grieving over Mark?"

She flinched at her brother's name. "Not that you would know." They'd left her to do everything after Mark had been shot. She'd arranged the funeral, sorted out probate, done the paperwork because of course he hadn't written a will, and then put all his stuff in storage until the state could rule on who should get his things.

"Don't be too hard on them. Everyone grieves differently."

Dot's temper flared. "They never cared about him when he was alive, so why would they start now?"

Lindsay sighed. "I know. I'm trying to give them the benefit of the doubt."

Lindsay saw the good in everyone. Dot envied her a little, but she had seen too much evidence proving people were inherently selfish.

As if on cue, her phone rang and she groaned as her mother's name appeared on the screen. With an apologetic smile at Lindsay, she answered. "Hi, Mum."

"Dot, when are we coming to dinner this month?"

She blinked in surprise. Since when had her parents offered to come to dinner? "I've been really busy. I'm not sure I'll have time this month."

"All this work around the treasure must be taxing."

The truth hit her. She wasn't interested in seeing Dot. She wanted to know what Dot knew.

"You should take some time out to see family."

Dot glanced at Lindsay. That's exactly what she was doing tonight, not that she'd ever tell her mother. "I'm sorry, I don't have time at the moment."

"Well then, if that's the case, why don't you tell me what the doubloon looked like? I'm dying to know."

The disappointment never went away. Perhaps one day she would stop expecting more from her parents.

"There was no doubloon, Mum. I need to go. I'll call you later." She hung up before her mother could say anything further.

Lindsay smiled sympathetically from the kitchen where she was making a single mug of tea. "I should get going," she said. "It's an early start tomorrow, and you need your rest." She hugged Dot, and Dot clung to her for a moment longer than she should. "Any time you need me, I'll be here."

Dot's vision blurred and she blinked to clear it. "Thanks for dinner."

"You're welcome." Lindsay squeezed her hand and closed the front door behind her. Dot exhaled, shaking off the heaviness which always came with dealing with her parents.

She settled on her couch with the tea, taking a small sip and then smiling at the taste. Lindsay knew exactly how much sugar to add. She closed her eyes and let go of the tension. She had to make time for the people she cared for. It wasn't a long list, but it had grown over the past year to include the extended Stokes family.

The thought brought her right back to Nhiari.

She checked her phone but there were no messages. Nhiari would spend her second night with her kidnapper. At least Dot knew she could take care of herself. She knew about bush tucker and where to find water thanks to her indigenous heritage, and Lee had been living in the ranges for months now.

She glanced at her backpack by the door. She really should go through the information she'd gathered and see if the discovery of drugs added anything to the picture. Then tomorrow she would drill the Stokes for all the information they had.

All she wanted to do was go to bed.

With a sigh, she got up, switched her music on and got to work.

Chapter 5

Sam's satellite phone rang as Oliver boarded the *Oceanid* from the tender. He'd spent the morning scanning the ocean floor and was keen to get in for his first dive.

"It's for you." Sam passed the phone to Oliver.

The waves pushed the boat up and he fumbled with the phone, almost dropping it in the water. Heart racing, he said, "Hello."

"You were supposed to call me last night."

Oliver almost wished the phone had ended up overboard. How had Lucas got Sam's number? "Morning, Lucas."

"What's this I hear about treasure hunters heading for Retribution Bay? Are you protecting my shipwreck?"

Oliver winced. *His* shipwreck, as if he owned it. Sam was helping Sherlock tie the tender to the boat, so Oliver headed for the cabin for some privacy. "We've seen no sign of treasure hunters yet."

"What about treasure?"

Oliver chuckled. "You know how rumours spread. I've been down there and haven't seen anything that looks like treasure. We're starting our grid search this afternoon."

"Why haven't you started it yet?"

"Conditions haven't been good for diving," Oliver replied. "I could barely see two metres yesterday." He didn't mention the drugs. Not that anyone had told him to keep it quiet, but Lucas would flip out if he heard of it. The risk of the police cancelling the dive while they investigated would really rile him up. "Conditions are great today," he continued. "The team is surfacing from the first dive now."

At the back of the boat, Suzyn and Andrew were inflating their BCDs as they surfaced. Oliver headed out to help. "I'll call you with an update this evening."

"Do that."

Oliver shook his head, pushing past his annoyance as he handed the phone back to Sam and helped Suzyn aboard. "How did it go?"

"Amazing," she said, prying off her fins. "I can't believe it's been down there, undisturbed, for three hundred years." She stumbled a little as she climbed onto the main deck and Oliver steadied her before turning to help Andrew, but he was already pushing past, heading straight for the bathroom. Oliver winced as the sound of vomiting followed. It turned out Andrew suffered from a severe case of seasickness. The only time he wasn't retching was when he was underwater. Hopefully he could handle tomorrow's forecast of smaller swells, otherwise it was going to be a miserable couple of weeks for him.

Andrew should have said something about it before coming.

This morning the four students had set up the grid they would work, while Oliver had used their scanning equipment in the tender to take photos of the bottom of the ocean.

Unfortunately the work hadn't kept him busy enough to keep his thoughts off Dot.

His visit hadn't gone to plan. He hadn't expected her to welcome him with open arms, but a smile would have been nice. He'd bought the biggest bunch of flowers he could find at Lindsay's prompting, and since she'd been an important person in Dot's life, he'd figured it was a good sign.

But Dot didn't want a bar of him.

Which was inconvenient. His plan had been to ask her how she'd been, find out why she'd ghosted him and then leave. He had more than enough on his plate right now without splitting his focus thinking about their past. This was his first expedition as lead, the first without his team, and the first with a bunch of newbies.

But he couldn't deny that his heartbeat had increased when she'd opened the door, hair damp from a shower, and wearing a short, bright emerald green dress which ended just above her knees, exposing her lovely legs. He touched the ring around his neck and smiled. She still loved bright colours.

"Want a drink, Oliver?" Suzyn's call had him blinking and glancing over.

The rest of the students had already dived on lunch like a bunch of seagulls.

"I'll be right there," Oliver replied.

Sam wandered over. "What's the plan for this afternoon?"

"Another dive, or maybe two, where we'll document the wreck, looking for identification." It lay at about ten metres deep, so they could stay underwater longer than if it had been deeper, though the students used up their air far quicker than he did. "Have you two got a good book?" He nodded towards Sherlock.

Sam chuckled. "We're used to waiting around. One of us will monitor you, while the other does work on the boat." He tapped the railing affectionately. "She's officially mine now. The season has ended, and the previous owner is moving away. I can make the adjustments I want to make without worrying about offending him." He smiled. "Plus I have to reapply for my tour licence which is going to take forever. I've got plenty to keep me busy."

"Great."

Occasionally they'd get a captain who grew bored and tried to make demands, even though they'd hired the boat for the duration of the expedition. Some had tried to make them head in early because of weather forecasts, so Oliver had studied weather charts and conditions and made a point of knowing a little about it so as not to be fooled.

He helped himself to a plate of salad and cold meat. There wasn't anything too heavy, which he appreciated. Sam had provided the food as part of the charge of hiring the boat, which made it one less thing he had to spend time on.

Somewhere in the distance, he heard the rumble of an engine. Both he and Sam glanced up at the same time. He strode to the side of the boat. A small aluminium dinghy was making its way towards them, a couple of fishing rods protruding at the back.

Were they coming over to see what was going on, or were they planning to fish the area?

Neither option was ideal.

Oliver ate his lunch while it approached. The dive flag had been set up above the wreck for the day.

The dinghy skirted the tour boat and dropped its anchor close to the dive flag. Two men on board started putting on dive gear. Shit. They had to be having a laugh. He placed his plate on the table. "Can I use the tender?"

"I'll drive you over," Sam replied.

They moved quickly and reached the dinghy as the men were about to go over. Oliver yelled to get their attention, and they hesitated. Would they ignore the hail?

Sam gunned the engine and brought them alongside the dinghy before the men could reach a decision.

"Hey," Oliver called, trying for jovial when he wanted to yell. "This area is temporarily off-limits for divers."

The man who replied was old enough to be Oliver's father and had grey hair and the tanned leathery skin of someone who had spent their life in the sun. "There's a dive flag right there."

Oliver nodded. "For my team. I'm from the Shipwrecks Museum. We're cataloguing a shipwreck."

"Really?" The man faked surprise. "I didn't know."

He wouldn't win any acting awards. "Yeah. Did you know it's illegal to remove anything from a shipwreck in Australian waters?"

"You don't say."

"Do you also know those rumours of treasure are bullshit?" Sam added. "There's nothing down there but anchors and cannons."

Oliver made a mental note to ask Sam how he knew. Instead, he smiled at the men. "You'll need to find somewhere else to dive for a few weeks."

"You don't own the ocean."

"No, but this is a temporary no-go zone if you don't have permission, and you don't have permission."

The younger man of the two tapped the older guy on the shoulder. "Let's go, Dad."

The older man growled. "Damned politics." He undid his BCD vest and dumped it on the bottom of the dinghy, making it rock. His son looked apologetic and waved as they sped away.

Oliver exhaled. "That's the first of many." He scanned the horizon and saw another boat heading their way. He swore.

Sam followed his gaze as they drove back to the *Oceanid*. "Sherlock and I can police the surface while you're under."

"Thanks." Hopefully the ex-army men would be enough to scare would be treasure hunters away. "How do you know what's down there?"

He grinned. "Penelope and I dived it after Georgie found it. We didn't touch anything, just wanted to see it for ourselves."

"Were you searching for treasure?"

Sam laughed. "Nope. I like to dive new places and Penelope is getting back into diving. It seemed like a good option."

Oliver studied him, looking for a lie, and couldn't find it. When they tied up to the *Oceanid*, Suzyn asked, "What did they want?"

"Treasure," Oliver said. He had planned to go back to town every night, but maybe he should talk to Sam about overnighting on the boat. That way he could keep an eye on things.

Andrew pushed open the bathroom door, his skin pale, almost green. Oliver cringed. He couldn't do that to Andrew, but he could buy a tent and camping gear in town and sleep on the island.

"Can the police protect it?" she asked.

He hadn't thought about Dot.

Sam answered. "They're stretched as it is right now. One of their officers is missing, and the storm caused a lot of issues in town."

"Missing?" Andrew asked. "How do you misplace an officer?"

"She was searching in the ranges for two children who were kidnapped," Sherlock replied. "People get lost in them all the time."

The students gaped at him, but Andrew said, "She mustn't be much of a cop then."

"She's an excellent officer," Sam said, his tone grim.

"All right, let's focus on the task," Oliver said before things got out of hand. "Gather around and we'll review the details of the next dive."

The last thing he needed was his students offending Sam and Sherlock.

"We've got a wreck to identify."

***

"They've sent the names of the officers coming up from the organised crime division," Martin said as he walked into Dot's office holding a piece of paper.

"Thanks." Dot scanned the names and swore. This had to be a joke. Of all the people they could have sent…

"Something wrong, boss?" Martin asked.

She shook her head and plastered on a smile. "It's fine. What time does the plane get in?"

"In an hour."

Great. Barely enough time to do anything before she had to be at the airport to pick them up. "Right. I imagine they'll want to look at what we found and then head out to the island to see for themselves. I'll take them if you can handle things here."

"Of course I can." Martin pulled himself up to his full height as if she'd offended him.

Dot smothered a sigh. She didn't have the energy to deal with his ego today. "Great."

She waited until he left and then glanced down at the list of names again. Rodney Taylor. She had hoped to never see him again. It didn't surprise her he was now part of the organised crime division. At the academy he had always bragged that he was going places. He didn't want to be a street cop for long. He was after promotion and excitement, and he hadn't cared who he pushed out of his way to get it.

Dot was glad Nhiari wasn't here. Rodney had tormented her all during the academy, and Nhiari hated him with a passion. Dot's dislike wasn't quite as violent, but it was close.

She could only hope he'd matured and discovered that treading on people wasn't the way to succeed.

Still, the thought of having to be polite and professional to him made her skin crawl.

She checked her notes on the case and then went into the evidence room to make sure everything was in order and to gather the items that needed to be sent to Perth on the next plane. Satisfied everything was correct, she finally drove to the airport to greet Rodney and his team, picking up the keys for their hire car when she arrived.

The three men who disembarked all carried themselves with the same arrogance, ignoring parents who were carrying children and a million bags, side-stepping couples who were taking selfies of their arrival and only when they stepped through the doors, did they look around for her.

Rodney's instant sneer confirmed all of Dot's expectations. She braced herself and smiled, holding out a hand. "Rodney. It's been a long time."

He frowned in mock confusion. "Have we met before?"

So that was how he was going to play it. He would have been given her name before he'd come here. "Dot Campbell. We went through the academy together." She smiled. "It's been a decade and we all forget things as we get older." Before he could retort, she turned to his colleagues and introduced herself. "I've arranged a hire car. Do you want to go to your accommodation first, or get straight to work?"

"We'll get straight to work," Rodney said.

Dot held out the keys. "Then follow me." She had expected at least one of the three officers would travel with her if only to ask questions about the case, but they all got into the hire car and tailed her back to the station.

Rodney greeted Martin and Pierre with courtesy, schmoozing in a way men did only with other men.

"Martin, why don't you show us where the evidence is?" Rodney said.

Dot forced her jaw to relax as she debated pulling rank. No, it would be petty. Martin could explain what had happened. "I'll be in my office when you're ready to go out to the scene."

Pierre was the only one who acknowledged her words with a slight nod.

It was incredible how Rodney made her feel so powerless in her own station. She entered her office and mentally shook off the hit to her confidence. She'd let him get to her at the academy, but she wouldn't let him make her feel inferior in her own town. He could go to hell. Sitting at her computer, she reached for the phone and rang the crime centre. "I've sent evidence on today's flight. How long will it be to get a result?"

"We've got minimal staff today and a bit of a backlog," the person answered. "Should have them by the end of the day on Tuesday or Wednesday."

She gritted her teeth to stop herself from declaring that her evidence was more important. They had their priorities.

She flicked over the incident reports from the past few days. Nothing particularly noteworthy, though the domestic reports from the Hamiltons seemed to have increased in the past month. She'd have to talk to Kristy, and convince them to go into counselling. It hadn't escalated to violence yet, but their arguments were heard all down the street.

Some relationships weren't meant to be.

Oliver popped into her head, looking refreshed and sexy like he had last night, with the beautiful bouquet of flowers in his hands.

Damn him for remembering her weakness. Flowers were such a lovely way of showing someone you were thinking of them, and gerberas were her favourite.

Her heart squeezed painfully, threatening to start feeling something for him again. She couldn't do that. It made her far too vulnerable, and she refused to be fooled a second time.

She exhaled.

But it was also quite likely that Lindsay had suggested it, manipulating him into coming to see Dot. The woman was the worst sort of matchmaker. Dot frowned.

She didn't want Oliver in her town, didn't want to keep running into him. It hurt too much. Maybe Sam could recommend they stay on the boat at the dive site. Then the only chance there'd be of her seeing Oliver was when he left.

That sounded like a good idea.

She lifted her phone to call when a report came in about someone speeding through town. "Pierre, Colin, can you see to that?"

The men left, though both glanced back at the evidence room as if they wanted to stay. It wasn't often they had visiting police in the station, and the drug squad was rare.

The others came out of the room and Rodney spoke. "Martin is going to take us to the island."

Like hell he was. Dot smiled politely but shook her head. "He hasn't been involved in this case like I have, and he's needed here. I'll take you." She grabbed her keys, waiting for him to argue the point, but surprisingly, he didn't. "This way."

This was her station, and she was in charge.

***

Oliver heard the boat as he finished his last rest break for the day. He smothered a groan and moved up to the top deck to get a better look at the next lot of treasure hunters. Sherlock was already there, and he handed Oliver the binoculars. "It's Dot with some others. They must be from Perth because I don't recognise them."

Oliver's heart jumped as he spotted Dot behind the wheel. Next to her was a man who looked kind of familiar. His hooked nose and dark, almost buzz cut hair tickled part of his memory, but he couldn't quite place him. His only run-ins with police had been when Dot was at the academy.

The memory clicked into place and he groaned. "Son of a bitch."

"What's wrong?" Sherlock asked, taking the binoculars back.

"The guy next to Dot went to the academy with her. He was an arrogant asshole, always trying to belittle and one-up the rest of the cadets, especially the women. Dot and Nhiari hated him."

"That's not good," Sherlock said.

No, it wasn't. Their antagonism towards each other had been legendary, but only away from the senior officers' eyes. Rodney was always the model officer when they were around. Which made him even more toxic.

Dot slowed as she approached the boat, and Oliver climbed down to the lower deck to see her.

Sam caught the rope as she idled the engine.

"I told you to take us directly to the island," Rodney said, glaring at Dot.

Dot ignored him and addressed Oliver instead. "When are you going under again?"

He smiled. Suddenly he was preferable to Rodney, though that wasn't saying much. No one was lower than Rodney. "Maybe twenty minutes."

She turned to Rodney. "Oliver and Sam discovered the drugs. Did you want to interview them?"

"I want to see the island first."

"We could show you where we found the barrel," Sam said. "Shouldn't take more than half an hour. You wouldn't want to hold up the researchers any more than you have to. They're on a tight schedule."

The man had a knack for being reasonable and non-confrontational. Seemingly harmless, though Oliver had seen how quickly he shifted to alert and ready.

Rodney hesitated, but it seemed like he couldn't come up with a reasonable excuse to refuse as he said, "Fine. Get on board."

Oliver called to his students, "Get ready for the next dive, but wait until I get back."

They all watched with interest as he climbed into the police boat. The idea of an undiscovered shipwreck was excitement enough for them, but add in the rumours of treasure and the drugs and it was probably more than they'd dreamed of.

He would have been fascinated at their age. Now, it was just a pain in the arse.

He smiled at Dot, but she had already turned her attention back to the wheel and was navigating away from the *Oceanid*. The bags under her eyes weren't as dark today, though her posture was just as tense, but that could be because Rodney was near.

Sam shook Rodney's hand as he introduced himself and said, "This is Oliver Anderson. He's leading the expedition."

Rodney's eyes narrowed, and he glanced between Dot and Oliver. Maybe he remembered the name. Oliver nodded at him. "Nice to see you again, Rodney," he lied.

When they reached the shore, Rodney took charge. "Where did you find the barrel?"

Sam took out his phone and checked the screen, walking with it for a hundred metres before he stopped. "Here."

"That's precise," Rodney said.

Sam smirked. "GPS."

"Then I guess you know where the drugs landed too." The challenge was clear.

"Yeah. I sent Dot the coordinates."

Before Rodney could speak, Dot said, "They're in the pack I put together for you."

Oliver kept his expression neutral, but inwardly he smiled as Rodney puffed up like a rooster on display.

"I don't have time to read everything. Take me through exactly what happened."

Dot stepped back and let Sam lead. Oliver added some information when he deemed necessary, but it was a laborious process as Rodney questioned them again and again, as if waiting for them to trip up.

Dickhead.

Oliver had done his own calculations last night based on the storm data and knew where he would dive to check if there were any more barrels, but he hadn't told Dot yet. No way was he telling Rodney.

Finally, after an hour of going through the same information, he'd had enough. "I need to get back to my students. We've told you everything."

Rodney glowered. "You're finished when I say you're finished."

Oliver smirked. Always the power play. He'd never met a man who lacked as much confidence as Rodney. Oliver almost felt sorry for him.

"Oliver doesn't need to be here," Sam said. "I found the drugs and can answer all your questions. He joined me on the island after his dive, as it was closer than swimming back to the boat."

Rodney hesitated and then nodded. "Take him back, Sergeant Campbell."

Dot stiffened but nodded.

Finally, a chance to speak with her alone. He waited until they were away from the others before he said, "Rodney hasn't changed, has he?"

She glanced at him. "I'm surprised you remember him."

Was she kidding? "He made yours and Nhiari's life a nightmare," he said. "Of course I remember him."

She moved across to the anchor and brought it back to the boat.

"I hope he doesn't give you any trouble."

Dot shrugged. "I can hold my own now."

"You could then," he said.

Her glare was laser hot. "Don't."

"Don't what?" he challenged. "Don't remember the time we were together? You want me to pretend that part of my life never happened?"

"Yeah. You've been doing a stellar job of it so far." She accelerated away from the shore and the engine noise blocked any retort he could make.

He gritted his teeth. She acted as if she was the wounded party here. That wasn't right.

She'd broken his heart.

He moved closer so he could shout, but she was already slowing, the *Oceanid* right in front of them. Too many ears around for a conversation which should be had in private.

He exhaled, breathing through his frustration. He wasn't finished with her yet.

Not by a long shot.

Chapter 6

After dealing with Rodney all day, the last thing Dot had the energy for was the hour-long drive out to the Ridge for dinner, but they had information pertinent to the case. Rodney had already dismissed her, so she had nothing else to do which couldn't wait until tomorrow. Besides, the Stokes family had been fighting Stonefish for longer than she had and had just as much at stake to catch them. She needed their information. With a heavy sigh, her fatigue causing her to drag her feet, she headed out of her office. "Where are we at?"

Colin was the only one who glanced up. "Clean-up is going well. Most residents have power again and the trees have all been cleared from the road."

Dot nodded, impressed. Colin had really stepped up after the storm, taking on more responsibility and working unaccompanied. "Pierre?"

"A couple of car park bingles this morning, and some arguments at the boat ramp this afternoon. Nothing major."

Nothing excited Pierre, though he'd been put out that he hadn't been involved in any of the Stonefish busts. He wasn't alone in that feeling. She and Nhiari had arrived too late due to the Stokes keeping secrets. Dot braced herself as she turned to the last man. "Martin?"

"Business as usual, boss."

She stopped herself from cringing at the nickname. It was his way of reminding her she'd got the promotion to sergeant-in-charge over him, although he'd worked in Retribution Bay most of his career.

"Great. I'll see you all tomorrow."

"Sarge, what are we doing about the search for Nhiari?" Colin asked.

Interesting that he should be the only one to ask. She sighed. "I'll call the State Emergency Service. We'll need to scale it back tomorrow and get the volunteers working on the next stage of cleanup."

Martin swivelled his chair around. "You haven't heard from her?"

"No," Dot lied, meeting his gaze. "But I have to put the town's recovery before one person. She would want it that way."

"What about the radio call you received yesterday?"

"Just someone messing around with the police frequency." She wasn't ready to let them know Nhiari was safe. Not until she knew who all the players were. She checked her watch. "I need to go. Any other questions?"

"Where are you going?" Pierre asked.

"Out to dinner," Dot said. "I'll see you in the morning." She walked out.

Dot stopped at home only long enough to get changed before she drove out to the Ridge. Penelope and Sam were driving with Gretchen, Sherlock, and Jordan. No room for her.

She could organise a lift with Georgie, but Dot liked having her own wheels and could use the drive to think. If she went with Georgie, her friend would talk non-stop.

As always when she drove into the sheep station, her

heart gave a pang at the angry-looking ram on the sign. She'd spent time out here when she dated Brandon during high school and had spent afternoons with his brothers, Charlie and Ed, drawing landscapes if Brandon was needed on the station. Charlie had been an excellent artist and the only time he had stayed still for more than a minute was when he was drawing or painting. Those memories were some of her fondest from her childhood. Brandon's mother, Beth, had been welcoming and nurturing, and seemed to understand Dot's need for the comforts of home.

Charlie's death had come as a shock to them all.

She blinked back the tears. Then Beth and Bill had died far too soon.

She swallowed hard, stopping to get her emotions under control and to let Lara's pet sheep, Flotsam and Jetsam, wander across the road to the next patch of grass. All the horses were in the horse yard and there were a couple of caravans in the campground, people already coming back to the area after the storm.

Maybe when this was all over, she could get back to Faith's horse-riding lessons and spend time at the Ridge riding with her friends.

Across at the large shed, a tarp still covered the section of the roof where panels had blown off.

The utes were parked outside, indicating the farmers were back for the day and she heard banging and voices in the shed. Rather than heading over, she walked up the steps of the verandah. Through the kitchen door, she spotted Lara doing homework and Ed sitting next to her, helping. Dot jolted. She'd forgotten Ed and Tess had come up from Perth to help clean up after the storm. She tapped on the door frame and let herself in.

Both Ed and Lara looked up at the same time and smiled. "Hey, Dot."

Dot smiled back. "Hey. How long are you up for?"

Ed shrugged. "As long as it takes."

"For what?"

"To clean up this mess. Plus, Tess wants to chat with the maritime archaeologist who is cataloguing the wreck."

Her smile faded at the mention of Oliver. "Why?"

"She's a history buff, and she's done a lot of research on the *Retribution* and the new wreck."

Her eyes narrowed. "What does she know about the new wreck?" They didn't even have its name.

Ed glanced away. "Not much. Just, ah, looking into missing ships of that era."

"Edward Stokes, what aren't you telling me?"

Lara grinned. "She's using her police voice, Ed. You're in trouble."

Brandon walked into the room. "That's the point of this evening, Dot." His presence no longer made her heart skip a beat like it had when she was younger. It had taken her time to recover from her heartbreak when he'd left without saying goodbye, but then she'd realised he'd treated his family just as poorly. Oliver had helped heal her heart before he'd broken it far worse than Brandon ever had.

"To tell you everything," Brandon continued.

As they should have months ago.

Brandon's wife, Amy, came in behind him and with her were Darcy's fiancée, Faith, and Ed's girlfriend, Tess. Dot smiled at her friends. "How are things out here?"

Amy switched on the kettle and turned on the stove to heat a soup pot. "There's still a lot of fencing to check, and we're waiting for supplies to fix the roof on the shed and replace a couple of panels on the house."

"Any news on the treasure?" Faith asked.

"Not yet." It had only been a couple of days since they had uncovered a chest full of treasure from the Dutch East Indies company. Dot had asked her colleagues in the south to make discreet enquiries about the ownership of such a find. She hadn't wanted word to leak it had been found, but Jordan had opened that bag of worms for her. She'd make some calls tomorrow. Right now, the treasure was still hidden in the cellar of this house, but it wasn't secure. The moment Stonefish saw an opportunity, they'd be back for it. Dot had considered moving it to a bank in town, but Stonefish had people everywhere. Chances were high they would steal it if she put it there.

There had to be somewhere secure it could go.

Darcy and Matt walked in, hanging their Akubra hats on the hooks by the door. Faith kissed Darcy and Lara waved. "Hi, Dad."

Darcy smiled. "Hi, pumpkin. How was your day?"

"Great. Faith and I went riding."

Georgie clattered up the steps from outside. "Guess what?" She flung open the door. Matt swept her into his arms before she could speak and kissed her. When they were done, Georgie fanned herself. "I've forgotten what I was going to say."

Dot chuckled. Definitely a rare occurrence for Georgie. She was glad all of her friends were happy, particularly after losing their parents at the beginning of the year, but she was conscious of being the only single person here.

Another car pulled up, and Sam, Penelope, Gretchen, Sherlock, and Jordan entered the now crowded kitchen. Jordan ran over to join Lara at the table.

"Take a seat," Amy called. "Dinner won't be long."

Brandon helped Amy with the food, placing bread and butter on the table, while Ed and Tess set the table and Faith passed out the drinks.

Dot felt a tinge of envy at the easiness of it all. This was a family. Sam and Sherlock had been Brandon's teammates in the army, and were as close as brothers, and the Stokes' partners were already part of the family.

Matt walked over. "Any news on Nhiari?"

In all that had happened, she'd forgotten to call Matt about his sister. "She contacted me."

"Quiet, everyone," Georgie called. "Dot has news on Nhiari."

Silence fell and Dot found herself the centre of attention. She cleared her throat. "Nhiari contacted me yesterday via the police radio. We used a code we made up at the academy. She's safe, and she doesn't want us to search for her."

"Why not?" Matt demanded.

Dot shrugged. "I don't know, but I trust her judgement."

"Could she have been forced to use the code?" Brandon asked.

"No. We've told no one about it." She stiffened. Except someone else had been there when they'd brainstormed ideas.

"Who did you tell?" Sam asked.

Dot exhaled. "Oliver knew about it." She'd shared all her secrets with him once.

Brandon and Sam exchanged a glance.

"I'll call the museum and the university tomorrow," Dot said. "Make sure he's here on merit." She took a sip of water, hoping it would settle the unease in her stomach. Maybe Sam was right about Stonefish having a hand in Oliver being here.

"We can feed him false information," Sherlock said. "Things that won't mess with his expedition, but that Stonefish might want to know. If they follow the trail, we know they've got to him."

It was as good a plan as any. The only people she trusted with information about Stonefish were Nhiari and the people in this room. "Tell me what you come up with."

"Where does that leave Nhiari?" Matt asked.

"Alive," Dot answered. "She'll check in when she can. She might have left me a message, but I haven't checked."

"Why not?" Matt demanded.

Dot cautioned herself to be patient. He was worried. "Because Organised Crimes arrived today and I've had to deal with them."

"How about we eat and then discuss things?" Gretchen suggested, glancing at her son, Jordan.

Yeah, it was a good idea not to speak about Stonefish in front of the children. They'd both been kidnapped to force their parents' hands, and the less they knew the better.

"The next time you speak with her, tell her to contact Mum and Dad. They're frantic."

Dot should have thought of it herself. "I will."

They chatted while they ate, Sam and Sherlock talking about the progress of the expedition. "We had several treasure hunters turn up today," Sam said, glancing at Dot.

She stifled her groan. "Did they give you any trouble?"

"Not really." Sam handed over his phone. "Recognise them?"

She nodded. "That's Isaac and Henrique Farnham. They're mechanics. I'll stop by tomorrow and have a word."

"I'd appreciate it," Sam said. "Oliver's talking about camping out there in case more try at night."

"By himself?"

"Maybe. One of his students has the worst case of seasickness, so he doesn't want to subject them to overnighting on the boat as well, but it would be more efficient to do so."

"Are you all right with that?"

Sam shrugged. "He's the client, and it works in our favour to make it hard for Stonefish to use the area."

"OK. Just don't engage with anyone. Call me."

Sam smirked but didn't agree.

She closed her eyes and let out a slow breath. These army men would be the death of her.

"Don't tease Dot, she's having a hard week." Penelope squeezed her hand. "They won't do anything foolish." She raised her eyebrows at Sam. "Will you?"

His smirk disappeared. "We'll be careful."

Not quite the same thing, but the best she would get.

When they finished dinner, Faith stood. "Lara, do you and Jordan want to go on an evening ride?"

Lara's eyes widened. "Yeah! Do you want to?" she asked Jordan.

"That would be cool."

"All right. Let's go saddle up."

Lara was halfway to the door when she spun around, causing Jordan to almost crash into her. "You're going to talk about stuff with Dot, aren't you?"

Clever girl.

"That's generally what we do when we invite friends over," Georgie said. "Talk about stuff."

Lara put her hands on her hips. "You know what I mean—treasure stuff."

Jordan perked up.

"It's nothing either of you need to hear," Gretchen said, and Darcy nodded.

"Enjoy the ride, pumpkin."

Both children dragged their feet a little as Faith shepherded them out of the house.

"She's smart," Sherlock said.

"I know," Darcy replied. "Smarter than I was at her age. I wish she didn't know about any of this."

"The quickest way to make them safe is to catch

whoever is behind all of this," Dot said. "To do that, I need to know everything."

Amy fetched two documents from a drawer and handed them to Dot. "These are how we found the shipwreck and the treasure."

She glanced down at the photocopies. The first one was a journal with Lilian Stokes's name on the front. The second was a captain's journal and dated from the sixteen hundreds. "Where'd you get these?"

"From the cellar," Georgie answered. "I found them about three months ago. Lilian's journal tells the story of how the *Retribution* was shipwrecked. Her husband, Reginald, found the captain's journal somewhere and was searching for the wreck and the treasure."

It finally made more sense. "You knew the Dutch ship was there when you found it." Dot flicked through the photocopy.

Georgie nodded.

Oliver would be thrilled to get a copy of the journal. "Do you have the original?"

"We have a translation. The original was stolen from Lilian in Cossack. They think some pearl divers who were on the ship took it."

"My ancestor Da was one of the divers," Tess said. "She didn't take it, but she came from Singapore."

Which was where Stonefish also had connections.

"The shipwreck survivors found some of the treasure, and there was a mutiny," Brandon continued. "Those who survived divided it amongst themselves, but Lilian suspected there was more."

"When they returned to the area after they'd been rescued, Lilian and the three convicts with her found the rest." Ed got up and put on the kettle. "Lilian and her husband hid their portion to help future family."

Dot shook her head. "How did you find it?"

"Sherlock figured out the clues in the journal,"

Georgie said. "The storm last week washed away a lot of the sand and uncovered it."

Dot had to get to the bottom of who owned the treasure. Technically it had been taken from the shipwreck before there were laws in place forbidding it. The Stokes were struggling financially, and she hoped they'd be able to keep a portion. It would be a shame for it all to end up in a museum somewhere. "It won't take long for Stonefish to regroup, especially if the treasure holds some kind of significance to them."

"Are you any closer to finding them?" Gretchen asked. "Did Kurt talk?"

Dot shook her head. "He said nothing, but I caught Myra Simpson on my way out of town." She enjoyed their looks of shock. It was nice to be the one who surprised them for a change.

Gretchen narrowed her eyes. "Did you arrest her?"

Dot nodded, understanding her anger. "She was being blackmailed by Stonefish."

When Dot didn't elaborate, Georgie said, "What did they have on her?"

"I can't say." They didn't need to know about the rest. It would come out during the court case.

Darcy scowled. "She endangered Jordan and Cody and ignored Lara."

"I can't tell you." Dot repeated as she opened her notebook and clicked her pen. "Let's start at the very beginning," she said. "Who did Taylor have connections with?"

The Stokes and Amy all scowled at the mention of the man who had caused the death of their parents.

Dot exhaled. It was going to be a long night.

Chapter 7

Oliver surfaced from his last dive and gave Sam the OK signal before inflating his BCD. Progress was slow, but steady, and he was pleased with his students' patience. They all worked in a line and visibility had improved so he could see the groups as they worked. So far, they'd uncovered some fragments of ceramics, and what looked to be some kind of wooden planks, newly uncovered by the storm.

He climbed aboard the *Oceanid* and lowered his vest to the ground.

"What's it like down there today?" Sam asked.

"Clear," Oliver answered. "Calm. Good conditions for a dive like this." The students were already standing around the table eating afternoon tea. Even Andrew was keeping food down today, though he'd thrown up the entire journey here. "Any issues topside?"

"A few boats came near, but they left after they saw us on board."

Good. Hopefully, Sam and Sherlock were enough of a deterrent.

Rajesh glanced over at the discussion. "A bunch of people approached us at the brewery last night, and we told them there was no treasure."

"Though there was one woman who thought Andrew was a bit of a treasure," Tom teased.

Andrew sniffed. "Don't be jealous. Older women recognise my maturity."

Suzyn rolled her eyes. "Or are desperate."

They all laughed. It was good to see the team was bonding.

Sam headed to the top deck to steer them back to town. Oliver needed to decide whether they should stay on the boat. There were only so many dives they could do in a day, they had more room in the house to work, and it wasn't a long trip out and back. However, Andrew wasn't as sick with the calmer weather.

Andrew ran to the bathroom and Oliver winced. Maybe staying on the boat wasn't the best option.

There'd been expeditions when he'd longed to have solid ground under him at the end of the day. However, the thought of treasure hunters messing with his site niggled at him. And there was a little voice in the back of his head that said if he stayed on the boat, he wouldn't run into Dot.

Stupid really.

He'd never let his feelings affect an expedition before.

The indecision plagued him, adding constant stress in the back of his mind as they unpacked the boat.

Back at the house, they collated their work. Suzyn turned her laptop around, showing a photo she'd taken. "I'm pretty sure this is some kind of wooden plank. It's shaped differently to the coral and appears as if it was uncovered recently, maybe in the storm."

Oliver reviewed it and nodded. "Looks like it. You can retrieve it tomorrow and we can test it. Knowing the type of wood might help us narrow down which ship it is."

Tom pointed to one of the printed photos of the

ocean floor. "I found some glass and ceramics here."

"And also here." Rajesh pointed.

Oliver looked at Andrew to see what he would add, but the man said nothing.

"I've got a list of ships that went missing in that era around Australia," Suzyn said. "I'll check which ones mention wood as cargo."

They continued discussing what they'd found until someone knocked on the front door. No one made a move to open it.

Oliver sighed. Probably another curious local. He opened the door and stepped back, his heart skipping a beat. Dot stood there in her police uniform, shadows under her eyes from fatigue, but her back straight and her face expressionless. Once upon a time she would have greeted him with a huge smile and a massive hug. He resisted the urge to instigate it, knowing he'd be rejected. And that hurt more than it should.

"Oliver." Dot nodded. "This is Tess Lim. She has some information which might be helpful to your expedition."

He blinked, glancing towards the young Asian woman next to her who was holding a journal and some photocopied papers.

Tess's smile was a little shy. "I'm studying history at uni and have a particular interest in the *Retribution* shipwreck as one of my ancestors was on board."

Oliver smiled politely. The two wrecks weren't related, but it was nice of Dot to help a friend. "We're actually studying the other shipwreck near the *Retribution*."

Tess nodded. "The *Avontuur*."

Oliver blinked. "We don't know the name of it yet."

Dot's smile was a little smug as Tess handed him an old, brown, leather-bound book. "It's all in this journal."

Confused, he took it and carefully opened it, wincing

at the crack of the spine. The front page stated, '*Avontuur. Captain's Journal. 1690*.' His heart leapt and then fell again. "The *Avontuur* went down further south near Shark Bay." Still, the journal was a valuable find.

Tess shook her head. "That was a lie to hide its actual location."

He stiffened. He was used to people peddling tales to involve themselves in expeditions, but he hadn't thought Dot would stoop to messing with his work. "Where did you get this?"

"It's a long story," Dot said. "Have you got time?" The seriousness of her tone paused Oliver's anger.

He exhaled, noting the sincere expressions on both of their faces, and then nodded, backing away from the door to let them in. "Come in." He led them into the kitchen. The table was covered in their notes, but there was a spare chair. "Clear some space."

Suzyn smiled. "Hey, Sergeant. Do you know how the joey is?"

"Donna said he's doing well when I called this morning."

Oliver was surprised Dot knew. Didn't she have enough on her plate dealing with drugs, storm clean up and would-be treasure hunters?

Tom tidied his notes into a neat stack. "Have we done something wrong?"

"No," Dot answered. "Tess has some information."

Oliver gestured for them both to sit. Tess took a chair, but Dot remained standing. Oliver placed the journal on the table. "Tess found a journal which belongs to a ship's captain, and she believes it is the journal from our shipwreck."

"How would it have survived then?" Andrew asked.

Tess cleared her throat. "The ship was carrying treasure for the Dutch East Indies company, but it was blown off course during a cyclone. It wrecked on

Retribution Island." Her voice grew stronger. "They salvaged what they could and cobbled together a boat to take them to Batavia."

Oliver frowned. "The Dutch East Indies company searched for the *Avontuur* and never found it."

"That's because the captain lied about the location," Tess said. "He wanted the treasure for himself, so he led them to Shark Bay because it was a similar shaped gulf to this one."

"Did he go back for the treasure?" Rajesh asked.

Tess shook her head. "He was arrested for theft."

Oliver flicked through the journal. "What about his first mate? Surely he knew where it was."

Tess handed over some documents. "The first mate died before they could ask him. According to the notes on the trial, no one else knew, or if they did, they weren't talking. Maybe they also wanted the treasure for themselves."

Her research was meticulous. She had copies of the original Dutch court proceedings with their English translations, and the sources were attached to the documents. Tess wasn't some wanna-be historian, she was the real deal. His body tingled with cautious excitement. "Didn't the journal give him away?"

"The court didn't have it. The documents suggest it went down with the ship, but the captain must have hidden it."

"How did you get an English translation of it?" he asked.

Tess glanced at Dot, who nodded. She handed over a photocopied document. "This is a copy of the journal of one of the original settlers of this area," she said. "Her husband had the original journal and the translation, but she didn't know where he found it. Reginald came to Australia on the *Retribution* searching for the treasure."

Oliver frowned at the name. Lilian Stokes. Why did

the name ring a bell? It wasn't Lindsay's surname, but he'd heard it before in relation to Dot. It suddenly clicked. "Is this Brandon's ancestor?"

Dot nodded.

"When was that?" Suzyn asked.

"1870."

"Surely he didn't think the treasure was still there," Andrew scoffed.

Tess shrugged. "It was worth the look. The captain said he and his first mate hid the treasure one night on the island. With the first mate dead, only the captain knew where it was, and his journal doesn't mention him telling anyone else."

"So Reginald ended up shipwrecked on the same island as the *Avontuur*?" Oliver asked. How ironic.

Tess handed over the final document. "This is the official manifest of what was on board the *Avontuur*."

Oliver's mouth dropped open at the list of coins and jewels. This was the real treasure. He scanned the pages listing spices, valuables, clothing, and wood. His breath caught. If they could corroborate the wood remnants Suzyn had found, they might be on to something. "Brandon's family had this journal for a hundred and fifty years and said nothing?"

The young woman shook her head. "They only just discovered it, along with their ancestor's journal."

She wasn't telling him something. "Are they the ones who found the wreck?"

This time it was Dot who answered. "Yes."

Which meant they'd had the journal for several months. "Was the treasure still there?" Perhaps that explained the rumours.

"No. They took nothing from the wreck. The woman who found it understood the importance of leaving it undisturbed." Tess gave him a small smile. "She told me, because she knew I'm into history, and I've been researching it since then.”

Suzyn reached for the journal, having found a pair of white cotton gloves somewhere, and Oliver handed it to her. “This is incredible.”

“So, what happened to the treasure?” Andrew asked.

“The *Retribution* survivors found it and there was a mutiny,” Dot said. “Those who weren’t killed split it amongst themselves.”

It was resignation rather than disappointment that filled Oliver. Wrecks had usually been plundered. It was a shame, but hardly surprising.

Whatever the case, Oliver wasn’t getting any sleep tonight. Not until he’d read everything Tess had brought him. “Can I get your number?” he asked Tess. “In case I have questions.”

She told him. “If you need a hand with further research, I’m happy to help.”

She had an eagerness he recognised from his own time as a student. “Why don’t you come out with us tomorrow?”

She smiled. “I’d love to.”

He gave her the details and walked them to the door, conscious he had said nothing meaningful to Dot. “I really appreciate you coming forward.” He glanced at Dot. “Thank you for bringing Tess here.”

Dot nodded but said nothing. They both turned to go.

He needed to focus on his job, but he couldn’t with the ghost of their relationship getting in the way. They needed to talk, just the two of them.

“Dot, wait!” Oliver bit his tongue as she glanced at him. What excuse could he use? “I, ah, wanted to discuss the security of the wreck with you.” He cursed his hesitation. He felt like an awkward teenager around her. “Are you free tomorrow afternoon?”

Her lips pressed together. She was going to say no.

"Please," he added. "I could do with some advice and local knowledge."

Dot stared at him for a moment before sighing. "Call me when you get back to shore. I can't guarantee I'll be free."

The rush of relief reaffirmed he needed to clear the air with her. "Thank you."

The two women got into the car. He waited at the door until they drove away, then rubbed his chest. Tomorrow.

All he had to do was wait until tomorrow and he'd get the answers he needed to put their relationship behind him and move on.

A little voice in his head taunted him as a liar, but he ignored it and instead went inside to discover what other treasures the journal held.

***

Dot tugged her hair as she drove away from Georgie's place after dropping Tess there. It had been another day of small issues; a vehicle crash—minor with no one hurt, alleged shoplifting from Brown's newsagency, some drunk and disorderly at the brewery at lunch time, and an ex-boyfriend who was getting aggressive with the girl who had dumped him. Everything came with just enough paperwork to keep her busy until it was time to finish for the day and she hadn't reviewed the notes she'd taken at the Ridge the night before.

Then there was the whole seeing Oliver again. He was genuinely grateful for her bringing Tess to him. His plea to speak with her tomorrow had been one she couldn't ignore.

She didn't want to spend time with him. Every moment in his presence reminded her of what they'd had, and what he'd tossed aside at the first better opportunity.

She couldn't let herself be sucked in again.

Dot peered in her fridge and spotted no groceries of note. When was the last time she'd done a proper grocery shop? Lindsay could probably tell her. She'd have to make time to get some food this week. She was living off nuts and fruit, the only things she had time to eat while working.

There were a couple of eggs, some ham that smelled OK despite being several days past its use-by date, and a block of cheese which would be fine to eat if she cut off the mould growing on the sides. She shook her head.

Pathetic.

She'd always envisioned herself adulting much better than this. Hell, she'd been more of an adult when she'd lived at home with her parents, buying the groceries and cooking everyone dinner several times a week.

Dot rubbed her eyes. It had been easier to get the groceries since she'd worked at the supermarket. Lindsay would organise her shopping if she asked, but it seemed too much of an imposition. Dot was supposed to have her life together by now.

Her dreams at the academy had involved working with her best friend by her side and coming home to Oliver every day. They would have dinner together, and maybe by now, they'd have a couple of kids to expand their family and she could shower them with all the love she had to give.

At least her work life was on track. In charge at the station in her hometown, working with her best friend, and feeling as if she made a difference. Until Stonefish turned up to make a mockery of everything she stood for.

The personal portion was incredibly dismal. She'd become so standoffish that she didn't like any physical displays of affection. Hugs made her realise what she was missing and made her yearn for more.

And there was no more for her.

Men were either intimidated by her job or wanted to use it for their own advancement. She'd stuck to the occasional hook-up with a tourist in town who didn't know who she was.

She learnt she could only rely on herself for happiness. Trying to please people led only to being hurt.

She beat the eggs with far too much vigour and poured them into her no longer non-stick frying pan. It would be more like scrambled eggs than an omelette by the time she was finished, but it was food.

Occasionally, she and Nhiari would hang out, and they had a girls' night with the rest of their friends once a month. But most nights it was this, coming home to an empty house and scrounging in the fridge for something to make for dinner. She could rarely be bothered to cook for one. Then she'd sit in front of the TV until it was time to go to bed, too tired to concentrate on reading a book. Lately all she had the energy for was listening to music to unwind.

Dot scraped the mess of eggs onto a plate and sat at the kitchen table. Damn Oliver for coming back into her life, and making her think 'what if?' He'd left her so easily, so she should be grateful he'd done it then, and not before she'd been even more invested.

Who was she kidding? She'd been thinking about rings and weddings when he'd suggested they move in together. Foolish.

And still she couldn't say no to him when he'd asked to speak with her, his puppy dog eyes full of hope.

To be fair, his request was to do with her work, so she could hardly say no, but the traitorous little leap of her heart when he'd asked needed to be squashed.

There was no happily ever after for her.

She washed her dishes and then spread her notes over the table. The Stokes had given her some valuable information, bits and pieces that hadn't come out during her investigations but formed a more complete picture. She could be mad about it, but it wasn't worth the time. She added items to her timeline, recording where people were on specific days, and going through police reports to review what was happening in town.

Her phone rang and she scowled, picking it up. Then she saw who it was. "Nhiari."

"I'm fine," Nhiari said. "I'm working on something with Lee, but no one can know."

"It's a dark night." Dot waited for the response.

"But the stars are shining," Nhiari responded.

Dot exhaled. "You went willingly with him?"

Nhiari laughed. "I wouldn't say that, but it's fine. I think someone in our team is working with Stonefish."

"Yeah. I spoke with the Stokes last night and they filled in some blanks. I'm collating the information now."

"Can you send it to me? I can't keep my phone on for long in case it gets tracked, but we should share information."

"Yeah. Is there somewhere I can drop a hard copy?"

"Hang on." Murmuring in the background. "How about at the lighthouse?"

A great suggestion. She needed a dose of lighthouse serenity. "I'll watch the sunrise tomorrow."

"All right. We're close, Dot. It won't be long."

Dot hoped she was right. "Take care—oh and call your parents. Matt said they're frantic."

"Will do."

She hung up, then checked the time and called Matt.

"Have you heard from Nhiari?" he asked.

"Yes. She's safe."

His exhalation was loud. "When is she coming back?"

"I'm not sure, but it sounds like she's on to something. I don't think it will be long."

"Thanks, Dot."

"Your big sister can take care of herself, Matt. She'll be fine."

"I don't like not knowing where she is. It's hard convincing Mum and Dad she'll be all right, without telling them what's going on."

"I told her to call them."

"Great. Thanks, Dot."

She went back to her notes with renewed energy. She had to get the information collated by morning so she could give it to her friend.

It was midnight by the time she finished her notes and photocopied everything. She blinked rapidly. There had to be a pattern here, but right now she was too tired to see it.

Her yawn almost cracked her jaw and made her eyes water.

She'd get nothing more done tonight. She took photos of all her scribblings as a backup and placed the copies in an A4 envelope for Nhiari.

On her way to bed she stopped by the vase of flowers and inhaled the sweet scent of the rose, unable to help herself. They really were beautiful and she hadn't been able to bring herself to throw them out just because Oliver had given them to her. It wasn't their fault. The tiredness eased and she smiled.

Tomorrow. She'd find the pattern and put an end to Stonefish once and for all.

***

Dim light glowed on the horizon as Dot headed out to the lighthouse the next morning. She had tucked the envelope under her jacket so it wasn't visible to anyone who might be watching. On the drive, she wound down the window and breathed in the cool morning air, allowing it to wash over her face. She should do this more often. One advantage of living on a peninsula was she got to witness the sun rise and set over the ocean. It never ceased to centre her, make everything in life fall into perspective.

It was late enough in the season that the lighthouse car park was empty. She inhaled deeply and stretched as she got out. The glow on the horizon was brighter now and soon the sun itself would appear. Birds chirped as they fluttered from bush to bush, greeting each other and the day. She wrapped her arms around her to ward off the chill and turned in a circle, scanning the horizon. She and Nhiari used to leave each other notes in the rusted, old, metal box on the other side of the wooden logs which marked the edges of the car park. The box might have been used for storage at some stage in the past.

Dot wandered over. No one could have followed her here. The land was flat and any car on the road could be seen or heard. But that didn't mean Stonefish hadn't set up cameras around Retribution Bay. They seemed to know everything that was going on before she did.

She crouched to do up her shoelace, turning on her phone torch to see what she was doing, and to shine the light through the gap in the side door of the storage box. A few cobwebs, but it was dry. She slid the envelope through the gap and then stood, hopping up on the storage box to sit and watch the sunrise. She stuck her hands in her pockets and breathed deeply again.

This was her favourite place. Her safe space. As a kid, she'd bike out here and sit in the lighthouse's shade, looking out at the ocean or Retribution Bay. She could get out of the house, where she was ignored, and pretend her parents would be missing her and counting the hours until she came home. As she grew older, she'd stay later and later wondering whether her parents would grow worried and search for her, but they never did. Often they thought she'd been in her room all along.

Nhiari would sometimes take her family's motorbike and ride along the base of the ranges, through dirt tracks, and meet her. Or Mark would pick her up and take them both to the beach to swim. He'd understood her need to get out of the house and had encouraged her friendship with Nhiari. Perhaps he wanted to make sure she had someone else she could rely on so there was less pressure on him, or to get her out of the way so she didn't know what he was up to.

Or perhaps he was just being a good brother.

She really didn't know and now she never would.

She squeezed her eyes closed and allowed the grief to fill her. When she'd moved to Perth, she'd been the one always calling Mark to stay in touch, and after Oliver had left she'd stopped doing even that, deciding if he really cared, he would call her.

He never had.

It had cemented her understanding that no one really wanted her, that she wasn't worth being around.

Exhaling, she pushed away the pain and then opened her eyes. As she took in the view, she spotted a familiar boat motoring along the coast. She shook her head, not surprised her parents were already out fishing, getting a couple of hours in before they had to go to work. They'd had to spend the weekend cleaning up from the storm, so they'd missed their fishing days.

Dot tried not to let it bother her, but the small pang of rejection was always there.

The reminder of rejection led her thoughts to Oliver. The one time she'd brought him to Retribution Bay, she'd brought him here, and told him what the place meant to her. He hadn't understood her need to get away, because his family had been supportive, such wonderful caring people who had embraced Dot as part of their family almost immediately. She'd loved them, loved their weekly dinners, and embraced his parents and sister as if they were her own. Maybe that's why he'd left her. Maybe he'd felt too much pressure from her. All she'd wanted was someone to love her and she'd been pathetically eager to please. Though fitting in with his family had been easy.

Dot sighed and shook away the thought. It didn't matter now. She'd come up here to clear her head and review the information she'd put together last night. There had to be a clue, some kind of pattern.

Month by month they'd uncovered more heads of Stonefish, but like a Hydra, they kept growing back. Nhiari had said they were close to putting an end to this. Dot prayed the information she'd collated would help. The results for the fingerprints they'd found on the drug barrel hadn't come through yet, so she'd have to call this morning and follow it up. It was times like this she missed being in the city with access to so many more facilities.

A light travelled along the road down below, coming from town. Someone was up early. Possibly an angler heading to the boat ramp on the western side of the peninsula. The light wound around the coast and then slowed as it reached the lighthouse road where it turned.

Damn it. She didn't want company.

The sun was already above the horizon, so whoever it was had missed the show.

Should she go back to her car, or wait? They might drive up, realise they were too late, and leave again.

Her muscles tensed as she read the words on the side of the bus. It was Sam's, the one he'd loaned to Oliver. Really not what she needed this morning. She hopped off the box and strode over to her car as the bus pulled up.

Suzyn, Rajesh and Tom jumped out, their voices loud in the morning.

"I told you we'd miss it if you didn't hurry," Suzyn

complained.

"It's not fully up," Tom replied.

"Hi, Sergeant Campbell," Rajesh said.

She nodded, wishing they hadn't acknowledged her. "Morning."

A car door slammed, and she braced herself as Oliver walked around the other side of the bus. His hair was tousled as if he'd just run his hands and a little bit of water through it to tame the bed hair. He'd thrown on a dark singlet and board shorts and looked much more like a sexy surfer than a lecturer. Damn him. Her heart fluttered traitorously.

"Morning. Sorry for disturbing you." His smile was a little uncertain, as if he wasn't sure of her reception. "Pipe down. You're ruining the moment."

His students fell silent. It was impressive they paid him so much attention.

Dot shifted closer to her car, ignoring her rapid heartbeat. "I was just leaving."

"Please stay. I know how much you enjoy the sunrise."

He remembered. Her surprise only served to spread the flutter of her heart down to her stomach. The sensible part of her shouted danger, but it was whisked away as the memory of their holiday to Retribution Bay swept in. They'd sat in the dark, on the same box where she'd just sat, his arm around her as she'd told him about all the time she'd spent here. The sun had gradually brought light to the world and Oliver had asked her to move in with him. She'd never had a more perfect moment.

Tom coughed, and Dot blinked. They were waiting for her answer. She nodded. "All right. Enjoy." She walked back to the box and Oliver herded his group further away from her, but their low voices carried.

Now wasn't the time to be caught up in the past. Who

had suggested they come out this morning? It seemed an odd thing for the research team to do when they had limited hours to work on the wreck. Was someone working for Stonefish and had seen her leave?

She rubbed her face. The paranoia wasn't a pleasant feeling, but she'd seen how Stonefish used people. Oliver arriving now was far too convenient. Which reminded her she still needed to call the museum and find out who was paying for the expedition. When she'd called them to tell them Georgie had found the shipwreck, they had thought it would take a year to get someone out to look at it.

The speed at which they were here spoke of Stonefish manipulation.

Dot checked the time. She should get back. Rodney would be there early, and she wanted to avoid his snide remarks as much as possible.

She pushed off the box and walked back to her car. The others were at the end of the lookout, pointing out some late season whales who were frolicking off shore. Oliver glanced back and when he noticed her, he strode towards her.

Damn it.

Could she get into her car in time? No, they'd made eye-contact. She couldn't ignore him. What she had to do was pretend her heart didn't ache with longing when she saw his easy smile.

"Leaving already?"

"I need to get to work."

"Sorry about before." He seemed genuinely apologetic. "We meant to get here early, but Tom is pretty slow to get going in the morning."

Oliver used to take his time in the mornings as well. There'd always been distractions. She pushed away those particular memories and asked, "What made you come today?"

He rubbed the back of his head. "I mentioned it yesterday when they were talking about things they could do in their down time. Suzyn was keen and encouraged the others, and only Andrew said no."

She stiffened. "You suggested it?" He couldn't have possibly known she was coming here. Unless someone had tapped her phone.

"Yeah. I remembered how nice the lookout was when you brought me here." His warm smile stirred her insides, made her want to step closer, into his bubble.

Did he also remember it was where they'd agreed to move to the next stage of their relationship? She wouldn't ask. "It is nice." She gave a polite smile. "I have to go."

He shifted aside so she could get in the car. "I'll call you this afternoon."

She nodded. "See you later."

It wasn't until she turned onto the main road that her hands relaxed on the steering wheel and her heart rate slowed. Oliver had always had a magnetic quality. It had been that way from the first moment they'd locked eyes across the room at a party. He'd made a beeline towards her, and she'd believed in kismet. Everything had seemed possible when she was with him.

They'd spent almost every night together, either at his place or hers until she'd graduated and Nhiari had got the job in Carnarvon. Then she'd turned down the job she'd wanted to stay with him and he'd accepted the position on the expedition team overseas.

The betrayal had eviscerated her.

The proof her love wasn't enough. That *she* wasn't enough reason to stay. That he didn't care enough about her to discuss it before he'd said yes.

When he'd left, it had been like losing a part of herself.

Her hands clenched around the wheel again and she exhaled, relaxing her hold. When she was with Oliver, she had to remember this feeling. Remember those days when getting out of bed had taken all her willpower. He had dumped her without a second thought, and would do so again if she let him in.

She wasn't going through that again.

Chapter 8

Oliver exhaled slowly as Dot drove away, and he rubbed the ache in his heart. That moment when he'd turned and seen her walking back to her car was so like the moment he'd first seen her. He'd been pulled towards her and hadn't been able to resist this time any more than he had the first time. She magnetised him. The moments they'd had together rushed over him like a flashback in a movie; dancing with her at a nightclub, the way her head tilted back as she laughed; wrapping his arm around her while she cried at the cinemas; walking hand in hand along the beach at sunset after a nice meal out together.

And she'd walked away from it all, as if none of it had mattered.

"Somebody's got a crush." Suzyn's sing-song voice shocked Oliver from his memories.

"What?"

"You've been gazing after the sergeant since she left," Suzyn said. "Are you going to ask her out?"

Heat rushed to his cheeks. "I'm focused on the shipwreck and keeping you lot out of trouble." He grinned and gestured to the bus. "Get in. We've got work to do."

He went around to the driver's side, but her words resonated with him. She was right. He wasn't as over Dot as he'd thought. He couldn't ignore the yearning to take her into his arms, or ask her about her day. This emotion swirling inside of him spoke not of indifference, but of want.

Suzyn sat in the front seat and the two guys sat in the seats behind him. "She seems nice," Suzyn continued as if he had said nothing.

"She's pretty cute as well," Tom added. "A bit short, maybe."

"She's the perfect size." Oliver winced as his students laughed. He'd walked right into that one, but Dot had been conscious of her height for a long time. "I'm sure she would have no problem restraining a suspect."

"You want to be her suspect?" Rajesh teased.

Oliver groaned, even as his cheeks kept their heat. Now was not the time to remember the role play they'd done when Dot had first got her handcuffs.

"Is she married?" Suzyn asked.

"No."

"Then what are you waiting for?"

He did not want to talk about his love life with his students. "We have a history. Now enough about the sergeant. Where should we start our dives this morning in light of the new information we received last night?"

"We should look for the cannons," Tom said.

Rajesh shook his head. "Nothing should change. We need to be methodical and continue our process as before."

Oliver let his students debate the merits of both as they drove back into town, glad they were distracted.

But one thing he knew for sure. He wasn't leaving Retribution Bay without talking to Dot. He needed to find out once and for all why she'd refused to give them a chance.

And convince her to give him one now.

***

Dot was at her desk by six-thirty, working through her notes on Stonefish. She'd told the others not to disturb her unless it was an emergency. Her timeline was shaping up nicely, and a few patterns were emerging. There were a couple of people she needed to visit.

She checked the time. Still only eight o'clock, but she had her museum contact's mobile number. As she reached for the phone someone knocked on her door. She sighed and called, "Yes?"

Colin poked his head in. "Sorry, boss. There's a Ryan Kilpatrick here to see you. I told him you weren't to be disturbed, but he reckons you'll want to see him."

Dot grinned. "He's right. Send him in."

Colin raised his eyebrows, but went to let Ryan in.

Dot dialled her contact at the museum. "I have a couple of questions about the research group going over the new shipwreck."

"Oliver's one of our best," the woman gushed. "He's so experienced. We were thrilled when he moved back to Perth and took up the role with us and the university."

"Is the museum funding the dive?" She waved at Ryan as he walked in and gestured to a chair. Tall and lean with an easy smile, Ryan had become a fast friend when she'd started at the academy. She'd even had a small crush on him until she'd met Oliver and then everyone else had vanished from her radar. Dressed casually in a T-shirt and board shorts, he still looked as good as ever.

"No. A philanthropist called offering to sponsor it. His son is taking Oliver's class, and his only condition was for his son to be part of the expedition."

Dot perked up. "What's his name?"

"Lucas Fitton. He's on the board or owns Zhēnzhū

Corporation."

She made a note to follow up later. "Does that kind of thing happen very often?"

The woman laughed. "Never. I wish it did."

Interesting. "Did you choose Oliver as the lead on the expedition?"

"Lucas requested it, but it was our choice as well. With the university students volunteering, and Oliver's experience, it made perfect sense."

It did, which was a relief, but she'd still follow up Lucas's details. "Thanks for your help." She hung up and smiled at Ryan. "I was going to call you. I couldn't remember when you were due up here."

"Yesterday." Ryan studied her. "You look terrible. Have you been sleeping?"

She snorted. "Nice way to greet an old friend."

"You've been under a lot of stress."

She gathered her notes together and put them in a backpack. "Let's go get coffee and we can talk."

He raised his eyebrows. "Coffee that bad here?"

"Yeah." She walked out and called to the others. "Just ducking out to get coffee. Everyone want the usual?" They nodded and she left with Ryan. "Are Hannah and Felix with you?"

"Yeah. They're back at the park. I don't want them involved in the police stuff. Where's Nhiari?"

She exhaled, but it felt good to have someone she could talk to. "It's a long story. As far as everyone knows, Nhiari has been kidnapped by someone working for Stonefish."

Ryan stopped walking. "What?"

Dot waved away his concern. "She's fine. We just can't tell anyone else that."

"You don't trust your staff?"

"I think at least one of them has to be involved."

Ryan swore. "That's rough. What can I do to help?"

She hesitated. "Did you get an answer to your enquiries about who owns the treasure?"

Ryan laughed. "That depends on who you ask. State says they do, federal says it's theirs, and the museum says it belongs to the people and should be displayed behind glass." He shook his head. "Then, of course, the Netherlands will see it as theirs because it came from a Dutch ship."

Dot groaned. "So they were no help." She clenched her hands into fists. "The Stokes really need the money, but it will probably be months or years before this is settled."

"Where's the treasure now?"

"Hidden."

Ryan raised his eyebrows.

"It's not that I don't trust you. The less you know, the safer you and your family are."

He nodded, not arguing the point. "So what's new?"

"Do you remember Rodney Taylor from the academy?"

Ryan groaned. "Pompous prick who would throw you under a bus if it meant he got ahead."

Dot nodded. "He's with Organised Crime now. We discovered a large haul of drugs. He's still up here, so be on the lookout so you can avoid him."

"He was an entitled prick back at the academy." Ryan shook his head. "The way he treated you and Nhiari, they should have failed him on the spot. I guess he hasn't improved?"

"No." She smiled, appreciating his defence of her both then and now. She dealt with insults and derision because of her gender and height, but Nhiari copped it for being indigenous, and the taunts had been far worse than those Dot had had to endure.

"So talk me through what's happened since the treasure was uncovered."

"Two boys were kidnapped, a woman was taken at gunpoint, Nhiari became a hostage, and we arrested two people for the crimes."

"This reminds me of the situation in Blackbridge last year. Any ideas who is behind it?"

"Someone else in town must be either in charge, or high on the ladder," Dot said. "Kurt was in town for weeks without being seen."

"Has anyone talked?"

"No one who had any helpful information. Those who were being blackmailed only knew their blackmailer, and those more involved are terrified of talking."

"So why now?" Ryan asked. "Stonefish seem well connected. They might have been doing this for years. Why is it all coming to light now? For us in Blackbridge, the patriarch running the show was ill and his children made a mess of things while trying to take over."

Dot considered the people around town. "I can't think of anyone in a similar situation. It all started when Stonefish tried to buy Retribution Ridge."

"Could the owners have been involved with Stonefish? They died, didn't they?"

Dot was impressed he remembered. "Yes, but I can't see Bill or Beth being involved. They loved the land and their kids."

"Loved it enough to do anything to protect them?" Ryan asked.

Her muscles tightened at the suggestion, but she had to put her emotions aside. She sighed. "It might be worth investigating, though none of their kids will like it."

"Will they hinder you?"

She shook her head. "They wouldn't dare."

"Anyone who lives alone, or has an isolated property?"

"Most properties which aren't in town are isolated," Dot said. "You know what it's like."

He nodded.

They arrived at the coffee shop and Dot greeted Tammy and ordered the coffees.

"Has the treasure been found yet, Dot?" Tammy asked. "We've got a few people asking questions about where the wreck is."

Dot smothered her groan. "I hope you're telling them it's out of bounds," she said. "I've got enough work to do without dealing with trespassers."

Tammy looked slightly guilty, which didn't surprise Dot in the least. "Is there really treasure?"

Dot shook her head. "People have to stop believing in get rich quick schemes. Even if there'd been treasure, someone would have found it long ago."

"So it might still be there?" Tammy asked.

The woman didn't know when to give up. "The team from the museum has found no traces of it, so I would say no."

Tammy turned her attention to Ryan. "I haven't seen you around town before."

Ryan gave her an easy smile. "My family is here for a holiday."

"How do you know Dot?"

"We're friends from way back," Ryan said. "Do those custard tarts taste as good as they look?"

"Better," Tammy said. "I make them myself."

"I'll take one."

By the time Tammy had bagged the tart, and a cream doughnut for Dot, the coffees were ready. Dot collected them, and they headed out before she could ask more questions.

"A gossip, or looking for information?" Ryan asked.

"Who, Tammy?" Dot frowned. "I don't think she's malicious."

"She'd be in a good position to hear what's going on in town, and insistent enough to get the information she wants."

"So would most of the shopkeepers in town," Dot said. "Pretty much everyone has to stop at this complex at some stage on their journey, if only to buy milk." He had a good point though. Stonefish seemed to have eyes and ears everywhere and Tammy would be a good suspect. So would Lindsay.

Dot sipped her coffee, trying to wash away the bad taste in her mouth, and gasped as the milk scalded her tongue. "Damn."

"Do you want me to look at your notes?" Ryan asked.

He'd be impartial, but he also wouldn't understand all the relationships around town. Still, the temptation was strong. "You don't want to work on your holiday."

"I mentioned I might help you. Hannah understands. Besides, you could recommend some spots we can visit. Felix wants to camp on the beach or in the bush. I used to take him all the time when we lived in Karratha."

"There are some great spots near the beach on the other side of the ranges," Dot said. "And some friends have a campground on their sheep station. They'll take you horse riding."

"Sounds great. How about you leave me with your notes now, and we can catch up for dinner?"

Dot hesitated as she considered the way Stonefish got to innocents. For all she knew, Ryan could be compromised. "Head out to Turquoise Bay today," she said. "There's some great snorkelling." They arrived at the police station. "I'll meet you at seven at the brewery."

"The notes?" Ryan asked.

"It's fine. Thanks for the offer, but I'll manage."

He frowned, but nodded. "OK. See you at seven." He crossed to a white four-wheel drive and drove away.

Dot sighed and entered the police station to find Martin and Pierre preparing to leave. "What's happened?"

"Got a call about a crash near the boat ramp."

She handed them their coffees. "Keep me informed."

Colin glanced up from his computer when Dot handed him his coffee. "All my reports are up to date."

"Good work." He was an enthusiastic rookie, always looking for something more to do. Dot suspected Retribution Bay hadn't lived up to his expectations about police work until the Stonefish crimes started happening.

"Do you need a hand with the kidnapping report?" Wide-eyed and eager, but Dot's trust was at an all-time low.

"I've got it. Can you do an audit of the supplies? We've been through a lot of evidence kits over the past week and I don't want us running out when we need them."

His face fell. "Are you sure there's nothing else I can do?"

"I'm sure." Her phone rang, and she stiffened when she saw Sam's name on the display. "What now?" she barked.

He didn't laugh like he normally did. "Someone's disturbed the shipwreck. A cannon is missing and Oliver's furious."

"I'll be there as soon as I can." This wasn't how she wanted to spend her day.

"Do you need help?" Colin asked.

She didn't want to leave Colin to deal with things by himself, but only one person needed to go. "No. Stay here in case anything else comes up. I'm going out to the shipwreck. Someone has pillaged from it. Can you put together the snorkelling gear for me?"

Dot dashed across to her house to change into her bathers, and by the time she returned, Colin had everything ready. "Thanks."

On the drive to the marina, she called the lab. "Any results on the evidence I sent?"

"They're next in line. I'll send the results as soon as I've got them."

It was a long shot, but if the fingerprints from the drug barrels were on file, it would be a huge help to the case. She loaded the gear into the police boat and headed south into the gulf. The sun had a bite to it today, warning that summer would soon be in full swing and they'd be dealing with forty-degree days and very short tempers around town. She slathered on suncream rather than getting into her stinger suit immediately. There was a chance she wouldn't have to get in the water.

The *Oceanid* anchored not far from the island and the blue and white dive flag was out, indicating people were underwater. Dot pulled up alongside and Sherlock tied her craft to theirs. She grabbed her backpack and climbed aboard, Sherlock giving her a hand. He seemed to have no problems with his prosthetic leg any longer. Tess and Sam stood around a table.

Dot frowned. "I forgot you were going to be here."

Tess smiled. "I'm calculating the wreck plume based on the weights of the goods we know were on board." She tucked her black hair behind her ear.

"That's great." Tess had been unsure and timid when Dot had first met her, and it was nice to see her confidence grow. "How long have the others been down?"

Sam answered. "They should surface any minute. Oliver noticed the damage at the end of his first dive and wanted to go down again and expand his search area to see if anything else had been damaged."

At least she wouldn't have to speak to him yet. She could do her own investigation. "I'll get my things."

Chapter 9

Oliver forced himself to breathe slowly as he swam past the disturbed wreckage. Coral had been ripped and there was a gaping hole where a cannon from the seventeenth century had lain.

Vandals, thieves, bastards.

He'd known this was going to happen. He should have listened to his gut and not allowed himself to be distracted by his own desires to see Dot. Andrew's seasickness had given him the excuse he'd been looking for. He'd put his own feelings before the job.

Foolish and unprofessional.

His anger at the vandals and himself simmered as he took a final photo and then surfaced. His students were already on board and the police boat was tied up next to the *Oceanid*. Dot was here.

The excited skip of his heart only increased his anger. She'd shown no interest in him. His delusion that she felt anything had led to his loss of focus and the cannon being stolen.

He hauled himself aboard and took off his equipment, glaring at Dot. She wore a stinger suit, the fabric clinging to her skin, showing her curves. So beautiful. The rush of jealousy as she smiled at something Sam said fuelled his temper.

Don't be stupid.

He brushed the excess water from his hair and strode over. "You're too late."

Her eyebrows raised at his abrupt tone. "For what?"

"To stop the theft. You knew treasure hunters were swarming the town, and you did nothing to protect the site."

Sam cleared his throat, but Oliver didn't look at him as he waited for Dot's response.

"I understand you're angry—"

"Of course I'm angry. The cannon was irreplaceable. It's probably going to sit in some dickhead's man cave and he'll brag to all of his friends about it."

"If he brags, someone will eventually have a conscience and tell the authorities."

Her calm, rational tone and the lack of expression on her face made him want to yell further. He wanted some emotion from her, even if it was to yell back at him. Anything to show she had feelings.

Sam shifted and Dot held up a hand to stop him from speaking. "What would you like me to do?"

He bit his tongue to stop from blurting out the truth. That he wanted her to care for him like she used to. He swore and spun around, stalking to the other side of the boat.

Get a grip.

He exhaled, trying to let go of the anger. When he turned, his students were staring at him with varying levels of discomfort on their faces.

Shit.

He exhaled again and walked back. "I'm sorry. I'm annoyed at myself for not listening to my gut."

She nodded. "How bad is the damage?"

"Bad enough." He let out another breath before

showing her the photos on his camera. Her arm brushed his as she stepped closer to see the camera display. Tingles spread over his skin and Dot's quiet intake of breath as she leaned into him and then shifted away told him perhaps she wasn't as indifferent as she appeared. Hope tempered his anger. "They've taken the cannon and damaged the surrounding area." He handed her the camera and allowed his fingers to brush hers as he did so.

Soft. Warm.

It took a moment before Dot pulled away. She cleared her throat. "Can you send those to me?" She gave him her work email address and then went over to her gear, where she radioed the station. "Colin, head down to the marina and check if anyone was there last night. We're looking for someone who might have seen people unloading a cannon, or people coming or going."

"Roger."

Her prompt investigation into the matter dissolved what was left of his anger. "You think they might have unloaded it immediately?" Oliver asked.

"Depends on whether they were opportunistic thieves or professionals," Dot said, her thumb rubbing the finger he'd touched.

He smiled.

"They'd need some good equipment to lift a cannon from the ocean floor, so they would have had a big boat with a decent range," Dot continued. "They may come to shore anywhere."

Meaning they'd never get it back, but the hope Dot might feel something for him, tempered his disappointment.

"I'll take a look," Dot continued. "Can you give me the coordinates?"

"You scuba now?" He'd tried for months to get Dot to learn to dive, but she'd freaked out and refused to try again.

She shook her head. "It's not deep. I'll snorkel."

She would struggle to stay down for long enough to do any kind of investigation. "I'll go with you." As she opened her mouth to argue, he added, "I can take you straight there, and you can share my tank when we go under."

She hesitated, the refusal on her face, before finally she nodded, her police mask sliding into place. "Let's go." She slipped on a weight belt and moved to the marlin board with the rest of her gear.

His gut clenched. This distance between them wasn't right. At one time she'd been the first person he'd thought of when he woke in the morning, the one he called any time he had news. Back then he'd been determined to succeed, to be one of the few people who had a career in maritime archaeology, and everything else had been secondary—except Dot.

But she wasn't the friendly, sweet, hard-working woman he remembered. Was that person still underneath her facade somewhere?

Sherlock had filled Oliver's tank and Oliver followed her into the water. Together they swam the short distance to the wreck. Dot took a few deep breaths and dived under, the weight belt keeping her from being too buoyant as she took photos of the disturbed site. Her movements were slow, calm, and nothing on her face showed she was scared. He hovered next to her, while she continued moving around the site, her gaze focused on the task at hand.

He frowned. How could she hold her breath for so long? She'd been down there for a couple of minutes. His muscles tightened as he held out the spare regulator to her, but she ignored him. He clenched his hands, resisting the urge to yank her to the surface. She seemed fine, still moving to get the best angles for her shots.

When she surfaced, she'd been under for almost four minutes. She took a deep breath of air.

"What the hell was that?" Oliver demanded, unable to keep the shock and fear from his tone.

She raised her eyebrow. "What?"

"The last time we went diving together you couldn't bear to be under water that long."

"A lot has changed in ten years, Oliver."

His name on her lips made him pause. It brought back so many memories of good times, laughter, love. He pushed down his fear as he floated closer. "Have you had free-diving lessons?"

That hesitation again before she nodded. "I enjoyed being able to stay underwater, but hated the weight of the tank and the amount of water on top of me. So I learnt free-diving and only snorkel at shallow depths."

It was just like Dot to take the bits she liked and find a solution. "That's great." They treaded water only inches away, the flow of water from Dot's strokes caressing him. He gazed at her, her brown eyes reminding him of strong dark tea. Her eyes always grew darker when she was aroused. "Really great."

She cleared her throat, stuck the snorkel back in her mouth and swam back to the boat.

Conversation ended. He frowned. He needed to stop her from walking—or swimming—away from him all the time.

By the time he reached the boat, Dot was stripping out of her stinger suit. Underneath was a navy, one-piece swimsuit which was cut just high enough to show off a little of her butt. He'd always loved running his hands over it and dragging her closer to him. She'd fit so neatly against him.

Dot glanced at him as if feeling his eyes on her, and then straightened, grabbed her bag, and went into the cabin to get changed.

Could she read his expression?

"What's the plan?" Sam asked him.

Oliver blinked. Right. He had an expedition to lead. "We'll go back to town, get our things, and return to stay out here until we're done."

Andrew groaned. "Do we have to?"

Oliver bit down on his annoyance. "Yes. I'm sorry you've not been well, but you can see what can happen if the wreck isn't guarded."

"Someone could come while we're in town now."

It would take an incredible amount of cheek to raid the wreck in the middle of the day, but Andrew had a point.

"I'm sticking around for a while," Dot said, coming out of the cabin. "I've got some work to do out here."

Oliver frowned, but it was Sam who said what he was thinking. "You shouldn't be out here by yourself."

"I'll be fine. My team knows where I am."

"Sherlock can stay with you," Sam insisted.

"Sherlock needs to help you with the boat," Dot replied.

"I'll stay." Oliver regretted the words, the moment they came out. Stupid. His feelings for Dot were what had got them into this mess. Still, he pushed forward. "My team can pack my bag, and we already have enough groceries for the week in the fridge."

Dot scowled.

"Great idea," Sam agreed. "If Dot needs to return earlier, she can bring you back with her."

"I'm doing police work. Oliver can't come with me."

"Let's chat." Sam motioned Dot away from the others and they stood at the stern of the boat, murmuring.

Although Sam hadn't been in Retribution Bay very long, he seemed to know Dot well. Oliver shook his head and smothered his jealousy. Sam had also told him about his partner, Penelope, and his tone was always full of love and admiration.

Finally they returned and Dot said, "Get what you need. You're coming with me." If her happiness about the idea could be rated from one to ten, hers would be minus ten.

Could she be any clearer in her disinterest?

Her body might react to him, but she didn't want him.

He needed to move on and stop hurting himself like this. Oliver grabbed his backpack, giving instructions to his students.

"It won't take us long to prepare the boat," Sam said as he handed them both a sandwich. "We should be back in a couple of hours."

"Great. See you then." He climbed into the police boat and grabbed the rope Sherlock threw him. They motored towards one of the other islands. "What do you need to do?"

She barely glanced at him. "I didn't have time to finish searching the islands the other day."

Despite the sun blaring down on them, the chill factor on the boat was extra high. Oliver sat in the seat next to Dot, but small talk would be too difficult over the engine noise, and he wasn't sure what he wanted to say.

Dot checked the depth of the water, peering over the bow to spot coral as they approached the first island.

"Want me to be spotter?"

She nodded. "I want to circumnavigate the island."

He climbed onto the bow and, using hand signals, navigated them around the first island with its sandy shore and dense bushes, and then onto the next, slightly larger island, further away from the shore. He peered onto the beach. "Are those footprints?"

Dot had binoculars out and was scanning the island. She nodded. "See if you can find us a way to the shore."

Further around on the end of the island, he found

them a gap in the reef. As the boat rubbed against the sand, he jumped off, pulling it further up, hoping Dot wouldn't strand him here.

Dot handed him his pack as she joined him on the shore. "You can stay here."

Fat chance. "I could do with stretching my legs."

"You'll follow police instructions."

Frustration filled him. "Drug smugglers are dangerous, Dot. I'm not letting you stumble on something by yourself."

Her gaze sharpened. "What do you know about it?"

Did she really suspect him? "I was there, remember?"

A definite eye-roll. "I'm capable and armed. You'll get in my way if I do run into anyone."

"You're the most capable person I know," he retorted, as his earlier anger returned with a vengeance. "You're determined to think the worst of me, but I've done nothing wrong." His pulse raced. It was time to lay it all out. If this didn't work, he'd accept there was nothing between them anymore. "I loved you once and I *still* care for you, Dot. I don't want you going into danger alone."

Her eyes narrowed. "You never loved me," she spat, walking away.

She'd gone too far. He grabbed her arm, stopping her. "Don't you tell me how I feel. It was *you* who wouldn't give us a shot. *You* ghosted me and I had no way of knowing why. I loved you more than I'd loved anyone in my life."

Her eyes widened, and then narrowed to slits. "Don't you dare blame our breakup on me. *You* left me. Your job was more important than our relationship."

Shock pierced him, and he shook his head. "I wanted to do long distance, but you didn't even consider it."

Her hands closed and opened as if fighting the urge to punch him, and she took a moment before she replied.

"We had just agreed to move in together," she stated, her voice even and viciously controlled. "I turned down the job I wanted in order to stay in Perth with you. And the very next day, you tell me you're leaving to spend a year overseas. You didn't even discuss it with me. Tell me, how is that love?"

Oliver had no words. He couldn't remember anything about Dot being offered a position. "What job?"

She took a step back, shaking her head. "I had the choice between a place in Carnarvon, or a place in the city. I chose Perth, despite hating living in the city, for you."

He remembered her often complaining about the noise, the traffic and the people, but he hadn't paid attention to it. "Carnarvon wouldn't have given you any career progression."

She laughed. "I didn't want career progression. I wanted to be closer to home."

His muscles tightened as he defended his actions. "Why? Your parents never cared where you lived."

Hurt flashed across her face. Shit. What a way to convince her he was right.

"They didn't, but I had others who did. It might make no sense to you, but I love Retribution Bay. I love the ocean and the ranges, and I love the people here." She spoke with passion for the first time, her arms waving like they used to when she was younger and less controlled. "I love the quiet, the space, the landscapes. I was never happy in the city. I only stayed because of you."

He opened his mouth to speak, but she kept talking, on a roll now.

"I talked to you about my job options, and you convinced me to turn down the job in Carnarvon so we could be together. Then the very next day you announced you'd accepted the job in Papua New

Guinea."

"That was a once in a lifetime opportunity. I wanted to continue our relationship. You ghosted me."

"Because your job was more important than I was," Dot said. "I've lived with being second-best all my life. I wasn't doing it again. Not with you. I thought you were different." Her voice broke. "I was wrong."

This time when she walked away, Oliver didn't stop her. He couldn't. He was stuck in place as if her words were chains holding him down. The flash of realisation almost knocked him on his arse. Finally he understood why Dot had cut him off. And to his older and wiser self, it made perfect sense.

He was an imbecile.

He'd been self-absorbed, so cocky about what he wanted, he hadn't thought how his actions might have affected anyone else. His childhood had been full of love and acceptance and support.

Dot's on the other hand…

He vividly remembered the night she'd confided in him. It was a couple of months after they had started dating. They were lying in bed, in the dark, talking, getting to know one another. He'd wanted to know everything about her, so when she'd brushed off his question about her parents, he'd pushed for more information.

"They're parents," she'd said. "They did their bit for the world by procreating and couldn't wait until I moved out."

He hadn't been able to comprehend it. They'd never been to a school assembly, or sports carnival, they'd never let her have any friends sleep over, but she could go to as many as she liked. They barely remembered her birthday. They'd been disinterested and absent.

He closed his eyes as he remembered his vow. "I'll never make you feel like that. You will always be my centre." He'd meant every word, but probably didn't understand the depth of her feelings on the matter.

Stupid, idiotic boy.

That night she'd also told him about Brandon, her boyfriend from high school, who had left town without saying goodbye. That had wounded her as well, but she'd understood he'd been grieving for his brother who had just died.

Oliver's behaviour would have been the ultimate betrayal. She'd opened herself to him, trusted him, confided in him, and he'd tossed her trust aside for a career opportunity. He hadn't discussed it with her, hadn't even considered how she'd feel, too excited about the lucky break.

It was no wonder she hated him.

His stomach swirled with nausea. He'd been so sure he was the injured party, so righteous in his need to tell her she'd broken his heart, when really he'd been the one to stomp hers into the ground.

He fought the urge to run after her as she strode away, back straight, arms swinging, her entire posture full of emotion.

She needed time to calm down.

He needed time to figure out how to fix this.

Was there any way she would forgive him?

Chapter 10

Dot didn't let her tears fall until she was sure Oliver wasn't following her. How dare he blame their breakup on her? She'd been so devastated she hadn't got out of bed for two days. Only Nhiari's threat to call Lindsay and tell her what had happened had been enough to get her to move.

She exhaled and dashed at the tears as she strode along the shoreline back to where she'd seen the footprints. She didn't have time for this distraction. Her focus had to be on the job. This island was the final one in the group, the only one she hadn't searched. Dot swallowed hard, repressing the emotions, putting up her wall of Kevlar. There'd be time to think about Oliver later, when she was lying in bed, trying to sleep. Right now, she needed to find clues.

She got her camera out of her bag and took photos of the footprints. Any trace of a boat had been washed away by the waves. The prints appeared close to the high tide line and then disappeared as they moved into the softer sand. Still, their direction was clear. She scanned the bushes and mangroves which grew on this side of the island. Nothing broken, nothing out of place. Also, no sound aside from the quiet buzz of insects and the occasional bird call.

Focused now, she walked closer, looking for a sign someone had been this way. The footprints could have been from a fisherman or tourist who'd been curious enough to explore the island. But the boat wouldn't have landed where the footprints began, unless it was high tide and the boat's hull was shallow enough to get over the reef.

Some limestone rocks peeked out from the bushes and leaves scattered on the ground. More than anywhere else.

Dot approached. A few broken branches. Carefully she lifted the remaining branches out of the way. The sand was firmer here, and another footprint was clear. Whoever it was had come this way. She took another photo as her heartbeat slowed and her focus narrowed.

A quick glance behind showed Oliver still with the boat at the other end of the island. Good.

Should she call dispatch? Procedure told her she had to, but she could almost guarantee something urgent would come up that required her to leave. Instead, she pressed forward, moving under the broken branches and into a dark hollow. She blinked so her eyes could adjust and then sucked in a sharp breath.

The bushes had been cut away, so only the top branches were still there, and a camouflaged net had been set up to hide the area further from flying eyes. Dot stood upright, but the net brushed the top of her head. Anyone taller than her—and that was most people— would have to stoop. The mangroves grew in the water, but again had been cut away to leave enough space for a small boat.

This is where Clark had hidden the dinghy the day he'd shot Mark.

But how did he get it in? The mangroves surrounded

the ocean side of the area.

Tamping down her desire to know more, she got out her camera, documenting everything before she stepped further inside. A small cave was filled with gear, but it was too dim for her to see the details from here. She finished taking her photos and put on gloves.

Surely something here would provide the information they needed to identify Clark. He'd remained unidentified aside from a first name for months. If they could identify him, they could identify the man in charge as before Clark had died, he'd revealed his father was Stonefish's leader.

Her radio buzzed. "Dot, do you copy?"

Annoyance filled her, and she pushed down her desire not to answer. "What is it, Colin?" She moved forward, eyes on the cave.

"Rodney wants to know where you are. He says he has information he needs to discuss."

She groaned. Rodney would need to know about this. "Tell him to go down to the marina. Sam will arrive there shortly. He can bring Rodney here." The cave was filled with tins and dry goods sealed in plastic containers, a small gas stove and a sleeping bag. She smiled.

"Dot, I don't have time." Rodney's entitled drawl came over the radio. "I've got a plane to catch."

"Cancel it," Dot said. "You're going to want to see this."

"Dot, I'm a very busy man. I have other cases to work on."

She didn't want to say anything over the radio. They already knew Stonefish listened in. "You'll get back to Perth and have to turn around and return. Trust me." She smiled, knowing he would hate having to trust her.

She took more photos but touched nothing. Rodney would be pissed off enough when he arrived. If she touched *his* crime scene, it would be worth an hour of berating and she didn't have the patience. Though she hadn't been impressed by his chain of custody so far. It was almost as if he wanted the evidence to be contaminated.

The thought made her pause. Rodney had always been the type to cut corners, to throw others under the bus if it meant he got ahead. Stonefish could have got to him. One of her friends in the organised crime division had said he'd insisted on being the one to come to Retribution Bay.

"This is ridiculous. I don't have time. You need to return immediately."

Was that a hint of panic in his voice? Dot's eyes adjusted to the dim light, and she scanned the cave again. Wait. There was a tiny reddish glow at the front of the cave, almost like the light from some equipment.

She switched on her torch and nearly missed the camera lens. She would have, if not for the light, because the lens was so well hidden. Security camera. Maybe one of those which turned on only when motion triggered it. Watching her. She pretended as if she hadn't seen it, while her mind raced.

Colin had radioed her just after she'd entered the area.

Her muscles tightened. Definitely someone watching her, someone who wanted her out of there.

But she'd found it now. It was too late to hide.

"Dot, I am your superior and you will follow my orders."

She laughed and rolled her eyes, knowing it would irritate him if he was indeed watching. "You're not my superior and I don't answer to you."

The only reason to want her to leave so desperately would be so they could clear it out while she was gone. She could play that game, but she didn't have any backup.

Her mind raced as she thought it through.

She would spot any boat heading this way if she went back to town, unless they came from the east, the side of the gulf which was uninhabited.

But that would mean someone was already out there.

She kept moving, trying for a casual perusal of the cave, but searching for more cameras. She didn't find any.

"Dot, don't be childish."

Irritation made her scowl. The other option was they would wait until she got to town and then hold her there for long enough to clear out the island. That made more sense, because Rodney could talk for hours about his own importance. But it would also mean she would lose all the evidence. There had to be fingerprints and DNA here, another chance to find out who was behind this.

If they were transmitting live, it meant there also had to be some kind of satellite signal. Could it be traced?

She made a big show of her irritation and sighed, taking a few more photos of the cave. "I'll be there in an hour."

Dot pushed the bushes out of the way and grabbed her gun as someone rushed towards her. She had it up and levelled before she recognised Oliver. He stopped short, eyes wide, hands raised.

"Fuck, Dot. It's me."

Slowly she lowered the gun as her heart clenched, the emotions rushing back, battering against the emotional wall she'd erected. She swallowed hard. "Sorry. I forgot you were here." Desperately wished he wasn't here making her feel things she didn't want to feel.

"You were gone so long I was worried something had happened."

"I'm fine." She couldn't think about Oliver's declaration that he still cared for her. He could be working for Stonefish. It might be some kind of ruse.

The thought centred her, helped keep her emotions

in check. She retrieved the satellite phone from her backpack and called her friend in tech crimes.

"You found something," Oliver said.

Dot nodded, monitoring his reaction while she waited for her friend to pick up.

Oliver glanced towards the bushes and then back at her, waiting patiently.

Finally he was listening to her.

"Amani speaking."

Dot moved away from Oliver. "It's Dot. I have a huge favour to ask and the fewer people who know what you're doing, the better."

"Shit. What's going on?"

She lowered her voice. "Can you trace a satellite signal?"

"Yeah. Where is it?"

"Same location as I'm calling from."

"Give me a minute." Keys clattered in the background and Dot checked the time. She needed her full kit to get as much evidence as she could. But maybe she could do it without Stonefish getting suspicious.

"Oliver, we need to go." She gestured for him to follow and then strode across the shore back to the police boat.

"I've got you on some island in the gulf of Retribution Bay," Amani said.

"That's right. There should be another signal on the island. I need it traced and then, if possible, disrupted."

"I'm on it. What are you working on?"

"An organised crime ring." Excitement built in Dot. "Get the anchor," she ordered Oliver.

"That's pretty big for your small town."

"I know, but I think I've finally got a break."

"The organised crime division not helping you?"

"They sent Rodney."

Amani groaned. "You poor thing. No wonder you

need my help." Some more tapping of keys.

"Tell me," she said. "Is the Oliver who is with you Oliver Anderson?"

Dot groaned. "Yes. It's a long story." She should have remembered Amani knew him. She glanced at the engine. "Any idea how to stop a boat engine from starting?"

"Dirty the carburettor," Amani answered.

Dot raised her eyebrows. "How do you know?"

"Ugh. I dated a guy who was into drag racing," she said. "I spent hours listening to him talking about engines."

Dot took another look at the engine cover. It would take too long to get the carburettor out.

"Got the signal," Amani said. "It's registered with a company who is always helpful. I'll give my contact a call and get a name for you."

Elation filled her. "Thanks. I owe you. Any chance you can disrupt the signal?"

"Not personally. I might be able to get the provider to do that, but I'd need justification."

"Don't worry about it." She'd make do with what she had. "Thanks for your help."

"I'll call when I have the information."

Dot turned the key on the boat and nothing happened. She frowned. Oh, the gear stick wasn't in neutral. She placed her hand on the gear stick and then hesitated. This was the answer. Oliver was at the bow, anchor in hand, ready for her to start the engine. She made a fuss of trying multiple things and then called, "The engine won't start."

"I can have a go."

She gave him a withering look. "Are you going to mansplain how to use an engine?"

He scowled. "I've been around a lot of boat engines. Maybe I can get it working."

"I can't let anyone who isn't authorised touch the engine. I'll call it in. Put out the anchor again." She grabbed the two cases she needed and when Oliver returned, she handed them to him.

"What are you doing?"

"I might as well do some work while we're waiting to be rescued."

"I'm good with engines, Dot. Let me look."

She gritted her teeth at his plea and shook her head, pocketing the key so he couldn't get any ideas. "Find a spot in the shade." She reached for the cases, but he didn't let go.

He studied her, his expression intense. "Have you called it in?"

His attention to detail was one thing she had loved about him. "Will do so in a minute." She tugged at the cases, their bodies so close she could feel his heat. She jerked hard, needing to distance herself from him, and he let one go.

"Why delay?"

Rodney would radio for an update any minute. She strode across the sand. "That's none of your business."

"It is if I'm stranded out here."

Dot glanced at him, saw his concern. Guilt filled her. "Please, trust me."

He met her gaze and nodded. "Always." He fell in step with her.

Her breath caught in her lungs. Instant agreement, instant trust. She'd done nothing to deserve it this time around, but there it was. It shouldn't matter so much. She swallowed hard as she increased her stride. She could obsess over it later. At the row of bushes, she stopped. "You need to stay here."

Her radio crackled. "Dot, how far out are you?" Rodney.

"Ah, having a little engine trouble. Just getting Oliver

to look over it." She winced at the lie and shot Oliver an apologetic glance. "We'll be on the way soon."

"Bullshit. You're disobeying my order."

"The boat won't start, Rodney. I'm fixing it as fast as I can."

The furrow on Oliver's forehead grew deeper.

"I'll send someone to tow you."

"Shouldn't be needed. Give me another ten minutes. Sorry, I won't catch you before your plane leaves." She pictured him swearing, and it made her smile.

"What the hell is going on?" Oliver asked.

Dot sobered. "I can't tell you, Oliver."

"Is this about the drugs?"

She nodded.

"Is it some kind of power play?"

"No." Why would he think that? "I need to process a crime scene. Stay here."

"Don't you need an eyewitness? An impartial observer or something?"

She didn't, but if Rodney was involved, he would do what he could to discredit her. But she also didn't want Oliver to appear on Stonefish's radar, which he would if they saw him on camera. Unless he was already working with them. She closed her eyes for a moment, hating that she couldn't trust him. "Stay here, please."

He nodded.

Dot returned to the hidden camp and made a show of setting up, setting her backpack directly in front of the security camera so it was blocked.

Then she got to work.

"What is this place?"

Dot spun, hand moving to her gun before she recognised Oliver. He stood a little slouched, his head pressing against the netting as he glanced around.

"I told you to stay out."

"I didn't like having you out of my sight."

She ignored the tug on her heart. He was here now. He might as well stay in the shade. Even if he was working for Stonefish, he knew she'd found the camp. Seeing inside didn't make much difference. "A hideout of sorts." She pointed to the patch of sand near the water. "Sit there while I process it. If you move, I'll charge you with contaminating a crime scene."

The mangroves reminded Dot she hadn't investigated them. She was certain Stonefish had hidden the dinghy here, but how had they got through the trees? She took off her shoes and waded into the water to the mangroves. Fake. The trees covering the entrance were plastic and fibreglass. She lifted one, which required a bit of effort, but it cleared a section to make way to the ocean. About half a dozen were fake. Genius. The island was so remote that few people would come this way, but even if they did, no one would look twice at the mangroves.

She replaced it, took more photos, and waded back to shore.

"It's a pretty complex set up." Oliver sat on the sand, his knees pulled up to his chest, arms wrapped around them. The posture was casual, but also sexy, reminding her of the days they used to spend at the beach together. Setting up a sunshade, taking a picnic, and spending hours in the water where their hands would roam. Heading back to his or her place, showering off the saltwater, still not having their fill of each other.

She'd thought anything was possible in those days.

"Dot?"

Her mind struggled to remember what he'd said… complex setup. She nodded, pushing away the unwanted memories. He had that right. But hopefully Stonefish's confidence at how well it was hidden had made them sloppy.

She needed a break.

She smiled and continued processing the scene.

Chapter 11

Oliver had so many questions, but he kept them to himself. Something big was at play here, something that had the potential to affect Dot's career if he understood things correctly. Now wasn't the time to talk about their relationship or demand answers.

He bit his tongue and settled on the sand to watch her work, his hand going to the ring at his neck. At one time he'd imagined giving the ring to Dot when he asked her to marry him. That had been back when he was sure they would work things out when he finished the expedition.

When it was clear they wouldn't, he hadn't been able to part with the ring. It was a token from his first expedition, and perhaps his sub-conscious had still associated it with Dot and refused to accept they were over. So it had become his good luck charm.

Dot was methodical, working one item at a time, fingerprinting everything, bagging the sleeping bag and then moving on to the boxes, which contained a drone and some kind of technical equipment. The camp was far too well set up for it to be somewhere a fisherman camped when he wanted to get away from it all.

The camouflaged netting added another layer of

intrigue. This was the kind of thing he'd only seen in movies.

This spoke of organised crime, of drugs, which could come with a lot of violence.

But Dot was ignoring Rodney's orders.

Sure, the man had been a toxic prick at the academy, but he called the shots in relation to drugs.

Didn't he?

Unease hovered on Oliver's skin. Just how much had Dot changed in the past ten years? "What do you do with all of this?"

Dot glanced at him, her brow furrowed. "We'll store it at the station tonight and take it to Carnarvon tomorrow. They'll process it or send it to Perth."

Another difficulty of working in a remote town. They didn't have the facilities they needed.

It was close to an hour before the sounds of an engine reached them. Dot glanced up. "Can you see who that is? It might be Sam back, but it also might be Rodney. I need another thirty minutes." She tossed him the keys to the boat. "If the gear lever isn't in neutral, it won't start."

No wonder she hadn't let him look at the engine. He grinned at the trust she perhaps unknowingly showed him by telling him the truth. "I'll make a great damsel in distress."

Their eyes met and Dot's smile made him feel as if he was ten feet tall. He would get her the thirty minutes she needed. Oliver brushed the bushes aside and strode along the beach, raising his hand to his eyes to shade them from the sun.

The *Oceanid* was lowering its anchor offshore, Sam behind the helm and Sherlock on the bow. Several other people were on deck. Oliver checked for a signal and found he had one bar. This island was closer to town than Retribution Island. He tried calling Sam, but the call failed, so he sent a quick text.

Take as much time as you can launching the tender.

He reached the police boat and waved. Up on the top deck, Sam glanced at his phone and then gave him the OK signal divers used to communicate with the boat when they surfaced.

Good. He got the message.

Oliver sat in the captain's seat and watched as people scurried over the deck. The person gesticulating wildly had to be Rodney, and Oliver could only imagine what excuse Sam and Sherlock had come up with as to why it was taking so long. He kind of wished he was a fly on the wall.

Finally, after about ten minutes, the tender launched with Sam at the tiller and Rodney on board. Sam took a slow, circuitous route to make it to the shore and by the time they arrived, about fifteen minutes had passed. Oliver leapt over the side and helped pull the tender up on the shore. "I'm so glad to see you," he said. "We're low on water and it's getting pretty hot out here."

"Where's Dot?" Rodney barked, his gaze going straight to the hideout. That was interesting.

Oliver gestured behind him. "I think she's gone to the bathroom." He grimaced. "Neither of us could wait."

Sam handed him a cold bottle of water. "What's up with the engine?"

Oliver shrugged. "Maybe the battery. It doesn't even turn over."

Rodney started down the beach and Oliver jogged in front of him. "Hey mate, where are you off to? We need your help."

"Sam can help you. I have to speak with Dot."

"Didn't you hear me? She's gone to the bathroom. It's going to be awkward if you find her." He turned to Sam. "Is it considered sexual harassment if you knowingly enter a room where a person could be naked?"

Sam shrugged, hiding a grin. "Rodney would know

the answer."

Rodney's face went red.

"I'm sure she won't be long," Oliver said. "And I'd appreciate help with the boat. Hopefully, by the time she arrives, it will be fixed."

Rodney pressed his lips together and then spun on his heels. "Let me look."

Oliver grinned behind his back, and Sam winked as they returned to the police boat. Oliver had made sure the gear lever was just out of neutral before the tender had arrived.

"Where's the key?" Rodney demanded.

"Oh, here." Oliver fumbled in his pocket as long as he could, dropping the key on the deck of the boat before finally picking it up and handing it to the man.

Rodney turned the key and nothing happened. He checked around the engine as if looking for switches and it was clear he had no idea what he was looking for. The man was too arrogant to admit to it though.

The radio on the boat crackled. "Rodney, can I get a hand over here?" Dot.

She stood by the entrance of the hideout and waved them towards her.

"You said she'd gone to the bathroom," Rodney yelled.

"I thought she had," Oliver replied. "I can help her."

"Stay here." Rodney included Sam in his glare. "See if you can fix the boat." He jogged across the sand towards Dot.

"Is she going to be all right with him?" Oliver said.

"She'll be fine. Want to tell me why she needed more time?"

Oliver pursed his lips. "I'll let her tell you."

Sam nodded. "Is the engine really dead?"

"I don't think so." He shifted the gear stick into neutral and turned the key. The engine roared to life.

Rodney glanced back, his expression livid, and Oliver switched it off again. "I'd forgotten how satisfying it was to take him down a peg or two."

"Did you do that often?" Sam asked.

"Not as much as I would have liked to. He hasn't changed."

"Have you?"

The question made him pause. Had he changed from the self-absorbed immature man who had broken Dot's heart? "Maybe. I hope so." He wanted to sit with Dot and discuss what had happened, but when would he have a chance? "Are my students on board?"

"Yeah, they're organising tomorrow's dives."

"Everything is arranged to stay on board overnight?"

"Sherlock's setting up the rooms at the moment."

Damn. It was what he wanted, but it meant he wouldn't see Dot again. Especially not if Rodney sent her home.

"Do you want to head back to the boat?" Sam asked.

Oliver shook his head, his gaze on where Dot and Rodney had disappeared through the bushes. "I'd rather wait for Dot."

Sam nodded and sat on a chair. "What do you know about Stonefish?"

Oliver frowned and glanced at him. "The fish? It's found up here, so you should be careful where you tread. Pain is supposed to be the worst on Earth."

"What about the company?" His gaze was focused and probing.

"Is that some kind of surf brand?" He shook his head. "I've never heard of it, but one of my students might have."

Sam smiled. "I'll ask."

Oliver checked the time. They could do a couple of dives this afternoon, but he couldn't shake the feeling not to leave Dot.

"What are you anxious about?"

"Dot." Oliver had been right about Sam. Beneath his laid-back attitude, the man saw everything. "Rodney was one of the few people who used to get under her skin and he knew it. He would look for reasons to get her kicked out of the academy, probably because she was his main competition." He glanced at Sam. "I'm half expecting only one of them to come back," he joked.

"Then let's get closer." Sam leapt over the side of the boat.

Oliver followed. "That will irritate Dot. She'll think we don't believe she can handle herself."

"You know her well," Sam said.

"I used to."

"And now?"

"We'll see." Oliver wasn't spilling his guts to a man he barely knew, but he appreciated Dot had someone who had her best interests at heart, someone who would protect her if he wasn't here.

They strode across the beach towards the hideout. "What's in there?" Sam asked.

Should he tell Sam? He was ex-military, so surely that gave him some kind of security clearance. And Dot trusted him. "A hideout with fake, moveable mangroves and enough space to hide a small boat."

Sam's gaze sharpened, and he swore. "That's how they did it!"

Oliver frowned. "What's been going on here?"

Sam stared at him for a long moment and then said, "The man who shot Dot's brother escaped in a dinghy, but no one found the dinghy afterwards."

Oliver's mouth dropped open. "Mark was shot? Is he all right?"

"He died."

Shit. Dot had idolised her brother when she was younger. She had hoped she could salvage their relationship when she went back to Retribution Bay.

Had she done that?

Either way, her brother's murder would have devastated her, and Oliver hadn't been there for her.

Her parents would have been useless. "How did she cope?"

"Brandon or Nhiari would be the best ones to tell you. I wasn't here for it."

"Brandon Stokes? He's back here?"

"Moved back at the beginning of the year."

Shit. Were he and Dot back together? Brandon had broken her heart when she was a teenager, but they might have rekindled something. He glanced at Sam, debating whether to ask the question.

"Brandon's my best friend. He got married a couple of months ago. He and Dot are friends."

Oliver nodded his thanks for the answer, despite the unasked question. "They were close once." At least she'd had someone who knew how useless her parents were. No wonder she was so intent on processing the scene herself. "Did she catch who shot him?"

"A few days later, he kidnapped a friend and was killed during the rescue."

"Dot killed him?"

Sam shook his head. "Dot wasn't there for it."

"Why not?"

"It's complicated, and a whole other story."

Maybe Retribution Bay wasn't the sleepy little backwater he'd thought it was. "Do you get much crime up here?"

"This year we have." Sam put his finger to his lips as they neared the bushes.

"I should have your badge for this," Rodney growled. "You've destroyed our entire operation because you didn't follow my instructions."

"If you'd included me in your plans, I wouldn't have,"

Dot retorted. "How was I supposed to know you planted the camera there?"

"Your team has a leak," Rodney said.

"I know! Why do you think I ignored you?"

Oliver's mouth dropped open. This sounded like serious stuff. Had Dot inadvertently ruined the organised crime division's sting operation?

"What were you even doing here?" Rodney said.

"Checking the rest of the islands for evidence. There were only two I hadn't searched because I kept getting called back to town." Dot's voice lowered and became less emotional. "Every time I get close to something, I get a call, so when you radioed, I figured someone was trying to stop me again. I couldn't let this evidence slip away."

Rodney swore. "You disregarded my order."

"I didn't know it was your camera. You could have been…" she trailed off.

"Are you accusing me of working for Stonefish?" Rodney's tone went low and menacing.

Oliver shifted forward, but Sam stretched his arm out to stop him. Annoyed, he glanced over.

Wait, Sam mouthed.

Oliver glared, but did as he asked. Stonefish. There was that name again. Sam had asked him what he knew about it. What was it? Some kind of company? His eyes widened. Maybe they were the ones behind the drugs, some kind of cartel. Which meant Sam had suspected him of being involved as well.

His skin prickled as things fell into place.

Kidnapping, murder, drugs.

Suddenly he wanted Dot out of Retribution Bay.

As fast as possible.

Chapter 12

Dot shifted, her eyes not leaving Rodney as she readied herself for an attack. Keeping her tone flat, she said, "I would be an idiot if I didn't suspect you. Stonefish have already proven they have contacts in the police. They have a way of making certain the right people are in place where they need them." She smiled. "But don't consider yourself special. I don't trust any of your team or mine."

"It sounds as if you *are* stupid," Rodney spat. "If you've worked with these people for years and never suspected a thing."

She refused to be riled. He wasn't worth it, and if what he'd said about the camera was true, then she had stuffed up. "We don't know that Stonefish has been in operation up here for years. The first contact came at the beginning of the year."

Rodney ground his teeth together.

This antagonism wasn't getting them anywhere. "What do you want to do now? Leave the camera and take the evidence? If Colin knows about the camera, then chances are high the rest of the team does too."

"I didn't tell him. I just told him to call you back."

Interesting. "I didn't tell them exactly where I am,"

Dot said. "We could leave the camera in place. Someone might return."

"Your team will know as soon as we bring in the evidence."

"So we don't tell them. We can ship it to forensics without them knowing."

He struggled for a moment before he said, "Fine. I'll deal with it."

Agreeing with her had to kill him. It would be satisfying if the case wasn't so important.

Dot bagged the drone and some of the other smaller items, putting them into her backpack to carry. She didn't like the idea of him having possession of all the evidence. She still didn't trust him.

She pushed through the bushes to find Oliver and Sam on the other side. Her annoyance peaked, but at Sam's friendly smile, she exhaled. No point wasting her energy being angry at them. They had heard everything. "Head back to the boat before Rodney sees you." She glared to put urgency behind her soft command.

"Need a hand?" Oliver asked, his expression guilty.

"No. Go." He was another issue she needed time to think about. She shook her head. Her focus had to be on the case.

Was Rodney telling the truth, or double-bluffing her?

The men walked with her back to the police boat.

"Rodney's not going to kill you?" Oliver asked.

"Not today." She refused to feel guilty about interrupting his trap. If he'd been honest in the first place, this wouldn't have happened. Leaving so much evidence unprocessed made no sense. Rodney could have set up the camera, but cleared the hideout and then he would have caught the culprit on film, but also had the evidence.

She glanced at Oliver. She'd fed Oliver a lie about the evidence. It would go straight to Carnarvon, whether she took it or Rodney did. But if someone tried to break into the police station tonight, she'd know he was working for Stonefish.

She hoped it was quiet tonight.

As she returned for the second load, she passed Rodney, who glowered at her, but said nothing.

When they were done, and Sam had taken Oliver back to the *Oceanid*, Rodney said, "I'll drive this stuff straight to Carnarvon police station when we get back to shore."

"Great idea. Want me to organise you some accommodation there?"

"Yes. I'll be back tomorrow."

She started the engine and cruised past Sam's boat. Oliver was suited up for his next dive. "You're set?" she called.

Oliver gave her a thumbs up. "We'll call you if we have any issues."

As much as she enjoyed hearing his voice, she hoped she didn't hear from him. She needed a quiet night to process everything.

The sight of the *Oceanid* moored off the wreck site should be enough to deter would-be robbers. It might also mess with any plans Stonefish had.

Win-win really, and she didn't have to be here.

She waved and increased her speed, travelling across the gulf, ignoring Rodney on the seat next to her.

Dot lifted her head and let the breeze wash over her face, hoping it would sweep away the muddiness and enable her to think clearly. The return trip was rough, and the boat jolted up and down waves. She glanced at Rodney. Pale face, sweat beading, death grip on the arm rests. He was going to be sick.

She reached into the side pocket and pulled out an emesis bag, thrusting it at him. He glared as he took it. No point slowing down. It would only make it worse and take longer for them to get back to the marina.

When they finally reached the channel in, she radioed the station. "On our way back."

"Need a hand?" Colin responded.

"Negative. Boat's fixed."

Next to her, Rodney exhaled and handed back the unused emesis bag. She was impressed. It must have taken an inordinate amount of willpower for him not to throw up.

"Is your car down here?"

He nodded. "Just near the gate."

Great. They wouldn't have far to carry everything.

It took about fifteen minutes to transfer the evidence to Rodney's hire car.

"I'll book your accommodation when I get back to the station," she said. "I just need to clean the boat."

"I'll be back tomorrow."

Dot waited until he drove away before she spent a few minutes making sure the deck was clean and then refilling the petrol tanks. Finally she headed back to the station.

Colin met her at the door. "What happened out there?"

"Engine wouldn't start."

"No, on the wreck."

She'd forgotten that was the reason she'd gone out there. "Someone stole a cannon. The team are going to overnight on Sam's boat, so they came back to town to get what they needed while I stayed to monitor things. Did you get any information at the marina?"

He shook his head. "No one saw anything. Have you seen the wreck?"

She nodded. "I dived to assess the damage. Not much of the boat is left, just the metal stuff."

"No treasure?" He raised his eyebrows in hope.

"Don't tell me you're buying into the hype as well," Dot said, but smiled to lessen the bite in her words. "Anything down there is the property of the government. If anyone asks, there is no treasure."

Which reminded her she needed to get the real treasure out of Retribution Bay. Her queries with the local banks had been unsuccessful. They couldn't arrange appropriate transport. "Where are Martin and Pierre?"

"Some issue out at a PAWS campsite. Someone down there saying they paid for days they didn't get because of the storm and wanting to stay now."

She sighed. She'd had to warn people about the approaching storm and advise them to leave. Asking those who'd thought they could ride it out for their next of kin details had convinced them the situation was serious and they'd stopped arguing and left. She could appreciate they wanted to return to the stunning location, but the sites were often booked out for months in advance.

"Where's Rodney?" Colin asked.

"He got called to Carnarvon. He'll be back tomorrow." She had to organise his accommodation. "I need to do a few things in my office. Let me know if anything comes up."

She debated shutting her door, but left it open so it didn't give the impression she was hiding something. After messaging Rodney where he was staying that night, she opened her backpack and discovered the drone inside. She'd forgotten about it.

She might as well review it while she had it. Smiling, she withdrew the memory card from the drone and slid it into her computer. Quickly she copied the data onto her hard drive and then returned the card to the drone.

She packaged and addressed it and put it on her desk for the mail run.

Then she clicked on the first video.

Two boys about five and seven years old ran around, shrieking as the drone rose in the air above them, and behind them an older girl, maybe ten, stood with her arms crossed. Dot frowned. Those kids looked familiar. She'd definitely seen them around town.

Colin moved past the door and she bit her lip to stop from calling out and asking him if he recognised them. No one could know she had the footage.

She paused the video at a place which showed their faces clearly and took a screen shot. She isolated the girl as well as she could and took a photo, sending it to Darcy. *Do you recognise her?* The girl was about Lara's age.

While she waited for an answer, Dot opened another program and searched to see if anyone had reported a missing drone. Two hits.

One person had lost the device in a strong gust of wind and was hoping someone would find it. The others were the Hamiltons, who had reported their drone stolen from their car. Darcy's answer came through. *Natasha Hamilton.* Lara's nemesis. Faith had mentioned the girl a couple of times when they'd spoken about pony club. She lived to put others down. Her mother, Kristy, wasn't much better. Faith said she was constantly flirting with Darcy despite being married. And it wasn't harmless flirting.

Dot watched the video on double speed, but it was only a long shot of the beach from the ocean.

The next shot was a few days later, taken from one of the car parks on the top of the ranges. The drone flew through the valleys and dips as if searching for someone.

The shot after that was taken from the lighthouse and the drone soared north, over the ocean where whales were frolicking and the *Oceanid* was nearby waiting with passengers on board. Kristy was in control of the drone and from the time stamp, the kids would have been at school. Then a killer whale appeared, and the drone recorded the hunt of the whale calf and its mother.

Dot paused, her finger poised to click the next video. She checked the dates of each one and then compared those dates with the police reports.

Her heart rate increased.

She went back to the first video. When the drone reached its peak, it did a very slow three-sixty-degree rotation. In the distance, towards the south, she spotted a boat. The police boat. It was the date she and Nhiari had been called back early because of a domestic disturbance at Kristy's house. The call had come in only five minutes after this video was taken.

The video of the ranges was the day Matt had been kidnapped.

Coincidence?

Not likely.

Dot clicked on the next video. This time it was a man in control of the drone and with him was Kurt, Gretchen's ex. As it rose off the beach, she recognised the island where she'd found the hideout. The drone flew south, over Retribution Island, and hovered high above the beach where the Stokes family were swimming. Gretchen and Jordan were there, as was Arthur, and they were playing in the water.

This was how Stonefish spied on the Stokes. This video was dated after the drone had been reported stolen, but Dot was certain the man holding the controls was Kristy's husband, Steven. It was hovering high enough that it wouldn't have been heard.

The Hamiltons owned a silver dinghy.

She exhaled. What was the best way to deal with this? She couldn't go after them without giving away she'd seen the footage. But she could monitor them. Their domestic disputes were legendary, but no one had ever been injured. Dot clicked on their file, lining up the dates. They'd started around January, right when the trouble with Stonefish started, and they always occurred in time for her team to be dragged away from investigating Stonefish further.

Maybe her team wasn't involved. Maybe it was just these two.

She needed to get word to Nhiari, though chances were good that Lee already knew they were involved.

She reviewed the rest of the footage and then took the packaged drone with her as she left her office. Martin and Pierre were back. "I need to run an errand," Dot said. "I'll be back in an hour."

Her stomach rumbled as she left the station. All she'd had was a sandwich Sam had given her. Just another normal day. She stopped by the cafe to get a cream doughnut and was on her way to the airport when Rodney called.

He should be out of mobile range by now.

"Something wrong?" she answered.

"Where's the drone?"

Her eyebrows raised. Interesting he should notice the drone missing now, when he should be driving straight to Carnarvon, not going through the evidence they collected. "I accidentally tucked it into my backpack when we were carrying things to the boat. I just dropped it at the airport to send to Perth."

"Sloppy work, Dot. I'll come back and get it."

"I've already signed the chain of custody."

Rodney swore.

"Don't worry. It will be loaded and in Perth before you even get to Carnarvon. They've got better facilities there."

"You need to do better, Dot." He hung up.

She accelerated, resisting the urge to use her flashing lights. She didn't want to cause talk, but she had to make sure the package caught the flight. Hopefully she wouldn't pass Rodney on her way out.

Where and why had he stopped?

Perhaps he'd simply realised he hadn't seen the drone when they'd loaded the car.

After dropping the drone at the airport, she called the lab to check the status of her fingerprints evidence.

"Dot, thanks for calling me back," the technician said. "I didn't want to give details to anyone except you in light of what I found."

Dot frowned. "Wait. You called the station? Who did you speak to?"

"Colin."

Who hadn't told Dot about the call, even though he knew she was waiting for it. "What did you find?"

"The fingerprints belong to Constable Colin Lipscombe. Did he touch the barrels without gloves?"

Dot's mouth dropped open and her stomach swirled. Not Colin. "No. He wasn't there."

The technician swore. "Sorry, Dot."

"Yeah. Thanks." She hung up, mind whirling. Colin had always been so eager, so willing to be involved. He'd said his dream had always been to be a police officer, and he'd proven to be a hard worker, always offering to do overtime and extra shifts for the experience.

What had happened?

She debated calling Rodney, but he should be well and truly out of mobile range by now. Plus, she wanted a chance to question Colin first.

She needed another officer with her. Without Nhiari here, it would have to be Martin or Pierre, and while Pierre was more likely to take a neutral stance, Martin was next in the chain of command. They needed to be on the same page.

When she arrived back at the station, all her officers were there. She called Martin into her office. "We have a problem," she said as he closed the door.

Martin raised his eyebrows. "Another one?"

"Colin's fingerprints were on the blue drug barrel we found."

He rolled his eyes. "The kid messed up again?"

Dot shook her head. "I took those fingerprints on site. Before the barrel came in, before any of you touched it."

His eyes widened. "Shit."

"We need to question him. The lab called and left me a message, but Colin didn't pass it on, so it appears as if he knows what they'll find. I'm not sure why he hasn't run."

"Nowhere for him to go, I guess," Martin said. "Stonefish get rid of people who know too much."

Dot exhaled. "Let's get this over with." She opened her door and Colin looked up from his desk. His face fell. Yeah, he knew what was coming. "Colin, come into the interview room, please."

His shoulders slumped as he glanced behind her at Martin and then stood.

It was going to be a long afternoon.

Chapter 13

Oliver couldn't focus on work. The idea of Dot in danger niggled at him like an itch he couldn't scratch, making it difficult to concentrate. She was in town where he couldn't see her, where he couldn't protect her. Not that she needed his protection. Not anymore. Back at university he'd been the one introducing Dot to Perth, and he'd felt important teaching her the ways of the big city. She'd needed him. Now, if anything, she'd be protecting him, but that was beside the point. He wasn't with her like he should be.

Like he should have been all of these years.

He wanted to say to hell with the shipwreck, let people take whatever they wanted, if it meant he could be with Dot.

Stupid.

She didn't even want to be near him. Sure, they'd had a moment before Rodney had arrived, a slight thawing in the frost, but it didn't mean Dot had forgiven him.

"Oliver?"

He blinked and glanced at Sherlock, who was obviously waiting for an answer. "Sorry, I'm off with the fairies. What did you say?"

"Are you going on the next dive?"

His students were waiting for him, already suited up and ready to go, except Andrew, who was floating in the water because of his seasickness. "Of course." Quickly he zipped his wetsuit and put on his scuba gear, running through his checks with Sam.

"She can take care of herself," Sam murmured.

Oliver didn't bother denying his concern. "I don't like this."

"None of us do. The quicker we can catch them, the better. You're doing your bit here. It might be Stonefish representatives who are taking from the wreck."

That didn't make him feel any better. He turned to his students. "You continue to take recordings of everything. I'm going to search for more cannons." They nodded and jumped in.

Oliver stepped into the tender and put on his fins as Sherlock motored him to the spot they'd identified as a point of interest. Sherlock had sent up a drone earlier in the day to look for other parts of the ship. After three hundred years submerged, there wasn't any of the wooden structure left of the ship, but they'd found manmade items, things of metal and glass in particular. And there weren't enough cannons for this type of ship, particularly when it had been carrying such precious cargo. The journal had mentioned they had been jettisoned in the storm to stop it running aground.

Sherlock slowed a few hundred metres from the main wreck site and pointed. "Down there."

From here it was a dark lump, but there were definite lines on the edges. Oliver smiled as his heartbeat increased in anticipation. This was what he loved about the job. The thrill of discovering something which had been lost for centuries.

Sherlock put the boat into neutral and then Oliver went over into the cool, clear water. From this distance, it was clear the objects beneath him were manmade. There were too many straight lines for it to be natural. He descended slowly, scanning the lines, noting the weed and coral growth and the fish schooling around. A few metres away was another line, and beyond that, another.

Oliver took photos, falling into a rhythm with only the sound of his breathing disturbing the peace. He reached out and touched the first cannon, rubbing some of the growth from it and seeing the tarnish underneath. He counted those in the clump and then followed the path of lines until he couldn't find any more. Eight cannons. It never ceased to surprise him that the ships were so well armed, but piracy had been alive and well in those days. He took measurements, recording them on his underwater notepad, and then checked his tank. Enough air to explore a little further. The main wreck was in front of him, and they may have jettisoned other heavy items in an attempt to save the ship.

Plus, he'd never explored the area where he suspected there could be more drug barrels. This was how he could help Dot.

He swam slowly, scanning left and right to find any other artefacts. Something to the left caught his attention, a movement which didn't seem right. He turned and spotted the culprit. At first he thought it was more weed floating in the water, but then he noted what it was attached to. A large, navy-blue barrel.

More drugs.

Satisfaction filled him as he took a photo and made a note of the GPS.

It appeared he would get his wish. He'd be seeing Dot again.

With that thought warming him, he headed for the surface.

***

"Why did we find your fingerprints on the drug barrel?" Dot asked Colin after she'd gone through the preliminaries of recording the interview.

Colin stared at the table in front of him, hands clenched together.

Dot glanced at Martin to check if he wanted to say anything. He shook his head. "How long have you been working for Stonefish?"

He cringed, almost curling inwards as if trying to hide, and pressed his lips together.

What had happened to the enthusiastic, law-abiding constable? "Did they threaten you or one of your loved ones?" She didn't know much about Colin's family. He'd brushed questions aside when she'd asked, and she'd respected his privacy, knowing she didn't like to talk about her family either.

Still nothing.

"Colin, the more information you can give us, the better it will be for you."

"I'm going to gaol," he said.

Dot tried again. "Did you know what was in the barrels?"

His thumb rubbed at a mark on the white table.

"Who were you working with?"

His stroke paused and then continued.

"Are they local?" A tiny flinch this time.

Martin was equally silent. Usually he'd be the one to jump in and demand answers when they questioned anyone. His patience was non-existent. Was he stunned by Colin's actions, or was he equally involved and didn't want Colin to confess?

Maybe he felt sorry for him. He had been Colin's mentor since he arrived and this had to be disappointing.

"Colin, if you weren't a willing participant, telling us what you know may help others from being in the same circumstances as you."

This time his gaze flicked to hers for a second and then down again.

"You promised to serve and protect," Dot continued. "You can still protect others by giving us information."

"But not himself," Martin pointed out.

Dot scowled. Now he speaks up, just in time to dissuade Colin from giving them information. "Colin knows he's going to gaol, but he can still help those who are vulnerable."

"Lee," Colin said. "It was Lee who gave me the drugs and helped me sink the barrels." He didn't look at either of them.

She sat back, surprised. "How did you meet up with Lee?"

"We met earlier in the year when all the stuff happened at the Ridge," he said. "Later, after we realised he was working with Stonefish, he approached me. Knew things about my little sister, said he would hurt her if I didn't help him." Colin kept his gaze fixed on the table, his words almost robotic, as if he'd practised what he would say. "I only did it once. Helped put the empty barrels out there. I didn't know what they were going to put in them."

Wait. He'd said Lee had given him the drugs. She filed it away and kept with the current questioning. "When?"

A hesitation. "August."

"Try again," Dot said. "Your prints would have dissolved by now if that were the case."

Colin glanced up, his gaze flicking to Martin and then back to her. Martin opened his mouth and Dot barked, "I'm waiting, Colin." She glared at Martin, daring him to speak, and he clenched his jaw tight. Good.

"Last week. Lee's a psychopath. Nhiari's probably already dead. He's been making me check the barrels every week."

Dot leaned back, surprised. "Do they get deliveries

that frequently?"

"It's only been about once a month, but I still have to check. It's like he didn't know when they were due in, or just enjoyed me doing his bidding."

"I thought you said he gave you the drugs."

Colin paled. "No. He took them from me—from the barrels."

Could Dot get hold of Nhiari and confirm Colin's story? She didn't like how he constantly looked at Martin for validation, but it could be because he was worried about Martin's reaction. "What did you do with the drugs when you removed them from the barrels?"

"Left them in the hide-out you found today."

Dot made a note, but her pen paused as realisation struck. Colin shouldn't have known they'd found the hide-out. Rodney said he hadn't told Colin, and she hadn't said what she'd been doing out there. She glanced up. "What hide-out?"

Sweat beaded on his forehead. "Ah…" Again he glanced at Martin.

"Colin, answer the question. What hide-out?"

"The, ah, one on the island you were at today."

"How did you know where I was today?"

"There's this thing called fleet tracker, maybe you've heard of it," Martin said.

She really wanted to gag the man.

"Yeah," Colin agreed. "When you said you were having engine troubles, I checked where you were. I figured you must have found the hide-out because you were gone so long."

Damn it. It was a reasonable explanation. "How many barrels are there?"

The change of tack made Colin blink. "Ah, a couple."

"A figure, Colin. You must know if you put them down."

"Six," he answered.

Which left five unaccounted for. "Are they still there?"

"As far as I know. I didn't want to risk checking them with those maritime archaeologists in the area."

"Do you know anything about the missing cannon?"

Colin shook his head. "No. I wouldn't do something like that."

As if stealing a historical artefact was worse than bringing drugs into the country. Some people had twisted morals.

A knock on the door and Pierre poked his head in. "Sorry to interrupt. We had a call from Sam. They've found another barrel out by the wreck site." He frowned as he saw Colin seated where a suspect normally sat.

"Tell him I'll be out shortly." She hesitated and then sighed. "And call Rodney." He'd be out of mobile range until he got closer to Carnarvon, which gave her a couple of hours head start. She turned back to Colin, disappointment heavy in her gut. "Colin Lipscombe, you're under arrest for aiding and abetting the importation of drugs into Australia."

***

Pierre wasn't able to contact Rodney before Dot headed back to the wreck site. She gave Martin instructions to find him when he arrived in Carnarvon with Colin, who would be remanded in custody there. Which left Dot with just Pierre to cover anything that came up in the meantime.

Dot needed to get hold of Nhiari. On her way out of the marina, she typed a long text explaining what was going on and asking her to get in touch. Then she sent Ryan a message to say she'd been called out and wouldn't make dinner.

Was it only this morning she'd had coffee with him?

She closed her eyes briefly, letting the wind blow over

her, hoping it would brush away some of her fatigue. They had to be getting close. How many more arms of the business could they have here in Retribution Bay? Surely the drugs were the last one. The evidence they'd collected from the hide-out might have something that would point her towards who was behind it all.

Maybe it was Natasha's parents. Steven had been good friends with Declan, and Declan had been quite involved.

She still hadn't figured out where the Singapore connection came in either.

But she was almost certain this part of the business had only been in Retribution Bay since the beginning of the year.

If only she had someone to talk to. Someone she trusted. She hoped Nhiari would call her soon.

As much as she'd relied on Sam, Brandon and Sherlock, they were civilians now and shouldn't be privy to police information. Besides, they'd go off half-cocked on some mission that would risk their lives, and she wouldn't know about it until bad things happened.

She had no one.

Oliver had once been her confidant, but she wasn't certain he wasn't a Stonefish plant. And again, he couldn't be told confidential information.

Her paranoia had isolated her from her colleagues, but at least she had proof she was right. Colin had been working for Stonefish. Were others as well?

She sighed.

What would it be like to have someone else to confide in? Someone to laugh with and come home to?

Seeing Oliver again had reminded her what she'd had, what she missed most about him. They'd had fun together and even if they were simply watching television together, there'd been a comfort being next to him.

She was lonely.

The realisation brought tears to her eyes, and she blinked them back. All her life she hadn't been someone people wanted to hang out with. After the academy, the breakup and Nhiari moving back to the bay, Dot had sunk further into herself, not willing to risk her heart again, knowing people would leave, knowing she wasn't enough to make them stay.

She should be used to it by now. She shouldn't want it so much.

Dot swallowed hard. Now wasn't the time to wallow in self-pity. She'd go out, take the barrel into evidence and while she was out there, she'd find the others. Colin had given her a rough map of where he'd put them.

Then tomorrow she'd meet Ryan for dinner and catch up with her old friend. Hear all the news about him and Lincoln and their small town of Blackbridge. Maybe she'd even arrange to visit when Stonefish was caught.

She wasn't as pathetic as she seemed.

The water was still choppy, and it took longer than usual to get out there. The sun was definitely on its descent, and she had at most two hours before dark. Not much time to locate, record and retrieve the drugs.

The *Oceanid* was anchored back closer to Retribution Island and a couple of lights were on in the cabin. Oliver grabbed the rope she threw to him. His wetsuit was pulled down to his waist, and a T-shirt covered his chest. A shame.

"Do you have coordinates?" she called.

"Yeah. I'll come with you. You might need scuba gear."

Her muscles tightened. "I'm sure I'll be fine."

"The barrel might be heavy. You can't hold your breath for that long and lift something heavy."

He had a point, and behind him Sam was approaching with his argumentative face. "Get your gear."

Oliver's eyebrows raised, but he didn't comment, just

hurried to fetch it.

"There're probably more barrels out there," Sam said.

"I know how to do my job," Dot replied.

He winced. "Yeah. Be careful."

She nodded and took the vest Oliver handed over the railing. By the time she'd placed it on the deck, he was on board, pushing off from the other boat.

Dot followed his directions to the barrel's location, then suited up and followed him into the water. A chain was wrapped around the barrels and connected to a mooring on the bottom weighing them down. It was in about fifteen metres of water and she would have to free dive to get close enough for photos. She took the shots and, as she was getting close to needing to surface, Oliver tapped her on the shoulder and handed her his spare regulator.

Their eyes met, and she registered his concern. Maybe he was telling the truth. Maybe he did care for her still. Her fingers brushed his, their warmth adding to the swirling emotions inside of her.

She nodded her appreciation, took a breath of air, and continued her investigation. When she was satisfied she had the information she needed, she took the keys Colin had given her and unlocked the chains, holding the barrel steady, but there was no need. It didn't move. She tried to lift it and shifted it a few centimetres off the bottom but it was too heavy for her to lift it further. She had to rig a pulley system like Colin had explained.

Dot gestured to Oliver that she was surfacing, and they both headed up.

Dot took a couple of deep breaths as she reached the surface, and retrieved the ropes to pull up the barrel. Oliver stayed in the water, floating nearby. "What's the plan?"

"We're taking them with us."

"Them?"

"There's four more."

Beneath his mask his eyebrows raised. "How do you know?"

She just glanced at him, but said nothing.

"Right, you can't say. What are you doing?"

"Rigging up a pulley system to get it up." She finished attaching it to the boat.

Oliver lifted his hand. "Give me the end and I'll clip it to the barrel."

Dot shook her head. "I need to do it."

"It's foolish us both going under."

He was right. "Come back to the boat. You can pull." She could stay with the barrel as it was retrieved.

Oliver didn't argue. Such a welcome contrast to Sam. He climbed back to the boat, taking off his BCD vest and mask. "Do you want to take it?"

She shook her head. She showed him what to do and headed back down to the barrel. This had already taken half an hour. If she wasn't faster, she wouldn't get it done before dark and she didn't like her chances of finding the others afterwards.

In little time, the barrel was at the surface. They fell into a nice rhythm and the next three were found and retrieved within an hour. Only one to go.

This one was closer to an island, and the tide was going out, making the coral a lot closer to the surface. Dot manoeuvred the boat around the clumps and eventually found the last barrel in the middle of a circle of reef. The sun hovered just above the horizon, and it was harder to see below the surface. She turned on the boat lights, and Oliver handed her a waterproof torch. "Last one."

They worked well together. It surprised Dot, though maybe it shouldn't have. They'd always seemed to know what the other needed, but after so long apart, she'd figured they would have lost that connection.

She dived, taking photos quickly in the fading light, and then attaching the clip to the chain. This one had shifted in the storm, and the base was underneath a ledge. She needed to shift it away before they pulled it up. Rather than jerking on the rope to let Oliver know he could lift it, she surfaced and took a breath.

"What's wrong?" Oliver called.

"It's right against the reef. I don't want to break it further." But it wasn't likely she'd be able to shift the barrel herself. Before she could ask, Oliver was already suiting up.

"Give me a second." He jumped in and swam to her, turning around so she could do his buddy checks. After she checked the tank, he spun, and they were face to face. Too close. His blue eyes searched hers as if looking for something.

Nothing she wanted to examine too closely. She grabbed his regulator, checked the air was coming through and then backed away. "Let's go." She dived under, in too much of a rush to take a focused breath like she should, but she didn't want to surface again. If she did, he would know she was rattled.

She swam to the far side of the barrel to push it away from the reef. Oliver followed her, holding out his spare regulator.

Her heart squeezed. Damn him for knowing what she needed. She inhaled and then he swam to the other side to pull the barrel using the rope. Together they shifted it away from the reef, and Oliver gave her the regulator again so she could take a breath before he surfaced to pull up the barrel.

Her heart ached, and she stamped down on the feeling. This was the man who had destroyed her. He would leave in a couple of days when the wreck had been properly documented. This was not the time to open her heart again.

She couldn't go through that again.

The barrel shifted beside her, and she followed it to the surface.

Chapter 14

Oliver hauled on the rope, pulling the barrel to the surface, hating the fact Dot was down there without a scuba tank. It was an impressive feat, but one that made him deeply uncomfortable. His lungs burned from the exertion and the fact he was holding his breath too. He exhaled and sucked in another breath as both Dot and the barrel surfaced.

Dot removed her dive gloves and started the engine. The sun kissed the horizon and was sinking rapidly now. Around them more coral was above the water.

Crap.

"Ah, Dot, we've got a problem." He pointed to the coral and then scanned the shore of the nearest island. Yeah, definitely low tide.

Dot swore. "Why would anyone put a barrel here when it's not accessible all the time?"

"They might not have realised." He climbed onto the bow to get a higher vantage point.

"Can you see a path?"

He shook his head. "It looks pretty shallow. Hand me my mask and I'll check." Part of him wanted to say there was no way out, so they would be stuck here together until the tide turned, but he respected Dot's time. She had to get these barrels back to town.

He jumped in and circled the area, searching for a spot to get them over the reef without damaging it. The boat sat lower in the water now the barrels were on board, and he didn't like to think how many drugs were inside.

"Anything?" Dot called.

"No." He swam back to the boat. "We need another foot of water."

Dot swore. "High tide isn't until midnight."

Five hours away. He could use this to his advantage.

She radioed the station and reported the situation. Then she radioed Sam. "We won't be back until later. We're stuck in a coral atoll until the tide rises."

"Will the tender get you out?"

Dot glanced at Oliver.

"Only if you want to leave the barrels behind." An option he hoped she wouldn't take.

Her struggle was real, before she said, "No, but thanks for the offer." She shifted away, peering over the edge as if trying to make the tide rise.

This was the perfect opportunity for them to talk. He needed to discover whether he could fix his mistake. His heart pounding, he cleared his throat and said, "Dot, can we talk about us?"

"There is no us." Her voice was raw, but it gave him hope. She felt something.

"That's my fault. I realise that now." Nerves danced a drum solo in his stomach. "I'm so sorry. I was young and idiotic, and only thought about what I wanted."

She flinched, but didn't look at him, busying herself by digging through her backpack and bringing out a towel and her clothes to get out of her wet bathers. "It doesn't matter."

"Yes, it does." He clenched his hands to stop himself

from touching her. She needed the distance. "You were the love of my life. It broke my heart when you stopped taking my calls and responding to my emails." He sighed. "I should have realised that I hurt you. I should have stopped for a second and thought about how you felt, rather than making it all about me."

"It's in the past." She moved to the back of the boat, examining the barrels.

A tremor in her voice made him step forward and reach out, but he didn't touch her. Dot hated to show her vulnerability to anyone. "Is there any way I can fix it for the future?"

She stiffened, tension creating a force field around her as a no-go zone. Finally she said, "What would be the point? I live here. You live in Perth."

She was right, but the fact she hadn't said an outright no gave him hope. When he'd come here, he hadn't thought past getting closure on why she'd ghosted him all those years ago. Now he'd spent time with her, all he wanted to do was hold her in his arms again. They had both changed, but he saw the glimmer of the Dot he knew underneath her protective coating.

Could they make it work? The teaching hadn't been as fulfilling as he had hoped, and while the museum was a worldwide leader for shipwreck research, he missed being on the ocean.

There were enough undiscovered wrecks along Western Australia's coast that he could use Retribution Bay as a base, if he could find someone to pay him for his work.

And that was the hard part.

Though there was the publisher who had asked about him writing his memoir. He had plenty of journals to draw the information from, but any income probably wouldn't be enough to fund his work.

He'd sort out the details later. Right now he just

wanted to make it work with Dot. "The point is I still feel something for you, Dot. We work so well together, we understand each other. Don't you want to discover what we could be like together?"

Dot shook her head, still not looking at him. "I can't go through the heartbreak again."

This time he couldn't ignore the pain in her voice. Gently he touched her shoulder and turned her, pulling her into his arms. "I'm so sorry, Dot."

She froze against him for a moment before she melted into him, her arms coming around his waist.

Relief and a sense of rightness filled him as he rubbed her back. She fit perfectly in his arms, her head resting against his shoulder.

This was right. This was home.

He closed his eyes, trying to imprint the feeling of her in his arms into his memory. His chest tightened. He couldn't let her go. Not this time. Not now he understood what a colossal mistake he'd made. "We'll make it work, somehow."

She pushed away, dashing tears from her eyes, shaking her head and stepping as far away from him as she could in the small space. "We don't know each other. Not anymore."

He sat on a chair and patted the seat of the chair next to him. "We've got about five hours to start changing that." The sun had gone down and the glow of last light made Dot look like an angel. He searched for a topic that wouldn't get her offside before realising she could take almost anything he said the wrong way. He might as well start at the beginning. "When did you move back to Retribution Bay?"

***

Dot stared at Oliver, reining in the instinct to snap and snarl at him, to tell him to mind his own business. He

174

seemed genuine and a deeper part of her yearned for the easy conversation they'd always had. If she was brutally honest with herself, their breakup was partially her fault as well. She'd reacted defensively, had shut him out, rather than discussing her feelings like a rational adult. She'd had to protect herself, and she hadn't known any other way.

But over the years she'd seen too many couples have issues because of their lack of communication, because one party believed the other should *know* how they were feeling, rather than expressing it in words.

She didn't want to be one of those people, even when she knew how much his leaving was going to hurt her again. "Let me get changed first."

She took her time in the small cabin. While she removed her bathers she considered what she wanted to tell him. Did he really understand why his decision had destroyed her?

Finally, when she couldn't delay any longer, she joined him on deck and sat next to him. His heat radiated from him, taking some chill from the air. "I took the job in the southern suburbs," she said. "I worked hard for five years and was promoted to First-Class Constable. From there I worked in major crimes for a while and applied for the sergeant promotion when a job became available up here." She shrugged. "I got it, though Martin will tell you it was because they were trying to fill a quota, not because of my efforts."

Oliver scowled. "Martin sounds like an idiot. Who is he?"

"One of my team. He wanted to be in charge of the station." He didn't know about the things she'd done in Perth, which had made her more than worthy of the promotion.

"What about Nhiari?"

"She got the job in Carnarvon first and moved here a

few years later. She wasn't interested in being in charge." Nhiari just wanted to make a difference. Before Oliver could ask another question, she said, "What about you? What was the expedition to Papua New Guinea like?"

"Life changing." He met her gaze. "It helped me get through our breakup, because it distracted me during the days." His smile was sad, and she longed to ask him about his nights, but she was afraid of what the answer might be.

"I eventually settled on angry righteousness, and the wreck was stunning, a nineteenth century pirate ship with so much still preserved. It had sunk into the mud, which protected it." He shook his head. "I've never seen so much gold and treasure in my life. The rich red of the rubies, and the clarity of the diamonds. It was worth a mind-boggling amount in today's money." His hand clasped the necklace around his neck.

"Did it all go to the national museum?"

"We were each allowed to keep a small piece." He held out the ring to show her. "It's my good luck charm."

"Is that a real emerald?"

He nodded. "I've never had it assessed, because I don't want to know its dollar value. It reminds me how fortunate I've been." He smiled. "Did you follow the expedition?"

Dot clenched her hands as her walls went up. "It was all over the news." She exhaled, relaxing. "And I wanted to know how you were doing." Couldn't quite manage the disinterest she wanted to feel. Was close to obsessed with finding out whether the expedition had been worth leaving her, but when she'd read the reports, she'd realised she couldn't possibly compete with buried treasure and pirates.

He would know what they needed to do about the treasure the Stokes found, and maybe the Stokes could keep some small part of their find. "What did you do next?"

"We spent about a year cataloguing everything. A private investor was fascinated by the find and was willing to pay to have the whole thing properly catalogued."

It sounded like the dream situation. At university, Oliver had often ranted about the lack of money given to archaeology.

"The whole expedition garnered so much attention that the team was asked to do other expeditions around the world and a TV studio came on board. We went to Indonesia, the Mediterranean, South Africa and the Caribbean, before I decided to come home."

She couldn't compete with jet-setting around the world. Dot frowned. "You or the whole team?"

"Me. They're currently working on a wreck off the Thai coast."

"Why did you leave?"

He was silent for a long time. "The entire experience had lost its shine. So many people were involved in the dives that I never got the chance to do any of the research. I always loved the stories behind the wrecks, but we were handed dossiers and told to dive." He shrugged. "First world problems, I know. There are hundreds of people who would want the opportunities I had."

"It makes sense to me. You used to stay up all night researching, and then use coffee to get through your day."

He smiled. "You used to bring me my first cup."

Her heart squeezed. The memories were still so clear. At first she'd tried to stay up with him, help with his research, but she hadn't had the stamina, or maybe the interest, to last all night. She'd wait for him in bed before falling asleep. Initially she'd worried he was losing interest in her, but then she'd realised he'd simply lost track of time. It had been an endearing trait, and something she'd loved about him. She cleared her throat. "So, you got a job at the museum?"

He nodded. "Which came with the position at the university." He hesitated. "Job satisfaction wasn't the only reason I left." He tousled his hair. "I was lonely. I love my team, but they all had families to go home to."

Dot's heart squeezed. She couldn't touch that. Not yet. "You must have a lot of stories to tell."

"I've lost count of all my expedition journals."

"Have you ever thought of publishing them?"

He laughed. "I've had an offer, but I'm not sure anyone really wants to read my ramblings."

"You were always wonderful at expressing yourself. You'd capture everyone's attention at parties when you spoke of pirates and shipwrecks."

"Who wouldn't be interested in pirates?"

He was deflecting, which wasn't like him. Normally he took praise with grace, but perhaps the idea of writing a book was daunting. "Are you happy?"

He crossed his arms, rubbing them as the temperature turned cool with the sun below the horizon. "I've missed the diving."

Dot shifted and grabbed a spare towel, handing it to him. He wrapped it around his shoulders and sighed. "I need to be honest, Dot. One reason I returned was because of you."

She sucked in a breath, waiting for him to continue.

"Every woman I've dated couldn't compare to you. I don't know whether I'd idealised what we had, whether I'm remembering only the good bits, but with you it was… right."

Her yearning grew stronger. "That time of our lives was special, but we were on the cusp of adulthood, with no real responsibilities except attending classes and paying the rent. We didn't care about anything except the freedom we finally had."

He nodded. "But I also remember the excitement of finishing class and seeing you again. Those days when you and Nhiari would come and eat at the Chinese restaurant where I worked and would stay all night just so we could be near each other."

Dot smiled. "The owners eventually set a table aside for us."

He grinned. "Mrs Lam was a romantic."

And Nhiari didn't mind where they hung out. She hadn't been interested in clubbing or bars. They'd spent many evenings talking about the future and what they wanted to do in Retribution Bay when they both got jobs there. And Dot had always had the red bean buns for dessert.

The plan to move to Retribution Bay had always been when, not if, even after she'd met Oliver. So many ships had gone down off the coast, and he wanted to discover them. For a small, popular town, with only a few staff, Nhiari and Dot had both been certain they would end up there somehow.

And they'd achieved some of what they had planned.

"Mrs Lam said to say hi," Oliver said.

Her eyes widened. "I'm surprised she remembers me. When did you see her?"

"I go to the restaurant once a week now I'm back. Your table is still there, and I sit at it and tell them stories of my travels. We kept in touch. I'd send them postcards from wherever I was, and they pinned them all to a wall in the kitchen."

Oliver made an impression wherever he went.

"When I told her I was going to Retribution Bay, I asked her to teach me how to make those red bean buns you liked so much."

Her chest tightened. He'd remembered. It shouldn't mean so much. "And did she?"

He nodded. "She said it would win you back."

Mrs Lam had said it was a family secret, though they had treated him like a son. She hesitated before asking, "How is your family?" He'd taken her to dinner there every Wednesday night and they'd welcomed her with open arms.

"Dad's talking about retiring and buying a caravan to travel around Australia. Mum's not as keen on the caravan and she still loves her job, but she might reduce her hours so they can do short trips away."

"What about Jenna?"

He smiled. "She got married last year and is pregnant, due in about three months."

Dot's mouth dropped open. She still remembered Oliver's sister as a teenager, but of course it had been a decade. "What's her husband like?"

"He's a nice bloke. Treats her well. Absolutely dotes on her now she's pregnant and is driving Jenna a little mad."

She smiled. Jenna was fiercely independent as a teenager, always doing things herself, not wanting to ask for help. "I'm sure she'll set him straight."

Oliver laughed. "Yeah. The last time we spoke, she said she was going to talk to him."

Dot closed her eyes remembering the nights Oliver's dad would cook them all dinner and then they'd play cards or board games, or sit around and chat. Quality family time where everyone wanted to be in the same room together. It had devastated her to lose them as well as him. She doubted any of them would want to see her again. Not if Oliver had believed he was the wronged party. Oliver's mum would hate her for breaking his heart.

"I told them I was coming here," Oliver said. "Said I was going to look you up."

She glanced at him.

"Mum and Dad both said to give you their love."

Dot shook her head as tears came unbidden to her eyes. "They can't possibly mean that."

He held her hand. "They do. They were upset about our breakup. They thought we were perfect for each other."

"I didn't bring anything into your life." But he'd shown her how to love and be loved, how to let people in, how to have fun again.

"That's not true. You taught me responsibility, helped me to grow up."

She cringed. "That sounds boring."

"No," Oliver said. "I'd had such an easy life; hell, my parents were paying my rent and food." He squeezed her hand. "Then I met you. You were putting yourself through the academy, had only Nhiari for support, and felt completely out of place in the city. It made me realise how easy I'd had it, and how much I took for granted." He smiled. "I wanted to be a better person because of you. That's why I got the job at the Chinese restaurant and worked so hard at university. I suddenly realised my career wasn't guaranteed. I didn't want to rely on your income while I flitted from volunteer expedition role to volunteer expedition role. I wanted to support you. You made me a better man."

She stared at him. "I had no idea." Either that she'd influenced him so much, or that he'd been thinking so long term.

"I loved you, Dot. I wanted to give you the world. I didn't want you to struggle for anything, or be let down by anyone." He shrugged. "I guess I failed pretty badly."

"I'm not as needy now as I was then." The Dot of those days had wanted someone who doted on her. Now she understood how important it was to provide for herself and be independent.

"I can see that. I admire everything you've done with

your life."

It was difficult to swallow past the lump in her throat. This was too much, too fast.

She shifted away from him. "Tell me about you. Where are you living now?"

Chapter 15

Oliver swore inwardly at Dot's withdrawal. No, he had to be patient. He'd had months to think about seeing her again and what he would say. She'd had days.

He smiled, keeping things light. "I'm renting a two-bedroom apartment in East Freo, not far from the museum. It suits me for now." Did she understand that meant he was flexible, that he hadn't put down roots yet?

What else could he tell her?

"When I'm not working, I've been volunteering for an environmental ocean cleanup group. It's part beach cleanup, part education about the effects of plastics in the ocean."

"Did you see much pollution?"

"Yeah. Some expeditions we had to spend a day picking plastic out of the water before we could begin studying the wreck."

"That's sad." She squeezed his hand briefly. "I'll have to introduce you to Penelope and Georgie before you go. They have similar interests."

He smiled. "I'd like that." He slipped his hand into hers, hoping he wasn't moving too fast for her.

She left it there.

"I've been trying to figure out what else I can do. People are doing amazing things in the plastic recycling space and switching to more renewable items."

"I'm sure you'll find something." Her faith soothed him. She'd been his confidant and his biggest cheerleader. He'd missed that.

Though he didn't want to spook her, he wanted to talk about more important things. "Do you want to tell me about Mark?"

She stiffened, almost pulled away, but he stroked her arm and she settled again. "What do you know?"

"Sam mentioned he was killed a couple of months ago."

"Yeah." She sighed. "He got involved with the wrong people. I guess he was always looking for a quick buck, a way to get as far away from here as he could, but he only ever got as far as Carnarvon." She placed a hand on his knee. "He started animal smuggling. We discovered a few traps and intercepted a car transporting the animals. Then two civilians stumbled across them making the transfer. They called the police, but before we arrived, the buyer had shot those involved and escaped." Her hand trembled. "I found Mark lying in the dirt with a bullet through his forehead."

Oliver lost his breath. "I'm so sorry, Dot. That must have been horrific for you."

"It wasn't my best day. Brandon and Nhiari were there. They helped."

Always understating. "I'm glad you had someone." He wished it had been him. "How did your parents react?"

She snorted. "Mum shed a tear. Dad told me to arrange the funeral. Both were horrified when the news spread that Mark had been animal smuggling. It made them look bad to their friends."

He growled. The one time he'd met them, they'd

spent the whole two hours at dinner talking about themselves and their friends. They hadn't asked Dot how she was doing in Perth, or anything about the academy. Oliver hadn't suggested they return to say goodbye before they left.

"Do you see them much?"

"They come to dinner once a month."

But probably never invited Dot to their house. "Why do you keep inviting them?"

She shrugged. "Isn't that what families do? Yours gets together every week."

His eyes widened. "Yeah, but we like each other."

She choked out a laugh. "Good point." She sighed. "It seemed like the right thing to do."

"I can't imagine it's any fun."

"No. They only ask about me if they want gossip."

How incredibly lonely for her. "What else do you do?"

"I go to Faith's horse-riding lessons on Saturday when I can make it."

Oliver frowned. He couldn't imagine Dot riding. "That's different."

She glanced at him. "It is, but it's nice to do something different, something where I'm a student and no one's side-eyeing me to check my reaction."

"Why would they?"

"Because I'm a police officer. People don't relax around me. They always watch what they say, in case they get into trouble."

"Sounds like a lot of guilty consciences."

She shrugged again. "Maybe. The only people who treat me normally are Nhiari and Lindsay."

"What about Sam and Sherlock?"

A brief tension in her muscles before she relaxed. "The situation is complicated." She sat up. "Tell me about the shipwreck. What have you discovered?"

The abrupt change of subject and the absence of her warmth against his chest made him pause. He wanted to ask how the situation was complicated, but it probably related to her work. Pushing back his desire to learn more about her, he said, "Now we have the journal, it makes identifying the wreck much easier. Finding the cannons they jettisoned during the storm supports Tess's assertion the journal is from the shipwreck."

"That's good, isn't it?"

He nodded. "Yeah." There was one thing that had been bothering him. "Lilian's journal says she found the treasure but then hid her portion. Do you know if the Stokes ever found it?"

Dot didn't look at him. "You'll need to ask them."

"What do you know, Dot?"

She said nothing.

"This would be a huge historical find, one which would tell us more about the life of the period."

The water lapped against the side of the boat, rocking it gently. Finally she said, "I can't discuss this with you."

Meaning she knew something and was keeping it from him. He opened his mouth to continue his argument but she crossed her arms and leaned away from him. The movement reminded him she was a police officer. There were elements at play that he knew nothing about. Things above his pay grade. He let out a breath. "Will you tell me when you can?"

She nodded.

"Thank you."

"How did you pick your team?" she asked.

Oliver frowned. "The team diving with me now?" At her nod, he said, "Suzyn, Tom and Rajesh are post-graduates. They volunteered as soon as they heard about it."

"And Andrew?"

"His father donated to the expedition. He insisted

Andrew be part of the dive."

Dot stiffened. "Is Andrew a student?"

"First year. Started mid-year. The others aren't happy about it because he's not interested and there are others who would love the chance to be here."

"What's his father's name?" She got out her phone and opened a note-taking app.

"Lucas Fitton."

"Has he donated to expeditions before?" Brisk questions. This was Dot in police mode. What had triggered her?

"No."

"And Andrew has been enrolled, what, twelve weeks?"

"About that."

"How is he doing in class?"

"He gets average grades. Doesn't take part in discussions unless it's to say something negative." Oliver was used to putting up with student attitudes and demanding donors. It was part and parcel of the job.

"What does Lucas do for a living?"

"He's in shipping or some sort of export business."

"You know him well?"

"Not really. We had a couple of meetings before I came up here."

"Did the company finance the expedition, or him personally?"

"He did."

She flicked to a web page and then swore when she noticed she had no reception. "Can you describe him to me?"

He retrieved his phone from his backpack. "I've got a photo. We took a bunch at the dinner he held." He scrolled through until he found them and passed the phone to Dot, pointing to Lucas. "That's him."

She pressed a couple of buttons and shared the

photos to her phone and then examined them closely, enlarging the photos to see who was in the background. She sucked in a breath as she zoomed in on the face of a guest. "Who is that?"

He took the phone from her and squinted, trying to make out the slightly blurry face. "I think he might be one of Lucas's executives. Thought himself a bit of a photographer, so had a camera in front of his face most of the night."

"Do you know his name?" She'd gone still, almost poker faced, as if she didn't care about the answer, but her body positively vibrated with tension.

"Lee something. I asked him to send me the photos so I could do a couple of social media posts, but he hasn't sent them through yet."

"Do you have his email address?"

"No. I gave him mine. I was going to ask Lucas for it."

Dot said nothing, but sent the photo to someone else.

"Who are you sending it to?"

She pressed her lips together. "Nhiari."

"Isn't she missing?"

Dot nodded, not looking at him. "Habit." She spent a few more minutes reviewing the photos and then put her phone away.

Oliver frowned. She was lying, but he didn't pry.

"Tell me about teaching. Do you enjoy it?"

Her question distracted him. He pressed his lips together. "Sometimes. So many students don't understand the laborious nature of the work. It's a lot of documenting and research, and depending on the depth of the find, it can be really short dives where you don't have time to see everything. It requires a lot of patience and delayed gratification." Something which was in short supply it seemed.

"Why teach then?"

"It was a requirement of my job at the museum. The museum provides a lecturer for the year."

He'd thought it would be fun. His university days had been amazing, and he'd soaked up everything he'd learnt, wanting to be the one who made a career. But with the advance in technology, so few people turned up for lectures and the only reason people were at the tutorials was because attendance formed part of their grade.

"You'd be an excellent teacher," Dot said. "You were great at explaining things to me."

He smiled. "You were interested." He tapped his fingers on the bottom of the boat. "I'm not sure why some of them are studying maritime archaeology. Take Andrew. I'm fairly sure his dad is making him. Lucas mentioned he came from a family of ocean-faring people and was adamant Andrew was part of the expedition."

"Does Lucas have any other sons?"

"Not that I know of."

"Did Lucas take part in the planning?"

"No, but he's called every day for an update since we've been here."

"Did you tell him about the journal?"

"Andrew did. I thought Lucas was going to drop everything and come here, but I asked him to give me a couple of days."

"Have you confirmed the identification yet?"

"I'm ninety-nine percent certain it's the wreck from the journal, but I was hoping to confirm it tomorrow by finding the ship's bell. It should have the name on it." He slipped his hand back into hers. "Did you get any leads on the cannon?"

"No one saw it come to shore at the marina, but there are other places it could have been taken." She glanced at him. "Does Lucas have a boat?"

He frowned. "He wouldn't steal from an expedition he was sponsoring."

"Sorry, that wasn't what I meant. My brain went off on a tangent."

"He has a pretty big luxury yacht," Oliver said. "That's where we had the launch dinner." He chuckled. "The man doesn't understand how good he has it. He has staff to take the boat wherever he wants it and then helicopters in for a few days. Meanwhile we're in a boat a quarter of the size, with far more people on it, and we stay out for weeks sometimes."

"He made his money in shipping?"

"Yeah."

Dot was silent, staring across the other side of the boat but a million miles away. Oliver stayed quiet. She'd often done that when she was working through something, and he didn't want to interrupt her thoughts. The faster she worked out who was smuggling drugs, the safer she would be.

He slid his arm around her shoulders and she tilted her head up towards him. It felt as natural as breathing as, without thinking, he bent his head and pressed his lips to hers.

Her gasp was followed by a quiet moan. Heat flooded his body as he drew her closer, needing her body against his. His head fought with his hormones to take it slowly, be gentle, show her how much she still meant to him.

He inhaled as his hands swept up her back and cupped the back of her head.

Her lips nipped and tasted as if relearning his, cautious but also insistent. He needed more, so he teased her mouth open. The same drugging taste of Dot. All the memories came flooding back of the nights when they'd spent hours kissing and exploring each other's bodies, learning what the other liked or didn't like. Figuring out how to make the other gasp and beg.

He smiled against her mouth as he remembered something and then slipped his hand under her shirt and ran his fingers lightly up her ribs to her breasts. He was rewarded with Dot's groan of passion. She'd always had sensitive nipples. He'd spent so much time pleasuring them into peaks with his fingers and mouth.

Dot pulled away and got to her feet, moving to the back of the boat. "Wait. I can't think."

Neither could he. He stood to go after her before the shock of cold air helped clear his head. His heart pounded and all he wanted to do was drag her into his arms again. He swallowed hard, trying to find something witty to say. "I'd say we're still compatible in this way."

Her quick smile sent a surge of affection through him. "We got that bit right at least."

Suddenly she spun around, looking into the dark. In the distance a boat engine hummed, getting closer. Sam and Sherlock knew they were waiting out the tide, so it had to be someone else. He shifted to his feet and looked around for the source.

The *Oceanid* had her lights on and people were on the deck, but the noise wasn't coming from that direction. It was coming from town, but wherever the boat was, they were navigating by the faint light of the moon, and it was impossible to spot.

Dot reached for the binoculars on the dash of the boat. Slowly she scanned the area and then swore. "I can't see it."

"Neither can I, but the sound is toward the barrels."

Dot nodded. She placed her hand on her radio and then hesitated.

"What's wrong?"

"There's no backup to call." Her frustration and defeat were clear.

"What about Sam and Sherlock?"

She shook her head. "The boat is likely the drug smugglers, in which case they're probably armed. I'm not sending Sam and Sherlock into that."

"So what do we do?"

"*We* don't do anything. You get down on the deck and stay hidden until I tell you to come out."

He bit his tongue to stop himself from arguing. "And what will you do?"

"I'm still working that out."

Chapter 16

Dot glanced at the scuba tank still on deck. It was an option, though not one she liked. All she needed was to get close enough to see who was on board and get a photo. The tank would allow her to get close, assuming the boat headed for each of the spots the barrels had been submerged. The closest one was about fifty metres away.

But in order to record their actions, she needed light, which would make her an easy target. She wouldn't be able to get away quickly if they spotted her, and the tank only had about fifty bar in it. It was too dark to navigate around the coral reef without a torch.

Her only other option was to use the spotlight on the boat. It should throw light far enough, but again, they were sitting ducks. She'd learnt recently it was possible to sink a boat using bullets.

The nearby island was a hundred metres in the opposite direction. Oliver could swim there before the smugglers arrived and be out of the way. She could flick the lights, take photos with her camera and then slide over the side and use the boat for cover if they started shooting at her.

There was also a slight chance the boat was full of idiots who didn't have the correct lighting on their boat, but it wasn't a risk she was willing to take. Not with Oliver's life.

"You need to swim to the island," Dot murmured, her voice sounding loud in the night.

"Why?"

"Because this boat is going to become a target, and I don't want you shot."

He shook his head. "What about you?"

"This is my job, Oliver. I need to see who these people are. I have to stop them. You'll get in my way."

"I'm not leaving you."

Frustration filled her. "You'll distract me. My full focus needs to be on what they're doing, not where you are. You'll endanger me if you stay."

He glanced towards the island and then back at her.

"Please, Oliver. Trust me. Let me do my job." She had to get Oliver somewhere safe.

He growled. "I don't like this."

"I know. The tide isn't high enough yet for them to get to me, and any gunshots will alert Sam and Sherlock." She hoped the sound of the *Oceanid's* tender would be enough to make the smugglers run.

The boat engine idled as they stopped at the first location. Time was running out.

"Go."

Oliver pulled her close and kissed her. Heat zipped through her body and she clung for a second before pushing him away.

"Stay safe." Oliver zipped his wetsuit and slid into the water, using strong breaststrokes to head for the island. The reef would slow him down in places, but he would make it.

Dot got out the camera, using a towel to hide the light from it. Either the smugglers hadn't noticed the navigation lights on the police boat, or they didn't care. Maybe they had heard the radio call that the police boat was stuck until the tide turned.

The dinghy moved to the next location and then the next. Dot glanced to the island and, in the darkness, she made out movement on shore. Oliver was safe.

She readied herself as the sound came closer. The spotlights pointed in the right direction, and her camera was ready. Someone on the boat had turned on a torch, making it easier to track. If they started shooting, she'd go over the side.

The engine idled and Dot pictured them searching for the last barrel.

Now.

She flicked on the spotlight and raised the camera, zooming in to the silver dinghy with two people on board. She took photo after photo as the man at the side of the boat stared straight at the light like a startled kangaroo. From this distance it was hard to see clearly, but he had no distinguishing features and he wasn't a local.

Damn it.

The captain at the wheel glanced across. "Get down!" He had the build and colouring of Steven Hamilton.

The man finally clicked out of his trance and ducked.

Dot grabbed the loud hailer. "This is the police. You are surrounded. Turn off your engine and put your hands up."

She took a photo of the boat's name before the captain gunned the engine, speeding away into the night. She swore.

They'd scared easier than she'd expected. No weapons, no attempts to fight.

Across the way, the *Oceanid's* spotlight came on, scanning the water. Perhaps she should have used them, but she didn't trust the radio was a secure form of communication.

She switched to the right channel. "All good, *Oceanid*. You can stand down."

"What the hell, Dot?" Sam said.

Dot didn't answer, aware of those who could be listening. Instead, she checked the photos she'd taken.

A few grainy and blurry ones, but there were a couple of sharp ones in the mix. Hopefully enough to get a good resolution shot of the men.

She checked the time. Another hour before high tide, but perhaps there was enough water to get over the reef.

A splash of water had her turning, hand on her gun. She swivelled the spotlight to find Oliver was almost back at the boat. He waved and she moved the light so it wasn't shining directly at him and instead at the reef nearby to check how deep it was. The coral which had been evident above the water was now submerged.

"Throw me my goggles," Oliver called as he got closer. "I'll check."

She waited until he looped around the boat, examining the reef. As he climbed onto the deck, he nodded. "We're good to go."

Dot handed him a towel, ignoring the sliver of disappointment. She switched on the main light and the bright beam cut through the dark, ending their private interlude. She needed to get back to reality. But where were they going from here? "Thank you for doing as I asked." She felt a little foolish now for making him leave the boat, but at least he was safe. She pulled the anchor in.

"I never thought Retribution Bay was dangerous."

She glanced at him. "Anywhere can be dangerous if the wrong people get involved." She started the engine. They'd cleared the air between them and now she had a crime syndicate to end and he had a wreck to examine. Anything else would have to wait until later.

Using the spotlight to illuminate the water, she picked her way back to the *Oceanid*. Oliver put his hand on her arm. "What are you doing now?"

"Heading back to town. I might catch them at a boat ramp or the marina."

"By yourself?"

Her muscles tensed. "I don't have a choice." She slowed the boat as she came alongside the *Oceanid*. Everyone was on board watching them and Sam grabbed the rope Oliver threw him. "What's going on, Dot?" Sam demanded.

"Police business," she answered. "I need to get back to town."

"Dot…" Oliver just looked at her.

"Thank you for your help." She couldn't reveal her feelings here. Not with so many eyes on them. She wasn't certain how she felt anyway. "You'd better warm up so you don't catch a cold."

His indecision was clear in his furrowed brow, and she waited for him to say something inappropriate, something that would reveal the intimacy of their earlier talk. Her hands clenched on the steering wheel.

"I'll see you when I'm back in town."

She nodded. "Good luck with your expedition."

Finally, he climbed aboard and she faced Sam's stony expression. "You're not coming," she said.

He growled, but threw the rope back to her. "I'll be in touch."

She had no doubt, but she wouldn't be bringing him further into this mess. "Have a nice night."

She sped away. She had a boat to catch.

***

"What the hell happened?" Sam demanded as Dot sped away.

Oliver didn't answer immediately. She was going after

the boat, alone. The criminals hadn't stuck around, or fired shots, but Dot shouldn't be facing them by herself. Oliver hoped they'd made a clean getaway.

"Are you all right, Oliver?" Suzyn asked, her arms wrapped around herself. Tom and Rajesh stood next to her, but Andrew was not on deck.

Oliver was still dripping wet after his impromptu swim. He nodded. "Sorry about waking you. Everything's fine. Go back to sleep. We'll be starting early in the morning." He wanted to get this dive finished and his students away from this mess.

He waited until the three of them dragged their feet back to their quarters and then turned to Sam and Sherlock. "Give me five to shower. Where's my bag?"

Sherlock showed him and Oliver headed for the shower.

Swimming away from Dot was the hardest thing he'd done. It went against everything he believed in. A man was supposed to protect his family. He stilled as the realisation settled over him. She was his family. The reason no other woman could compare with Dot was because he was still in love with her. She had been his other half, the yin to his yang, the mask to his fins. OK, so he wasn't a poet, but he recognised this emotion swirling around inside of him. He had never stopped loving Dot.

Now he only had to convince her to love him again.

He stared in the direction Dot had gone.

Dot thought Lucas, or Lucas's colleague, might be involved somehow. He would review all his interactions with the man for any information that would help Dot. Something might point to who was behind this.

He dried himself and dressed, heading onto the deck to find Sam and Sherlock waiting for him.

"The cabin," Sam said and closed the door behind them.

Sherlock poured three mugs of tea and handed Oliver one. "Noise carries at night, so keep your voice low."

"What happened?" Sam asked.

Oliver hesitated. The two men seemed to know more about what was going on than he did. "We got stuck by the low tide," he said. "The last barrel was under the reef so it took us a while to get it up."

"And just now?" Sam prompted.

The man wasn't normally this impatient. "We heard a boat. It wasn't running lights, but it was going from spot to spot where the barrels were. Dot made me swim to the island in case they fired on the boat."

Sam flinched. "Good idea."

Oliver raised his eyebrows. "You've had experience?"

"My partner's boat was shot up when she was trying to stop poachers on the reef. It sank in the middle of a shark feeding frenzy."

Oliver's blood chilled. Sharks didn't normally bother him, because it was rare they were after a feed, but he'd seen some frenzies before and that was when all bets were off.

"What happened next?" Sherlock asked.

"Dot turned on the spotlights and hailed them. They took off, I swam back to the boat."

"And Dot's gone after them on her own," Sam said and swore.

"I don't like it either, but it didn't seem as if they were armed." It was his turn for questions. "What's going on here? Why are poachers shooting up boats, and children being kidnapped and drugs being smuggled? Retribution Bay was a quiet tourist town."

Sam and Sherlock shared a look. "Up to you," Sherlock said.

"All we know is a company called Stonefish Enterprises is behind it, but no one can trace who that is. Each time we catch someone, another branch pops up."

"How long has this been going on?"

"All year."

No wonder Dot looked so exhausted. "Is Nhiari being missing related?"

"Yeah. The man who has her works for Stonefish."

"Lee is the only one we know of who hasn't been caught yet," Sherlock added.

Oliver jolted. "Lee?" He got his phone out. "This guy?" He showed them the photo that had interested Dot.

"When was this taken?" Sam asked, his body tensing.

"A week ago at the expedition launch dinner."

"So he hasn't been up here the whole time." Sam frowned and stared at the table.

"Who do you know him as?" Sherlock asked.

"An executive with Lucas Fitton's company. He's the man funding this dive."

Sherlock dragged across his tablet. "What's the company name?"

Oliver told him and waited while Sherlock searched. "Shipping," he said. "He's filthy rich through shipping all over the world." He glanced up. "The base is Singapore."

That obviously held some significance for the two of them.

"Is this the first dive Lucas has funded?" Sherlock asked.

"Yes. He has a particular fascination with this wreck. He's called almost every day." Oliver shrugged. "We're lucky he offered to pay for it otherwise it might have been months or years until we got the funding to examine it." Oliver was thankful to him. It enabled him to go back to doing what he loved, but now he wanted to know Lucas's motives.

"Have you met Lee before?" Sam asked.

"No. He came to the kick-off dinner to take photos, but he didn't really talk to anyone."

"Did Lucas know about you and Dot?" Sherlock looked up from the notes he was taking.

Oliver paused. "Yeah. He asked me if I knew of anyone living in Retribution Bay and I mentioned her."

"How did he react?"

Lucas's smile had seemed a bit off at the time. Almost smug. "He seemed pleased." Was that why Lucas had asked for Oliver to be on the expedition?

"How did you get this expedition?" Sam asked. "It's not the team from the TV show."

"I left my team. Got tired of the travel and having no real base. I reached out to the Shipwrecks Museum, and they offered me a job which came with teaching at the university." He'd thought it another lucky break, but maybe Lucas had been behind that as well. A movement outside caught his eye as Andrew walked to the bathroom. "Andrew only enrolled this semester. He's not particularly interested in class."

"What's he been doing while he's been here?" Sherlock asked.

"He does what I tell him, but he's not enthusiastic about it." The sounds of retching came from the bathroom. "And he's seasick all the time."

Sam tapped his finger on the table. "Has Lucas contacted you?"

"Every day." Oliver rolled his shoulders. "He's been pretty intense. I thought it was because he has history in this area."

"What history?" Sherlock's gaze was razor sharp.

"An ancestor was a pearl diver, and he was on the *Retribution* when it sank."

"I knew it," Sam said. "He's got to have the original journal."

"But why would he leave it this long to find the

wreck?" Sherlock argued.

"Maybe he already searched it, but couldn't find the treasure. Or perhaps he only just found the journal, like the Stokes did."

All at once everything clicked into place. The treasure that had been found, Lilian's suspicion the pearl divers had stolen the Dutch captain's original journal—Lucas's ancestor. The rest of the treasure was still out there.

"Lucas would have a copy of Lilian's journal by now," Oliver said. "Andrew would have sent it to him. He'll be trying to decipher the clues."

"It doesn't matter," Sherlock said.

Why not? Oliver's mouth dropped open. "You've already found it. Those rumours of treasure are true."

Neither man said anything, but their silence confirmed it.

"Where is it? It belongs in a museum. It needs to be catalogued."

"If Lucas has as much influence as he seems to, how quickly do you think the treasure will be stolen from the museum?" Sam asked.

"The museum has excellent security," Oliver said.

"If he's behind Stonefish, he'll have contacts, and he has a sense of ownership," Sherlock pointed out. "His ancestor was almost killed in the mutiny. Surely he feels he deserves a piece of what caused it."

"He's got more money than he can ever spend," Oliver said. It was difficult to wrap his head around the idea the man could be involved in these shady dealings.

Sam nodded. "But people do stupid things all the time."

"If Andrew is telling his father everything, then it gives us an opportunity," Sherlock said. "We could feed him information that will help us catch them."

Which would mean Dot was out of danger. "I'm in. What do I need to do?"

Chapter 17

Dot yawned, trying not to dislocate her jaw at the same time. Her eyes might as well be filled with sand and every step required focus. She sipped her coffee as she pushed through the back door to the police station. She shouldn't have spent several hours last night searching for the damned boat, but she hadn't been able to resist. She'd sped back to the marina, got Pierre out of bed to help her unload the barrels, and then driven the police car to all the nearby boat ramps, hoping to find it.

No such luck. By the time she returned home, she desperately needed to sleep.

This morning she'd work on the photographs and if she had no luck, she'd send them to a colleague she trusted.

She yawned again and then waved at Pierre and Martin, who were already at their desks. All that was left of her team. "Thanks for your help yesterday."

"You don't know when to leave things alone."

She tensed and turned towards the spare office she'd allocated to Rodney. "Morning, Rodney. I didn't expect you back so soon." And would have made sleep a priority if she'd known she had to deal with him.

"Those barrels should have been left in place so I could investigate them properly."

"Those barrels would have been gone this morning if I hadn't collected them," Dot countered, in no mood to play nice. "A boat went to get them last night."

"And you didn't stop them?"

"I couldn't, but I got photos." She walked through to her office, placed her coffee on the table, and took the camera out of her backpack. Rodney stormed in.

"Show me the photos."

Dot glared at him. "Give me a second." As his face went red she added, "Did you have time to question Colin in Carnarvon?"

"Stupid kid. He didn't know much."

"What did he know?" Dot connected the camera to her computer and turned both on.

"He went out every week to check the barrels. If they were heavy, he'd notify Lee."

It was interesting Lee was involved. Dot suspected Georgie had been lying about what had happened when Matt had been kidnapped a couple of months ago. Lee hadn't been mentioned, but there had definitely been another set of footprints at the scene. And Georgie showed no signs of remorse for killing a man, if that was indeed true.

Was Lee on the outer with Stonefish and didn't know when the drugs were being delivered? Or was it because he was in hiding up here that he couldn't get decent communication channels?

"Anything else?"

"He spent a lot of time apologising and swearing he didn't want to do it." Rodney sounded bored.

Her computer recognised the camera connected and opened the folder. Dot copied the photos she'd taken last night to her hard drive and then opened the first one. Dark and blurry.

"That will be a real help in identifying the boat," Rodney said, peering over her shoulder.

Dot ignored him and clicked on the next photo, an equally blurry mess. She clicked the next and found one in focus. Good. She zoomed in, but the light wasn't good enough to make out the writing on the side of the boat. She wrote an estimate of the boat size and description to search the boat database before clicking to the next photo. Jackpot.

Cersei.

She opened the boat registration database and searched, scrolling through the results. Hamilton. Kristy and Steven Hamilton. More than enough evidence to pay them a visit. Satisfaction filled her. Finally she was getting somewhere.

"Do you know them?" Rodney asked.

Dot nodded. "They're known for their domestic fights, but they only seem to argue when it drags us away from investigating Stonefish further. I've never seen a bruise on Kristy, however they break some furniture or glass and yell loud enough to concern the neighbours." She'd thought it odd when the arguments had begun at the beginning of the year. The two had always seemed to have a good relationship. Now it made perfect sense. "Let's go bring them in."

"This is hardly enough evidence to tie them to the drugs. They could argue they were fishing."

She hadn't shown him the drone footage yet. Bracing herself for his displeasure, she clicked on another folder. "This is enough evidence." She played the video of Steven watching the Stokes.

"Where the hell did you get this?"

"From the drone in the hideout." As he sputtered his displeasure, she continued, "I took a copy of the footage before I sent it to Perth."

"That's highly inappropriate. I'm lead on this

investigation. You should have told me."

"A lot has happened since yesterday." She didn't want to waste time arguing. "Shall we bring them in?"

"Them?"

Dot clicked on the other drone video. "This was taken on a day we were investigating Stonefish." She pointed out the police boat. "We got a call shortly after about a domestic disturbance at their place. They argue when they want to stop us from investigating something."

"One drone video isn't proof."

It wasn't, but she was certain she was on the right track. Still, she bit her tongue and asked, "What would you like to do?"

"I'll bring Steven in for questioning."

"Shall I come with you?"

"I can handle picking up a suspect."

"He might be armed."

"He'll be at work. He's not likely to carry a gun at a shire building."

"True, but he'll recognise me and won't know you." She locked her computer and took her vest out of her locker. "Shall we go?"

She walked out before he responded. "We've got a lead," she told Martin and Pierre.

"Who?" Martin asked.

"Steven Hamilton," Rodney answered.

Damn him. Rodney knew she thought there was a leak in the department. He should keep this quiet. But maybe he figured Colin had been the only one.

Both men raised their eyebrows. "He's always got the flashiest things," Pierre said. "But I figured they paid him well at the shire."

"He doesn't seem the type." Martin's gaze darted to the phone on his desk and then back. "What's the lead?"

"Photos from last night. Dot caught him going after

the drug barrels."

"Must have been desperate when he heard about Colin."

"How would he have heard about Colin?" Dot asked. "We were the only ones who knew. Colin didn't mention working with Steven."

Martin shrugged. "Probably saw him being driven away. Doesn't take much to put two and two together if you see a police officer in the back seat of a police car."

"Let's go," Rodney said and gestured Dot to follow him.

Her shoulders tensed as she left the room. The paranoia was back. Rodney was impatient, but her question was relevant, and for him to interrupt her seemed suspicious. It wasn't until Rodney pulled up in front of the shire building requiring no directions that something else occurred to her.

"How did you know where Steven works?" He'd never met the man and the Hamiltons hadn't been on their suspect list until today. He wouldn't have met him during the investigation because the shire hadn't been involved.

Rodney glared at her. "You might think I sit around doing nothing, but my team has investigated people in positions of power in Retribution Bay."

It must be nice to have those kinds of resources. Dot scanned the building. Just the double front doors as the only exit from this side, but there were rear doors leading out to a staff car park. "I'll go around the rear."

"He's not likely to run for it. He doesn't know we're coming."

She didn't care. Her gut was telling her to go around the back. "I'll catch up with you." She strode around the side of the building, ignoring Rodney's curses behind her.

No exits on this side of the building, but as she

rounded the corner to the back, the door was flung open and Steven strode out. Average height, slim build but getting a middle-aged paunch, and neat, dark hair. Very similar to the boat captain last night. He made a beeline to his car and hadn't seen her.

Dot smiled and jogged over. "Steven! Can I have a word?"

He whirled around, eyes wide. The recognition hit, and he reached into his jacket. Dot grabbed her gun and levelled it at him. "Freeze!"

Steven hesitated, glancing behind her.

She couldn't afford to look. His hand was still underneath his jacket. "Very slowly show me your hands." Her heart raced, her finger hovering on the trigger and her focus narrowed to his every movement.

"Sergeant Campbell, relax. I was reaching for my phone." Slowly he withdrew his hands and held them high.

Dot lowered the gun. "Where were you off to?"

"Family emergency. Natasha's sick at school and needs to be picked up. Kristy is busy."

"I'm sorry, but it will have to wait. I need to ask you a few questions."

His face screwed up as if in pain. "My baby girl is ill. She might need to go to the hospital."

"I'll call the school when we get to the station," Dot said. "Please come with me."

"Can't whatever this is wait?"

"No." She tucked her gun away. "This way."

That hesitation again, but then he sighed and walked over to her. "Let's make it quick."

Rodney came out of the back door and spotted them. He scowled as he joined them.

"This is my colleague, Detective Rodney Taylor, who is with Organised Crime," Dot said.

"Detective, I was just explaining to Sergeant

Campbell that my daughter is sick and needs to be picked up from school. Can we talk later?"

"Afraid not," Rodney answered. "We'll make sure your daughter is taken care of."

They drove back to the station and when they arrived, Dot called the school and spoke to the principal, Jenifer Fredericks, about Steven's daughter.

"There's no one in the sick bay," Jenifer said. "As far as I know, Natasha Hamilton is in class."

"Could you please check for me and call me back?"

"Of course. Won't be long."

Dot fetched the printed image from last night and a notebook and joined Steven and Rodney in the interview room. The recording device hadn't been turned on yet, so Dot switched it on and did the preliminary introductions before sitting on Rodney's side of the table. She handed Rodney the printout and gestured for him to take the lead.

"What were you doing last night?" Rodney asked.

"I went to the brewery with my family for dinner."

Interesting he should be at the brewery where Dot had planned to go with Ryan and Hannah. Had she mentioned her plans to anyone? It might be a coincidence.

"What time did you leave?"

"About seven o'clock. The kids needed to get to bed."

Dot jotted notes as Rodney asked, "Did you go out again afterwards?"

"I went fishing."

"Where?"

"In the gulf."

"Which boat ramp did you use?" Dot asked.

"The southern one. Heard the fishing was good down there."

The boat hadn't headed in that direction, but it was possible he'd swung back around after he left. The southern boat ramp was the one she hadn't checked, and he could have towed the boat to town before she arrived at the marina.

"Is this you?" Rodney handed over the photo.

Steven squinted at the image. "It's hard to see. It might be."

"It's your boat though," Dot said, pointing out the name.

"Yeah."

"And you were on the boat last night?" she continued. When he nodded, she asked, "Was anyone else with you?"

He glanced at Rodney and then shook his head. "No."

Dot's phone rang, and she answered it, moving away from the table as she did so.

"It's Jenifer. Natasha is in class and has been fine all morning."

Dot smiled. "Thanks for your help." She hung up and sat back down.

Steven glanced at her. "Good news?"

"Yes. Who called you to tell you about Natasha?"

"Kristy. She usually gets the calls from the school, but she's on an excursion with Joseph's class today. They're snorkelling around at Turquoise Bay."

Someone was lying. "You'll be happy to hear Natasha is fine. She's not ill and has been in class all morning."

Steven nodded, but a slight film of sweat beaded on his forehead. "That's great news. Kristy must have got the wrong message. Phone signal can be a little spotty in places."

"Did anyone else use your boat yesterday?" Rodney asked.

Steven blinked as if surprised by the question. "Not that I know of."

"What time did you get back?"

"About..." he took his time thinking about it.

"Eleven o'clock."

Impossible. They'd seen the boat around that time. "Are you sure?"

"Yes. Kristy wanted me home by midnight and she was surprised I was so early."

Dot really wanted to get Kristy in an interview room.

"How do you explain this photo taken at ten fifty last night?" Rodney placed another photo on the table. "Who is this with you?"

Steven didn't answer.

"Why did you run when Sergeant Campbell asked you to stop?" Rodney continued.

Steven glanced at the table, his fingers tapping a beat. He opened his mouth and closed it a couple of times before saying, "I'm sorry. I thought I'd got the zoning wrong, and I was fishing in the wrong area. I'd be in so much trouble at work."

"What is your job at the shire?" Dot asked.

"Town planning."

Fish zoning fell under Parks and Wildlife, but still he would know the gulf had only a few areas at the tip where you couldn't fish.

"Getting caught would make you look the fool," Rodney commented.

Steven nodded. "I'm so sorry. I should have dealt with the issue, but Kristy's talking about me running for Shire President next year. I can't have a stain on my record."

He'd have more than a stain by the time Dot was through with him.

"Tell me when you met Kurt Webb," Rodney asked.

Steven blanched but shook his head. "Who?"

"Kurt Webb."

Dot was impressed Rodney didn't elaborate further.

"I don't know who that is."

Rodney showed him the image taken from the drone.

"Jog any memories?"

Steven clenched his hands together on the desk. A single drip of sweat followed his hairline down his face. "No, he doesn't look familiar."

"This might help." Rodney opened his tablet and showed Steven the drone footage.

He gaped as if he couldn't decide what to say. "Our drone was stolen. We reported it missing."

"Thanks for reminding me." Dot made a note. "We can add making a false claim to the list."

"He made me do it," Steven shouted. "He saw the drone and then needed me to show him how it worked."

"Why don't you tell us how you met?" Rodney asked.

Steven licked his lips. "Well, ah, we were at the beach, playing with the drone, and he approached us. Offered to pay a thousand dollars cash for it." Steven shrugged. "It wasn't worth that much, so I agreed."

They both stayed silent. Steven looked between the two of them and then continued. "He wanted to be shown how to use it, but he had to be in the gulf, so I took him out one day. He chose the island and where to fly the drone."

Who did he think he was kidding? The shot was taken rising from the hideout on the island and zooming in on the Stokes family. Steven knew far more than he was pretending.

"Did he say anything about the Stokes?" Rodney asked.

"Just wanted to know who they were."

Steven wasn't doing a bad job of pretending to be an innocent party, but then he'd had time to prepare a story in case he was caught.

"Did the kids have to share a room while he was staying with you?"

It was a stab in the dark, but worth it when Steven laughed.

"He didn't stay with us. The kids never would have kept it quiet."

"Where did he stay?" Dot asked.

Steven sobered, realising he'd admitted he knew Kurt had been in town for a while. "I don't know."

Rodney sighed. "Can we stop playing games? Kurt told us you two were friends from university, and you called him to Retribution Bay with promises he would make it rich. He's not willing to take the fall for you."

Dot only just stopped herself from glancing at Rodney in surprise, and kept her expression blank. Was it true?

"That's bullshit," Steven said. "He inserted himself up here as if he was in charge and fucked up our plans."

She had to give Rodney his due. He'd got more information out of Steven than she had and Steven hadn't even realised it yet.

"What were your plans?" The question was almost menacing when Rodney said it.

Steven paled. He dropped his head to the table and said, "I want a lawyer."

***

Oliver groaned as he scanned the ocean and spotted a silver dinghy coming towards them. It was too early in the day to be dealing with treasure hunters. He tightened the strap on his scuba tank and headed to the top deck where Sherlock and Sam were. Sherlock already had the binoculars to his eyes.

"It's set up for a day of fishing, and there's only a woman on board."

That was a change. Usually the would-be treasure hunters were men.

The boat neared, but at about twenty metres away it slowed, moved parallel, the driver waved at their boat blowing a kiss, and then stopped at a distance from the dive area. Downstairs Tom laughed. "Andrew, isn't that the old cougar who tried to pick you up at the brewery the other night?"

"She's not old," came the retort. "Besides, older women are more experienced."

The others laughed.

Oliver smiled at the teasing as he headed back downstairs. It was nice to see Andrew interacting for a change. "Let's finish getting ready," Oliver called and returned to his gear. He yawned, but it didn't take long before he was on the tender with Andrew and Sherlock, heading for their dive spot.

Sherlock did his buddy check. "You forgot to turn on your air," he said, opening the valve on the scuba tank.

Oliver rubbed his hand over his face. He was sure he had. "Thanks, mate." His exhaustion from the accumulated lack of sleep was making it hard to focus. Maybe he shouldn't go down, but they were almost finished. They had two more areas to catalogue and if all went well, he could tell Lucas they were finished when he called this evening.

Then he could drive his students home and return to sort things out with Dot.

Last night she'd called Sam's satellite phone to say she was home safely.

Then he finally got some sleep.

"Oliver, are we going?" Andrew asked.

Oliver blinked and nodded, bringing himself back to the present. "Let's go." He rolled backwards off the tender and into the water, allowing it to close over him before kicking to the surface. He and Andrew were cataloguing anything found in the area between where the cannons were dropped and the rest of the wreck site. Other items may have been pushed overboard to stop the ship from hitting the reef.

He descended slowly, balancing the buoyancy in his

vest as he did so, and scanned the bottom. Nothing that appeared unnatural, but he gestured for Andrew to take one side and together they swam over the area.

A lot of fish swimming through the coral, a turtle grazing and a stingray swimming along the sandy bottom nearby. Nothing man made.

He checked on Andrew, who was disappearing out of the limits of Oliver's vision. Annoyed, he kicked over. They were supposed to stay within sight of each other, in formation, so they missed nothing. Andrew knew that.

He'd be glad when he didn't have to deal with the kid's disinterest anymore.

Andrew increased his pace, kicking hard as if he'd spotted something of interest. Oliver waved, trying to get his attention, but he didn't look back.

Damn it.

Oliver swam after him. He couldn't let Andrew go off alone. He had a duty of care.

Andrew must have seen an animal, a manta ray or something, because he couldn't have spotted anything to do with the wreck.

Anger built in Oliver as his lungs burned. He'd never seen Andrew move this fast. The kid would decide to go rogue today, when Oliver was exhausted.

Oliver slowed. Something about the word rogue seemed significant. As if he should pay attention.

His distraction almost cost him, as Andrew was a shadow in front of him. He kicked harder again to catch up, knowing he was burning through his air. Oliver was going to have stern words to Andrew when he caught up. He should know better than to be distracted by an animal when they had limited time on this dive.

Finally, when Oliver was about to call it quits and let Andrew go, Andrew stopped. There was a shape in the water beyond him, but Oliver couldn't see what it was. He caught up, grabbing Andrew's shoulder and checking what had so distracted him.

And stared at a woman pointing a spear gun right at him.

Chapter 18

Oliver stared at the spear gun, confused, his tired brain trying to catch up. Why was the woman pointing it at him? Andrew grabbed his arm and pointed to the surface where Oliver noticed the hull of a boat.

His confusion grew to concern. Something wasn't right.

This must be the woman from the brewery who'd driven past before they'd got into the water. But what did she want with him?

Was she part of Stonefish? Was Dot right about Lucas Fitton, and Andrew was carrying out his father's wishes?

But Lucas could ask Oliver what he wanted to know.

Andrew tugged him towards the surface, his expression determined and a little angry. The woman waved the spear gun at him and his body tensed.

Oliver checked his gauges. He'd burned through a lot of his oxygen chasing Andrew, so he would need to surface soon. He had no idea how likely the woman was to use the spear gun. And the way she was waving it around, she'd likely fire it without meaning to.

Perhaps if they could talk to each other, they'd clear up this mess. He made the thumbs up gesture for surfacing and slowly ascended. At the safety stop location, Andrew shook his head and kept him moving.

When his head broke the surface, Oliver inflated his BCD and took the regulator from his mouth. They'd come up on the northern side of the boat, so he couldn't see the *Oceanid*. Maybe there was a way to get Sam and Sherlock's attention though. "What's going on?" he asked Andrew.

"You need to get in the boat." The kid sounded angry and was already ripping off his fins and throwing them over the side onto the deck.

"Why?" Oliver asked.

The woman floated next to him, not saying anything, just pointing the spear gun at him.

"Because you have to."

He kept his smile friendly. "What I have to do is finish the examination of the wreck. I don't have time for delays."

"Get in the boat or I'll shoot you," the woman said, her tone firm, as she prodded him in the side with the tip of the spear.

Fear rushed through him, not so much from her but from her lack of awareness of where the trigger was. "Stop pointing it at me." Slowly he took off his fins, hoping the boat would swing, exposing them. "Would you at least tell me what this is about?"

"They want to know where the treasure is," Andrew said as he climbed onto the boat.

Incredulity filled him. "What treasure? We haven't found any."

"But the Stokes have," the woman said. "And you know where it is."

"I don't know anything."

"I heard you talking to Sam and Sherlock last night," Andrew said. "You were talking about the treasure."

Shit. How much had he heard? "We were talking

hypothetically. They asked me some questions about ownership, I answered them."

The woman swore. "You said they had it," she growled at Andrew.

He looked unconcerned. "They have it, Kristy." Nothing seemed to faze him. He didn't seem to care that Sam and Sherlock hadn't told Oliver where it was, or that he'd delayed Oliver's work.

"I'll be on my way." Oliver raised the hose ready to deflate his BCD.

"No!" Kristy looked left and right, checking no one was near. "I don't believe you. You're still coming with us."

"I'm no use to you."

"You're lying. You've been cosying up with Dot. That emotionless bitch will have told you something. Get in." She gestured for him to climb into the boat.

Oliver gritted his teeth at her assessment of Dot and, instead of retorting, examined the spear gun. Her finger hovered over the trigger and she had it poked into his side. It was difficult to move fast in the water, encumbered as he was with the BCD. She could fire faster than he could twist and push the gun away.

"Get in." She prodded him in the back again, her finger coming perilously close to the trigger.

"All right." He handed his fins to Andrew and moved around the side of the boat to the ladder. The top deck of the *Oceanid* was just visible and Sam was looking south towards the dive site. It was a reasonable distance away, and Oliver wasn't certain a shout would attract Sam's attention.

"Keep quiet and move," Kristy said.

She had to be a local if she knew who Dot was, but this was an aggressive tactic if she wanted the treasure.

Oliver climbed the ladder, moving awkwardly with the weight of the tank on his back. As soon as he was up, the woman followed. "Sit on the ground. Both of you."

Andrew had already removed his BCD and Oliver followed suit, but used the jacket as a back rest. Kristy placed the spear gun on the dash of the boat and grabbed her mobile phone. She swore and threw it back on the dash. "No service."

Oliver assessed his chances. Could he dive over the side before anyone stopped him? No one on the *Oceanid* would hear him over the engine and Sam or Sherlock might not be looking this way. He couldn't stay under water for long without his scuba tank and if Kristy got annoyed, she could shoot him with the spear gun and be done with him.

"What's going on, Andrew?" He leaned closer to the boy to be heard above the engine.

Andrew ignored him as they sped across the water.

Frustration filled him as he put together what he knew. Sherlock and Sam suspected Lucas. Andrew had been forced on the expedition, maybe even forced to study maritime archaeology by his father. But why? Anyone who had watched the reality TV show would realise Oliver always did things the way he was supposed to.

Maybe that was the problem. Perhaps as Sherlock suggested, this was about family history and Lucas didn't want it done by the book.

But what was Kristy's role in all of this? Was she part of the Stonefish consortium?

What would she do to him when she realised he really had no idea where the treasure was?

It wouldn't take long for Sam and Sherlock to notice they were missing. He checked his dive watch. Another ten minutes at the most and they'd start getting worried, because Andrew was always the first to surface. With today's calm waters, it would be easy to see underwater and if they sent up the drone, they would see they weren't there. The men would realise the boat was the only option.

So he needed to delay, or lead them into town where they'd be around more people.

Andrew lurched to his feet and spun, vomiting over the side of the boat. Oliver winced and shuffled out of the way to avoid being hit by any spray. Kristy slowed.

"Get down."

"You want me to vomit all over your boat?" Andrew asked, his voice weak.

Kristy swore.

"He gets seasick," Oliver told her and got to his feet to help Andrew to the front seat. The *Oceanid* looked smaller now and people moved on the deck.

"You get down." Kristy pointed at Oliver. "And you sit in the chair. Why did your father send you on a boat if you get seasick?"

Andrew said nothing, but sat in the chair and clung to the sides. Kristy handed him a bucket and then accelerated again.

Oliver stumbled back. There was no point diving over the side, as they'd be back around to get him before he went far. It was interesting Kristy knew Lucas. Perhaps his theory was right.

As he sat, he noticed the waterproof pen hanging out of the side of one of his BCD pockets. No one was paying him attention, so he slipped it and the notebook it was attached to out of the pocket. Using the jacket sides as a shield, he wrote a note for whoever found it and tucked it back inside.

Then he began to plan.

It wasn't too much longer before the boat slowed. Oliver peered over the edge as they approached an almost deserted boat ramp, with only a single car parked in the car park. Damn.

Kristy ordered Andrew off the boat to tie up and tried to call someone again. She swore. "There's still no reception!" She grabbed the spear gun, climbed off the boat, and gestured him to follow.

"What are we doing now?" Andrew asked.

"He's supposed to lead us to the treasure, but he doesn't know where it is," Kristy snapped.

"Then we take him back to town."

"We can't," Kristy said. "If Dot has been alerted Oliver is missing, she'll be checking all the boat ramps. She'll see us if we drive back to town."

Andrew shrugged as if he didn't care. Perhaps he didn't understand the charges that came with kidnapping. "Then we head out of town."

"I have to be home when my children finish school," Kristy replied.

Oliver's eyebrows raised. Kidnapper by day, mother by night. "Maybe you should arrange for someone to pick them up." He smiled. "Just in case."

The worry on Kristy's face gave him a pinch of guilt. At least she cared for her kids.

"Let's take him to Lee. He'll know what to do," Andrew said.

"Do you know where to find him?" Kristy asked.

"He'll find us. He always does." Again that nonchalance from Andrew.

Kristy nodded, determination crossing her face. She waved the spear gun at Oliver. "This way. Andrew, tie up the boat."

Oliver's body flushed with heat. "Stop pointing that at me. I'll go with you." He'd read about too many spear fishing accidents to be comfortable with her lack of respect for the weapon she held.

Kristy lowered it as Andrew said, "I don't know how to tie up a boat."

It happened in slow motion. "Can you do anything?"

Kristy complained. She raised her arm in annoyance, the spear gun pointing at Oliver again. The spear released, hurtling straight through Oliver's chest.

The jolt of the impact made him stumble back and warm, metallic blood filled his mouth. The air left his lungs, and he spat out blood, gasping, trying to breathe. Sharp stabbing pain with every inhale. He stared at Kristy and then looked down at the spear protruding through his chest.

Kristy paled and dropped the weapon.

"Shit, Kristy. What did you do that for?" Andrew asked.

"I didn't mean to!" She took a couple of steps back, panting in shock.

Oliver clutched the spear, trying to breathe gently through the pain. Warm blood ran over his hands.

"Are you…" Kristy swallowed hard. "all right?"

What a stupid question. He shook his head. His head spun and his throat tightened as his stomach threatened to lose its contents from the pain. He needed to sit. He stumbled to the jetty pylon and leaned against it, and then jerked back as the spear shifted. It must have gone all the way through. "Hospital," he gasped.

Kristy shook her head, her hands trembling. "No. I can't go back to town. We'll pull it out and patch it." She stepped towards him.

Was she completely insane? He held up a hand, fear coursing through him. "No!"

Kristy blinked and tied up the boat, moving automatically. "Andrew, help him to the car." She jumped on board to get some towels and a first aid kit.

No way was he getting in the car unless they took him to the hospital. The spear was about sixty centimetres long and protruded a decent way out of his chest. He pressed firmly against the wound and retched at the pain.

"This way." Andrew's hand shook as he gestured

Oliver to follow.

"I… need… medical help."

A flicker of concern crossed Andrew's face. He nodded, a little hesitant. "Then you need to get into the car."

Oliver blinked, trying to clear a path through the pain in order to think.

Andrew was lying. They wouldn't take him to the hospital, which meant he had to delay. Dot would have been notified he was missing by now. Sam and Sherlock would have called her immediately with everything that had been going on.

She might have a plane mobilising, or boats, or have her people searching boat ramps.

Someone might be on the way right now.

He wasn't certain how far out of town they were, but it couldn't be more than about thirty minutes.

Kristy threw him a towel for him to mop up the blood. The tight wetsuit would hopefully help to slow the blood flow.

"First… aid… kit." He held out his hand, his head spinning.

She passed it to him, not looking him in the face, and then strode to the white Range Rover to unhitch the boat trailer. She'd made up her mind, but what she'd decided, he had no clue.

Andrew stood by watching, his face pale, as Oliver fumbled with the zip.

"Reason with her," Oliver begged. "I'm… losing… blood. Hospital." Every breath was agony.

Andrew straightened and stepped further away. "I'm just doing what I'm told."

"Help me!"

He shook his head. "I can't. Dad would kill me."

Selfish little prick.

Oliver examined the contents of the kit and took out

the first bandage, wrapping it into a donut ring.

Kristy had unhitched the trailer and driven the Range Rover to the edge of the jetty by the time he was done.

"Get in," Kristy ordered through the open window. When he ignored her she added, "I'll take you to the hospital."

Bullshit. Oliver threaded the ring over the spear. His legs wobbled as the pain compounded.

She no longer had a weapon. They couldn't make him get in. He could wait here until help arrived.

He prayed Dot had been notified.

"Bandage," he said to Andrew.

The boy passed it over and Oliver made another donut ring.

"What are you doing?" Kristy demanded.

"First aid," Oliver retorted.

"We don't have time." She jumped out of the car and strode over.

The next part would be tricky. He couldn't do it himself. He studied Andrew. "Put… over… spear." He turned to give him access. "Wrap… bandage… around." Every breath, every word was torture.

Andrew nodded and did what he was told, making quick and remarkably good work of wrapping the bandage in place.

Kristy shuffled foot to foot impatiently. "Hurry, someone's coming."

Relief filled him as the rumble of a vehicle got closer.

The sun beat onto his head as he stepped forward and the nausea he'd been fighting was released. He vomited over the gravel ground.

Andrew yelled and leapt out of the way.

His head spun, and he sank to the ground, groaning at the pain.

He closed his eyes, focusing on his breathing, slow shallow breaths to calm himself, and applied pressure to the wound.

He fought the urge to sink into the darkness that called to him.

Dot was on her way.

He had to believe it.

He just hoped she wasn't too late.

***

Dot let Rodney do the formalities of remanding Steven in custody and when he returned, she asked, "Shall we bring Kristy in?"

He nodded. "Find out where the excursion is."

Dot called Jenifer back. "Can you tell me where the third graders have gone on excursion today?"

"We have no class excursions," Jenifer replied.

"No one has gone snorkelling on the reef?"

"No. I review the school schedule every morning, and nothing of note is happening. What's this all about, Dot?"

"I can't say," Dot replied. "Is anyone else allowed to pick up the Hamilton children?"

"I can check their file. Hold on." Clicking keys in the background and then Jenifer said, "Declan and Dominique Abdoo."

Declan was in gaol, but Dominique had been cleared of any involvement. "Thanks." She'd call Dominique if Kristy was arrested. She hung up and turned to Rodney. "There is no excursion."

"Let's go."

Dot wasn't sure what to make of Rodney's change of heart, allowing her to go with him. Perhaps he finally trusted her. Or he realised she wouldn't let Martin go with him.

They drove the short distance to the Hamilton house and the concrete slab where the boat usually sat was empty. "Boat's gone," Dot said.

"We'll check."

No one answered Rodney's demanding knock.

Dot opened an app on her phone and checked the marine traffic in the area. Not everyone had a tracker installed on their boat, but it was becoming more common, especially for those who fished kilometres offshore. No *Cersei*.

They would have to do this the old-fashioned way. "Do you want to start at the marina? It's the closest boat ramp."

Rodney nodded. "How many ramps are there?"

"Three on this side of the peninsula and another one on the other side." It would take them a couple of hours to check unless they sent Martin or Pierre. Or if she called some of her contacts. She dialled a number. "Hey, Penelope. Are you out on the water today?"

"Just heading out now," her friend answered.

"Did you notice a white Range Rover in the marina car park?"

"No, it's pretty empty today."

Dot smiled. "While you're out and about, if you see a boat called *Cersei*, can you contact me?"

"Sure. Is everything OK?" Penelope sounded concerned.

"Yeah. Don't worry about it."

Rodney waited for her to hang up before he said, "Are you mad? You can't tell people who we're after."

"Penelope won't tell anyone. She's the one whose boat was shot up and sank in the middle of a shark feeding frenzy." She wanted Stonefish caught as much as Dot did.

As they returned to the car, Dot called Sam.

"I was about to call you," Sam answered.

Not what she wanted to hear. "Me first. I'm looking for a boat called *Cersei*. Have you seen it down your way?"

Sam swore. "Yeah. That might explain it."

Unease grew in her stomach. "Explain what?"

"Oliver and Andrew are missing."

It took a second for his words to sink in. "What do you mean, they're missing?" She tossed her keys to Rodney. "Drive to the marina."

Rodney grunted but did as she asked.

"They went under thirty minutes ago, and haven't been seen since."

Dread made her nauseous, but, "Thirty minutes isn't long for Oliver."

"No, but he was diving with Andrew who chugs through his air in about twenty."

"Tell me everything," she barked.

"They were searching the area between the cannons and the main wreck. Just before we dropped them, a woman in the boat *Cersei* came near, waved at us and drove off again. It looked like she was fishing over by one of the islands. Tom teased Andrew about her because she chatted him up at the brewery the other night."

It had to be Kristy. "Then what happened?"

"We dropped them in the water and waited for them to surface. When the rest of the team surfaced after thirty minutes, Sherlock sent up the drone. There's no sign of them in the water, but the drone had little battery charge. Suzyn swore she put the charger on last night, but someone turned it off."

"And the boat?"

"Only stuck around for about twenty minutes."

Rodney parked at the marina and Dot got out, but hesitated. There might be no point taking the boat out. There was enough time for Kristy to have made it back to shore. "Which way did the boat go?"

"West."

Towards the southern boat ramp. Steven said he'd

used it last night.

"Have you searched the islands?" They might have run into trouble and gone to shore.

"Just using the drone. No sign of them. Oliver would do something to get our attention. He'd know we'd be looking for them by now."

Oliver wouldn't have suspected his team. If Andrew had led him away from the dive site, Oliver would have been annoyed, but he would have followed. He took safety seriously.

"I've got the drone batteries on charge. Might take another hour before I can send it up again, but we'll search the islands in the tender."

"Do that," Dot said. "Call me if you find anything." She hung up and grabbed the binoculars from the car.

"What's happened?" Rodney demanded.

"Oliver and Andrew are missing." Dot strode to the side of the marina, which overlooked the ocean, and scanned the horizon. When Rodney followed she added, "Kristy was in the area before they disappeared. She flirted with Andrew the other night at the brewery."

"That means nothing."

"No," Dot agreed. "However, it's a lead. All of this happened about thirty minutes ago, so if she was returning to a boat ramp up this way, we should see her by now." There weren't a lot of boats in the gulf today. Most of the tourists had left the area and those that were there didn't match the size of *Cersei*. She lowered the binoculars. "My guess is she's parked at the southern boat ramp. It's less distance from the wreck site, and fewer people are around."

"Or she might be out of sight here and going anywhere along the coast."

Dot didn't have time to argue. Oliver was in danger. She couldn't fail him like she failed Mark.

Her throat tightened as fear threatened to surface.

No, she wouldn't consider the option that he'd already been harmed. "We can get Martin to search the northern boat ramps while we go south." Why had Oliver been taken? He didn't know anything. Unless someone had told Stonefish they had been stuck on the boat together. Someone like Andrew. They might have thought she'd confided in Oliver.

Rodney got into the passenger seat. "Take me back to the station. I'll go with Martin."

Damn him. They were wasting time. She drove fast back to the station, radioing them to tell them what had happened. As soon as Rodney got out, she was on her way again, estimating how much time had passed.

By now Kristy could have got the boat out of the water, but she had only two directions to go; north back to town, and south out of town.

Dot switched on her lights and sped south. It would be difficult for Kristy and Andrew to lift an unconscious Oliver out of the boat, so maybe he was still conscious, and they had a weapon to keep him in line. He was sensible enough to do what they said.

The tightness in her chest was from more than adrenaline. She gripped the steering wheel as her hands trembled. This wasn't fear for herself, this was terror Oliver might be taken away from her again. Just when she'd got him back.

There was still so much to say to him. She wanted to see if they could make things work. She still loved him.

She exhaled, fighting back control. Think.

She tapped her finger on the steering wheel. It made no sense to take Oliver unless it was to use him as leverage against her. But what did Stonefish want with her? To scare her off the case? That wouldn't happen.

Just before Dot turned off the main road towards the boat ramp, she noticed a dust plume in the direction of the ranges. A car, but only rangers were allowed there.

She headed for the ramp, but radioed Parks and Wildlife. "Are any of your rangers in the southeast of the ranges today?"

Karen responded quickly. "Negative."

"Thanks." Dot was tempted to turn around, but she was almost at the ramp. She slowed as she came around the bend. The car park contained an unhitched boat trailer and closer to the ramp, a white Range Rover was parked in front of the jetty. Dot could see two people standing on the jetty next to *Cersei*, but it was impossible to see who they were through the car.

She radioed dispatch. "I've found the boat and its occupants. Send backup." Dot pulled to a stop, got out of the car, and drew her gun.

"Rodney and Martin are heading to you now," dispatch replied.

Good.

One person ran towards the car and came into sight. Kristy glanced Dot's way and her eyes bulged. Dot headed her off, raising her gun.

"Stop, Kristy."

Kristy stumbled to a stop and raised her hands high. "Don't shoot." She wore a T-shirt over her wetsuit, which was pulled down to her waist. No weapon in sight.

"Head back to the others." Dot could see around the car now. Andrew stood next to a kneeling Oliver.

Her eyes met Oliver's, saw the pain. Her gaze lowered and her breath left her.

A spear stuck out of his chest and the bandage wrapped around his torso was red with blood.

Shit.

Horror filled her and panic wanted to take control.

She couldn't lose him.

Chapter 19

Dot strode forward, calling into the radio. "Require ambulance to southern boat ramp. Man impaled through the chest with a spear." She assessed the situation, her heart pounding.

Oliver was conscious, bending drunkenly forward at the waist, his hands around the spear as if holding it in place. His weak smile gave her hope and allowed her to focus on the others.

Andrew stood next to him, watching her with a frown on his face.

He was still a suspect, though he didn't seem to be armed. He held a first aid kit in his hand and his wetsuit was pulled down to his waist.

Not a lot of places he could hide a weapon, but he could still hurt Oliver.

She kept her gun out but lowered as she called, "Andrew, raise your hands and step away from Oliver."

Andrew did as she asked.

Dot stepped onto the jetty, glancing at the boat. It appeared empty from where she stood, but someone could be hiding on the deck. "Is there anyone else on the boat?"

Oliver shook his head, but the movement was loose, uncontrolled. He was in a bad way.

"An ambulance is enroute." She didn't have time to waste. "Did Andrew help kidnap you?"

A nod.

She moved over to Kristy. "Kristy, you're under arrest."

Kristy shook her head. "You can't arrest me. I've got to pick my kids up from school."

The woman was a piece of work. Oliver was critically injured and all she cared about were her children. "Dominique can do it." Dot moved forward.

The woman frowned. "Why Dominique?"

"Steven's in gaol. We arrested him this morning."

Kristy went pale. "What for?"

"Drug smuggling."

She lowered her shaking hands. "No. He didn't do anything."

"That's not what the evidence says." She tucked her gun away and handcuffed Kristy and then moved to Andrew to do the same. She read them both their rights while assessing Oliver's pale skin and shaking hands. The bandages around the spear were a deep red, but there wasn't anything else she could do for him here. He needed medical help.

"You hanging in there, Oliver?" she called.

"Yeah." His voice was thready and his eyes fluttered closed.

Panic filled her. There wasn't a lot of time.

In the distance another car engine got louder. Whoever it was could help Oliver while she restrained the others. Unless it was someone from Stonefish.

She needed to work fast and get Andrew and Kristy in the police car.

"This is bullshit," Andrew said. "I only did what my father told me to do."

Dot glanced at Andrew. "Lucas Fitton?"

Andrew nodded. "He told me to get Oliver away from everyone else. He didn't tell me what was going to happen. Kristy was the one with the spear gun. She ordered us both into the boat."

"Don't pretend you're innocent," Kristy spat. "You were spying on the group. Trying to find out where the treasure was."

"My father made me take the stupid university course. He said he'd cut all my funding if I didn't do what he said. He blackmailed me."

Finally, someone willing to talk to the police. "You're saying you were coerced into participating?" Dot asked. The sound of a car engine came closer.

Sweat poured down Oliver's face and his breathing was shallow. Dot stepped towards him.

"Yeah," Andrew answered. "I didn't want to."

Dot brought her attention back to him. "What did he ask you to do?"

"Take Oliver's course. My father knew the museum would send someone to investigate the new shipwreck and he could make sure it was Oliver. He needed me to be his eyes and ears on the dive." Andrew scowled. "Further punishment for not being interested in the family business."

"And what is the family business?" Dot asked.

"Smuggling."

Dot glanced behind her as Rodney and Martin pulled up. Backup had arrived, but no ambulance. They could help Oliver while she listened to Andrew's confession.

"What did you smuggle?" she asked Andrew.

"Everything. Drugs, animals, people."

"Why Retribution Bay?"

Andrew shrugged. "Father's obsessed with the shipwreck and finding the treasure. Not even Clark's death changed his mind."

"Clark?" Dot asked.

"My brother. He was shot a couple of months back by Georgie Stokes."

Dot's heart lurched at the confirmation of Clark's identity. "Who else is involved with the smuggling?" Both Martin and Rodney approached, steps casual, as if they had all the time in the world. Martin had his hand on his gun.

"Help Oliver," Dot called.

Andrew's gaze was on the officers approaching. His brow furrowed, concern creeping onto his face for the first time. "The cops."

"Colin?"

"No. I don't know why Lee involved him." He nodded towards Martin, jerking on the handcuffs trying to loosen them. "But he is."

Dot's heart jumped, and she whirled to face him, her own hand going to her gun. Martin held up his hands. "Are you going to believe this kid? He'll say anything to save his arse."

"It's true," Andrew said. "I saw him talking to Father the night before we started staying on the boat."

"Lucas is in town?"

"Yeah. He's staying at a resort. Wanted to be close when the treasure was found."

Kristy watched Martin warily. Was it because he was a cop, or because she was afraid of him?

"Kristy, what do you know about it?"

She shook her head and kept her lips pressed together but stepped away from Andrew.

Rodney took hold of her arm and led her towards the police car. He was being remarkably docile. She'd expected him to barge in and take over the questioning so she could help Oliver.

Why was no one helping Oliver?

"Did you hear what your father said to Martin?" Dot

asked, trying to get to the bottom of this as she shifted closer to Oliver. It could have been an innocent conversation, or this could be Andrew's way of sowing distrust amongst her team.

"They were talking about Kurt and how much he stuffed up kidnapping the kids."

Martin lowered his hands. "That's enough of your lies."

Dot glanced behind to see where Rodney was. He was helping Kristy into the back of the police car.

"Father bragged about having someone on the local police force to look the other way," Andrew said, his words coming fast. "I'd bet it is him."

An accusation, but not a certainty.

"Shut your mouth," Martin ordered, pulling his gun and pointing it at Andrew.

Oliver was right behind Andrew and he shifted, but groaned, swaying precariously.

"Martin, lower your weapon," Dot said, reaching for hers.

Martin kept his gun on Andrew.

"That's an order, Martin. Lower your gun." Dot's heart thumped in her chest as she waited to be obeyed.

Dot shifted her gun to point more at Martin. There was no reason for Martin to want Andrew to stop talking if he was innocent and no reason for him to draw his weapon. Andrew was restrained and no threat to anyone. "Put your gun away and help Oliver," she told Martin. To Andrew she asked, "What else do you know?"

"A whole lot. I'll tell you everything. I took a copy of Father's files—"

The gunshot echoed through the still morning. Andrew fell back, a bullet hole through his head, in an almost identical position from the hole which had gone through Mark's head. Dot's pulse jumped and she pointed her gun at Martin as Martin shifted his gun to

Oliver.

"I'll kill lover boy here if you don't let me go."

Oliver straightened with a wince.

What the hell? Dot exhaled, her brain racing. Oliver was in real danger. Martin had nothing to lose by shooting him. She had to reason with him. "You shot your boss's son. Do you really think you'll get away with it?" Pounding footsteps behind her, but she didn't dare take her eyes off Martin to look at Rodney.

"I shot a liability. Lucas will reward me. He's been complaining about him since we met."

Dot's pulse raced. He'd confirmed Lucas was his boss. "Why do this?"

"What was the point in working my arse off if they gave my promotion to you?" he snarled. "At least this way, I can make money and make a fool of you."

How did he think this was going to play out? Even if she let him go, he'd be caught eventually. He'd just murdered someone in front of her.

No, he wasn't stupid. But how did he think he would get away? If she lowered her gun, Rodney would still stop him.

"Drop your weapon, Martin," Dot ordered, as Rodney stepped up next to her, weapon also drawn.

"Never gonna happen. You want your lover alive, you're going to have to kill me." He glanced at her, loathing in his eyes. Then he shifted to Rodney, and a smug grin followed.

Oliver shifted to the side and Martin's gun followed him.

Dot stared at Martin, but she was hyper aware of Rodney by her side. "You spent your entire career upholding the law and then disregarded it because you were looked over for promotion?"

"I did everything I was supposed to do. They owed me."

"I also did what I was supposed to do." He stood side on to her, not providing much of a target unless she killed him. Trying to shoot his hand would be a fool's game, but the biggest target was his head.

"Dot, hospital," Oliver whispered, his voice thready.

"Looks like I might not even have to kill him," Martin said. "Just delaying you will be enough." He laughed and shifted.

He turned to face her and Dot fired. Twin explosions of blood. One on Martin's right shoulder where Dot had been aiming, the other in the centre of his head. The gun dropped from his hand and his body collapsed, falling over the side of the jetty and into the water.

Dot spun to Rodney, but he was already moving forward to peer into the water. "Help Oliver."

She didn't need to be told twice, but her brain was still processing the shock. Rodney had killed Martin.

In the distance, ambulance sirens wailed. She slid her arm under Oliver's shoulder. "Can you stand?"

He nodded and grunted as he took his first step, leaning heavily against her. She didn't have the strength to carry his weight, and there was no way to bring the car closer.

She glanced at Andrew, the flies already buzzing around him. She'd have to come back for him.

"He's dead," Rodney declared.

"No shit," Dot snapped. "Help me with Oliver."

Rodney raised an eyebrow, but did as she asked. By the time they reached the car park, the ambulance pulled up, and the paramedics took charge.

One looked towards the jetty. "Does he need help?"

Dot shook her head, walking beside the gurney. "He's dead. We'll deal with him. Get Oliver to hospital." She squeezed Oliver's hand. "I'll be there as soon as I can."

His eyelids flickered open.

"Stay with me," she said. He was so much paler than

normal and his breath was thready. She couldn't lose him. She stood back as they loaded him into the ambulance. As the doors closed she whispered, "I love you."

Then she watched the man she loved be driven away.

Chapter 20

Oliver's head throbbed, the pain waking him from unconsciousness. The scent of disinfectant filled his nose, and the stark lights above him made him wince. Why was he in hospital?

He shifted and a sharp, stabbing pain spiked his chest, bringing back the memories. The spear through his chest, the bizarre kidnapping, Martin working for Stonefish and shooting Andrew. Martin being killed. Had Dot done that?

Sorrow filled Oliver. Andrew hadn't been particularly nice, but he hadn't deserved to die.

Vague recollection of being transferred to the ambulance and Dot whispering she loved him.

Was that a hallucination?

Where was Dot?

He turned his head, looking for a call button. There was a bag of blood next to him, feeding into an IV in his arm, replacing what he'd lost. A nurse walked into the room and her eyes widened.

"Mr Anderson, I didn't realise you were awake. How do you feel?" She lifted the back of the bed so it supported him, and he groaned.

"Sore. Where am I? Where's Dot?"

"You're at Retribution Bay Hospital and you're extremely fortunate to be alive. The spear missed all your vitals." She put a blood pressure cuff on the arm not connected to the blood transfusion and checked his vitals.

"Do you have a phone I can use?"

"If you're up for visitors, Sam Hackett and Arthur Hammond are here to see you. They might have one."

Dot must have called them. Oliver exhaled. "Please send them in."

The nurse finished his obs and then showed in the men. Both examined him, and Sam nodded his approval. "Feeling all right?"

"Weak and sore. Where's Dot? How are my students?"

"The students are back at the house," Sam replied. "All they know is you've been found. They don't know details. What happened?"

"Where's Dot?" He needed to see her, make certain she was all right. She'd shot another officer. There had to be ramifications. Probably the only reason he didn't have cops waiting to interview him was there was only one other left in Retribution Bay.

"She's dealing with everything." Sam grimaced. "As soon as we got word you'd been found, we headed back to the marina."

"So how did you get kidnapped?" Sherlock asked.

Oliver winced and recounted the story, ending with Dot and Rodney both shooting Martin. "I don't know who killed him."

"We haven't spoken to Dot yet," Sam said. "She'll be by when she can."

"Has anyone contacted Lucas to tell him his son is dead?" Sherlock asked.

"I don't know." But it was something Oliver should

do, even if Lucas orchestrated his kidnapping. Or maybe he should wait until he spoke to Dot. "Can I use your phone?"

"Use yours." Sam handed him a bag of his things.

He took out his necklace with the emerald ring and slipped it around his neck. Then he found his phone and sent Dot a text.

Hey. I'm awake. Can I call Lucas about Andrew?

Her response was instant. *Send me his number.*

He did so and the three dots wiggled as she wrote something else. He waited.

We have someone who will contact Lucas, but if you want to, go ahead. Tell him as little as possible. See if he's in Retribution Bay.

OK.

Before he could make the call, he received another message. *Be there as soon as I can. Xo.*

Oliver smiled. Good. He needed to see her, needed to find out whether she had actually said she loved him.

He stared at Lucas's contact details as the reality of what he needed to do hit him. He needed to tell a man his son was dead. The nausea in his stomach had nothing to do with his injury. Lucas might be in charge of a crime syndicate, but no parent wanted to lose a child.

He exhaled and hit the send button, wanting to get it over with. He'd been responsible for Andrew and it was his duty to inform his father.

"Where are you?" Lucas demanded. "Why is the boat back at the marina?"

Oliver blinked. The police mustn't have called him yet if he was concerned about the expedition. "Are you in town?" Maybe Andrew had been telling the truth, and Lucas was in Retribution Bay.

"Why would you ask that?"

"Because you know the boat is in the marina."

"Andrew told me."

Lie. But it definitely meant Lucas didn't know what had happened. Oliver pinched his nose. "There's been an incident."

"Is my son all right?" His concern was evident in the way the pitch of his voice raised. He didn't seem to notice he'd contradicted himself.

Oliver exhaled and closed his eyes, not wanting to break the news. He braced himself. "No. I'm sorry to have to tell you this, Lucas, but Andrew has died."

A harsh inhale was his only reaction for a long moment. Finally, his voice cold, Lucas asked, "What happened?"

Oliver hadn't considered what he was going to say. He could hardly tell Lucas he was the main suspect in the police case.

"The two of us were diving together this morning, and we came across a woman with a spear gun. She forced us onto her boat." He waited for Lucas's reaction, but the man was silent.

"She wanted the treasure and wouldn't believe me when I told her we haven't found any."

"What about those journals?" Lucas asked.

"They're hundreds of years old. It's likely the treasure was found and removed before now." Sam and Sherlock were listening.

"Then what happened?"

"The woman shot me through the chest with the spear gun. Sergeant Campbell caught up with us."

"How did my son die?"

"He was shot."

"By the sergeant?"

"No!" Hell, if Lucas thought Dot had anything to do with it, she'd be in real danger. "Backup arrived and one of her officers shot Andrew."

"Why?"

Oliver grimaced. "I don't know. I'd lost a lot of blood

by then and it was difficult to focus. I couldn't hear what they were saying."

"What was the officer's name?"

"Martin."

Glacial silence, then, "Where is he now?"

"He's dead too."

"Where is Andrew's body?"

Sam pointed to the ground. They must be able to hear what Lucas was saying.

"Here at the hospital. I imagine they'll need to do an autopsy or something. Someone might need to do a formal identification. Are you able to come up?"

A long pause. "I don't know. When are you going back to the dive site?" Lucas asked.

Oliver's eyes widened. He would have thought the expedition was the least of Lucas's concerns. "I haven't spoken to a doctor yet about when I'll be released." The curtain swung open and Rodney strode in. Oliver swallowed his groan. He'd forgotten about the man.

"I'll call you later." Lucas hung up.

Damn. He'd hoped to get more information from Lucas.

Rodney glared at the two ex-military men. "What are you doing here?"

"Checking on a friend," Sam answered.

"I need to ask him questions. Get out."

Sam glanced at Oliver for confirmation, and he nodded. "Can you tell my team I'll call them when I'm done here?"

"Copy."

Rodney waited until they left the cubicle and then demanded, "Tell me what happened."

It was going to be a long afternoon.

With a sigh, Oliver started his story.

It was what felt like hours later when a doctor walked in,

his posture straight, temples greying, and interrupted the interrogation. "Excuse me, Detective. I need to speak with my patient."

"We're not done here," Rodney barked.

Oliver's head thumped and his throat hurt from talking. "Could I get some pain meds?" he rasped.

The doctor nodded. "You'll need to come back tomorrow," he said to Rodney. "My patient needs rest. He's exhausted."

Oliver wanted to kiss the man.

Rodney opened his mouth to argue, and the doctor said, "Please leave." The tone brooked no argument and reminded Oliver of Sam and Sherlock. Military.

Rodney glowered. "I'll be back in the morning."

When he was gone, Oliver smiled at the older man. "Thank you."

"You're welcome." He wrote something on his file.

"How long am I going to be here?" Dot hadn't come in with Rodney, which had to mean she wasn't allowed to, or was busy elsewhere. She wouldn't choose to let him deal with Rodney without a buffer.

"You've lost a lot of blood," the doctor said. "I'd like to keep you in overnight and reassess in the morning depending on how your injury is healing." He smiled. "But when you get out, buy a Lotto ticket. The spear glanced off your rib, and only just nicked your lungs. Hardly challenged me at all."

Oliver frowned at him as a nurse walked in. The doctor showed her Oliver's file and then left.

The nurse waited until he was gone and then said, "Don't mind him. He's ex-military and has seen far worse injuries than yours. You're lucky he was here. He's due to go on holidays next week." She checked the monitors. "I'll get those pain meds for you."

Finally alone, Oliver took stock of the situation. His head was an uncomfortable combination of throbbing pain and light-headedness, and his chest ached, but the bandage wrapped around it was comforting. His students were safely back at the house and there was no reason Stonefish should go after them.

And then there was Dot.

He needed to see her, confirm she was all right. But she had a whole mess to clean up. He couldn't expect her to drop everything for him.

Should he discharge himself?

He wouldn't get far without a vehicle, and the only place to go was the house, where his students would want details.

He ran a hand through his hair. He didn't have the energy to deal with it, but he needed to call them. Although they were all adults, they were still his responsibility. He called Suzyn.

"Oliver, are you all right? I've got you on speaker."

"I'm fine, but they want to keep me in overnight."

"What happened?" Rajesh asked.

"Someone thought we'd found treasure and kidnapped me to find out where it was."

"What about Andrew?" Tom asked.

Shit. They didn't know. "I have sad news." He paused, giving them time to prepare themselves. "Andrew died."

Suzyn gasped and her voice wavered. "How?"

"He was shot. I've contacted his family. I still need to contact the university and museum, so please keep this quiet."

"Why was he shot?" Tom asked.

"I'm not sure. Things are a bit hazy."

"Why?" Rajesh asked.

Oliver sighed. "I was shot through the chest with a spear gun. I'm fine, but I lost a lot of blood and was a little out of it when Andrew was shot. They're keeping me in hospital overnight for observation."

"Do you need anything?" Suzyn said.

"Yeah. Stay at the house tonight. I think they've caught everyone, and you shouldn't be a target, but I don't want you in town." Maybe he should ask Sam or Sherlock to stay with them to protect them.

"OK. We'll visit you tomorrow," Tom said.

One call down, one to go. Oliver braced himself and called the museum. His boss was horrified, and wanted all the details, which Oliver dutifully told him, but eventually promised to call the university to tell them.

He hung up as the nurse returned with his pain meds. "Thank you."

He swallowed them and closed his eyes for a moment.

And drifted to sleep.

***

Dot hung up the video call with Perth. Almost three hours of interrogation about what had happened and what was going on in Retribution Bay. Rodney had left after an hour when Oliver had messaged to tell her he was awake. Rodney hadn't been required to repeat himself about what had happened.

She hoped Oliver had fared better.

Rubbing her face, she groaned and checked the time. Mid-afternoon. She wanted to visit Oliver, and she needed to track down Andrew's notes before Lucas claimed his things, but first she needed to eat. She exited her office and glanced around the vacant station. Pierre had taken Kristy and Steven Hamilton to Carnarvon gaol, which left her as the only officer in Retribution Bay. She prayed for a quiet few days. Head Office was sending more officers but couldn't tell her exactly when.

On her way to the hospital, she swung by the cafe to grab a cream doughnut. Not the healthiest of lunches, but she needed the comfort.

Lucas Fitton had checked out of his resort

accommodation that morning, which wasn't surprising. Stonefish had a way of disappearing. Though she might have to head to the ranges and investigate the dust plume she'd seen earlier.

Right now she wanted to visit Oliver.

They'd gone from having a moment only last night, to chasing criminals and being kidnapped. Not a great start to a new relationship.

If that was what this was. Oliver might have second thoughts after everything that had happened.

Nerves coalesced in her stomach as she greeted the nurse at the nurses' station.

"I think he's just gone to sleep," the woman said.

Disappointment filled Dot. "Mind if I poke my head in to check?"

"Go ahead."

He'd been put into a room with two beds, but the other bed was empty. She poked her head around the curtain to find him lying with his eyes closed, an IV still in his arm. Her heart clenched. A little colour had returned to his face, but he was still paler than normal.

She didn't want to wake him. Rodney had probably grilled him, and he needed rest, but she couldn't bring herself to leave. She slipped into the chair by his bed and put the pastry she'd bought for him on the tray table, before carefully removing her cream doughnut from its wrapper. At the crackle of the paper she paused, but the noise wasn't loud enough to wake him.

Dot consumed the treat while she watched him.

What was she going to do? He'd spoken about trying again, but was that even possible? She wasn't sure where she would be when this whole mess with Stonefish ended. Would she be considered a failure for not realising two of her team had been compromised, or would she be applauded for ending what was left of Stonefish? She only had Andrew's and Martin's word

Lucas was involved, and both were dead. She needed proof. Rodney said he hadn't heard Martin mention Lucas, and Dot couldn't remember if he'd been there, or with Kristy by the car when it had happened.

Then there was Martin's confession and Rodney killing him. There'd been no reason to shoot to kill, though Rodney had portrayed it as the only option to their supervisors.

And from the tone of her conversation with head office, she was treading on thin ice. Rodney had voiced all of his complaints about her behaviour towards him.

What would she do if she couldn't be a police officer?

The idea was terrifying. She'd worked so hard for it. She loved what she did, even when people drove her crazy sometimes.

She glanced at the man who had recaptured her heart. His fringe hung low, touching his eyelashes and she clenched her hands to stop herself from brushing it off his face. He'd always worn it long, more because he didn't have time for haircuts than any stylistic choice.

She used to love running her fingers through his hair in the evening when it was just the two of them hanging out.

They would talk for hours about everything.

Where would they be now if they hadn't broken up?

Stupid to think about what if. She should be thinking what could be.

If it was just her and Oliver and nothing else counted, she would want a relationship with him. She'd never stopped loving him. She could admit it now.

But life was more complicated.

There were careers and obligations to consider. They had to agree on a location to live, and deal with families. She was worried about seeing his parents again, though his father had been kind over the phone when she'd called them to tell them about Oliver's accident. They were catching the morning plane to Retribution Bay.

Something to worry about tomorrow.

She yawned, exhausted beyond belief, and stretched her legs out. Her eyes grew heavy, and she leaned against the bed.

She would just rest here for a moment.

"Dot?" The quiet question jolted Dot into wakefulness. She swiped at her eyes and looked into Oliver's blue, watchful gaze.

His skin was flushed with colour, and the intensity of his gaze warmed her.

Her heart galloped. She sat and stretched, wincing at the ache in her back. "Sorry. I didn't mean to disturb you." Her cheeks heated.

He smiled, looking bemused. "You didn't."

She examined him. Aside from the IV in his arm, and a slight darkness under his eyes, he looked the same as he had yesterday. She almost wouldn't know he'd had a spear sticking out of him not so long ago. "How are you?"

"Groggy. Tired. Hungry." He glanced at the tray table. "I don't suppose the pastry is for me?"

She smiled, passing it to him. "As long as you're allowed to eat."

He broke the pastry in two, offering her half. She took it with a smile. "Any pain?"

"Some throbbing, but it's manageable. What did I miss?"

Dot shook her head. He was lucky to be alive and he acted as if he'd stubbed his toe. "Kristy and her husband, Steven, are heading to Carnarvon gaol; Martin's and Andrew's bodies have been taken to the morgue; and Rodney is taking all the credit."

Oliver scowled. "Are you in trouble for shooting Martin?"

She hesitated before shaking her head. "There will be an investigation, but Martin died from Rodney's shot, not mine."

"And Lucas?"

She hesitated before admitting, "We can't find him."

"I called him earlier, but he didn't say where he was, though he knew the *Oceanid* was at the marina. He said he'd let me know if he was coming to identify Andrew's body."

They'd catch him. A billionaire shipping magnate couldn't hide for long.

Oliver finished his food and clutched Dot's hand. "Thanks for the rescue."

She ran a thumb over the back of his hand, liking that his grip was firm. "I'm sorry I didn't get there earlier. Why did Kristy shoot you?"

He laughed and then winced. "It was an accident. She was waving the spear gun around and it went off."

Stupid. She'd almost killed him. If the spear had gone a few millimetres in either direction, Oliver might be dead.

Her throat closed over. The thought of him no longer in her life made her sick. No, he wasn't dead. He was here sitting in front of her, looking very much alive. She swallowed, trying to keep the fear from her voice. "How long are you in here for?"

"At least overnight." He shrugged. "I might discharge myself tomorrow. I need to check on my team and finish the expedition."

He had to be kidding. "You can't go diving with your injury!"

He raised an eyebrow at her tone but said, "We'll see. My team might finish the rest."

She shook her head. "No. No *we'll see*. The doctor can't possibly clear you for diving yet. It's too dangerous. You were seriously injured—"

"Calm down, Dot." He squeezed her hand.

Her heart beat erratically as the fear fought its way to the surface. "You could have died." She choked the words out.

"It's OK. I'm OK," he soothed.

She inhaled a ragged breath and exhaled again, willing her pulse to slow. "Oliver, I…" What did she say? The thought of opening her heart again still scared her, but the thought of losing him altogether was truly terrifying. Before she could find the words, Oliver spoke.

"After this, I'll need to return to Perth, but university is over for the year, and the museum will give me some time off. I want to come back to Retribution Bay if you'll have me."

Her heart galloped. She couldn't take much more of this. "To talk about things?"

"No, to live."

Dot stared at him. This was happening too fast. "But your work and your family are in Perth."

"But you're here. That's all that matters."

She shook her head. "You love your job. You're so good at it. I saw it in every episode I watched." Her heart told her mouth to shut up. She shouldn't be trying to convince him moving to Retribution Bay was a bad idea.

He raised his eyebrows. "You watched the show?"

Heat filled her cheeks. "Maybe one or two episodes." Or every single season like the sad case she was.

"I was thinking about it before I woke you. I've got an offer for a book contract, and one of the producers might spin off an Australian version of the series." He smiled. "It would mean I'd still be away sometimes, but a lot of the research I would need can be digitised."

She couldn't let him throw away his career when hers was so uncertain. "I'm not sure where I'll be after this is all over," she admitted. "The tone from up high hasn't been great."

His eyes widened in outrage. "Your job is in danger? Who do I need to talk to? I can tell them how amazing you've been."

She held up a hand. "I can deal with it." But his defence of her made her feel all warm and fuzzy inside.

"I guess Rodney hasn't been singing your praises."

She chuckled. "No, he hasn't."

He squeezed her hand. "Whatever happens with both of our careers, we'll work it out. As long as we have each other."

The promise sang to her, luring her in with its sweet words.

"I won't let you down again." His earnest expression was hard to resist.

"You'll talk to me, discuss what is happening with your career?" she asked.

He nodded. "And you'll tell me what is happening with yours. We'll make it work, Dot. We were always stronger and better together."

She was silent, the final string of restraint plucked tight. Could she risk her heart again?

"I love you, Oliver, but I'm scared. I can't handle another broken heart."

"I've never stopped loving you." He fumbled with the necklace around his neck, unclasping it and slipping off the ring. He smiled at her. "When I chose this, I always thought I would one day give it to you. The bright green reminded me of your love of colours." He held it out to her.

"It's your good luck charm." But she couldn't resist reaching out and brushing a finger over the gem.

"I don't need luck if I have you." He smiled. "Please start a life with me, Dot."

His words snapped the last of her resistance and dissolved her fear. She wouldn't throw away what they had a second time. "All right." She leaned forward to kiss him. "Together," she murmured. "We'll do this together."

He slid the ring onto her finger and it fit perfectly.

Chapter 21

Dot's steps slowed as laughter floated out of Oliver's hospital room the next day. She would recognise that infectious laugh anywhere. Oliver's mother had arrived. She should have remembered they were coming, but she'd been called back to work early that morning to answer more questions from her supervisors.

She exhaled and braced herself as she stepped into the room. Oliver's parents sat facing him, and his mother was regaling him with a story about their new puppy.

Oliver's eyes widened and lit up when he saw her and his smile caused the others to turn.

Dot forced a smile, but before she could speak, Mrs Anderson jumped to her feet. "Dot Campbell. Don't you look amazing! It's been too long."

Dot was knocked back a step by the fierce hug that enveloped her, almost squeezing the breath from her.

"It's so good to see you. Oliver said you rescued him. You have my eternal gratitude."

Dot swallowed hard, willing the tears away. She cleared her throat. "Oliver's exaggerating."

Mrs Anderson let her go and stepped back.

"My turn." Mr Anderson opened his arms wide. "I've

missed my little pocket rocket."

Dot sniffed and stepped forward almost without conscious thought. His hug was firm but gentle and reminded her of all the debates they used to have in the evenings over games. When he let her go, she dashed at her eyes.

"Look, you've made her cry. I always said that was an awful nickname," Mrs Anderson said.

"Pish. She's just happy to see us."

The friendly banter burst through her walls and tears flooded from her eyes. "I have missed you," she whispered.

Both parents enveloped her in a group hug. "We missed you too," Mrs Anderson said.

"Hey, save some of that for me," Oliver called. "I'm the injured one, remember?"

His words made her smile, and she wiped her eyes. She moved over to him and gently hugged him, mindful of his ribs. "There's plenty for you." She kissed him.

Mrs Anderson clapped. "Perhaps you can convince him not to discharge himself yet."

Dot glanced at Oliver. "Actually, I'm here to spring him. There are a couple of things I need him for, if you can spare him for a couple of hours."

The doctor walked in and Mrs Anderson turned to him. "Is Oliver really OK to be discharged?"

He nodded. "He's healing well. All he needs is rest and to manage his pain. No diving though."

Oliver's scowl told her he'd argued about that already.

"Fine," his mother answered. "I've been wanting to snorkel the reef, so perhaps we'll go to the beach this afternoon."

Dot smiled. "How about you both come to my place for dinner this evening?"

"We'd love to," Mr Anderson said.

It didn't take long to discharge Oliver and Mr

Anderson helped him into Dot's car before promising to see them later. Dot waved and started the car, heading out of town.

***

Oliver smiled. Things couldn't get any better. He was no longer in hospital, Dot loved him and his parents had accepted her back into the family.

Not that he'd had any doubts about that.

Now he just had to finish the expedition, take his students home, and he'd be able to set the next stage of his life into motion.

They passed the *Thank you for visiting Retribution Bay* sign and he realised they weren't heading back to the share house. "Where are we going?" Oliver asked.

"To Retribution Ridge. It's the Stokes' place. There's something you need to see."

Oliver's heart jumped. "The treasure?"

"Wait and see." Her secret smile made him grin, and he stayed silent. Her reunion with his parents had gone better than he could have hoped for, and he hadn't even had to warn his parents to be on their best behaviour.

She seemed lighter, happier, and was smiling a lot more.

"By the way, I found your cannon," she said.

He shifted, wincing at the pain. "Where?"

"The Hamilton's shed. I don't know how they got it off the ocean floor, but it was sitting there right in the middle of the concrete."

"I'll need to arrange for it to be taken to Perth." He reached for his phone.

"The museum knows. I called them earlier and they're arranging transport in a couple of days." She smiled. "You can focus on talking your students through the last of the expedition."

"Thank you." He settled back and tried to get

comfortable.

They chatted about his parents on the journey out until Dot turned into a gravel driveway with a picture of an angry-looking ram on the gate.

"We're here." She pulled up at the quirky homestead where several utes were parked outside. His chest twinged as he shuffled out of the car.

A blue heeler gave a half-hearted woof from where he lay on the verandah but didn't move to greet them. Oliver didn't blame him. The sun had a real bite to it today and the heat enveloped him the second he got out of the car.

Inside the homely kitchen sat an extended family with a pot of tea and scones on the table. They all turned to look at him. Sam and Sherlock were there, as was Tess, but the others were strangers. Dot made the introductions.

Brandon and Darcy Stokes both had chocolate brown hair and tanned skin from working outside. Ed and Georgie, the other two siblings, had more light brown, almost blond hair. Then there were the partners; Amy, Faith, Tess and Matt, and with Sam and Sherlock were Penelope and Gretchen.

It would take him a little while to get everyone straight.

Two kids ran in, the girl calling, "Are we going to show him now?"

Darcy shushed her. "This is my daughter, Lara and Gretchen's son, Jordan."

Oliver smiled and shifted a little, his chest giving him some discomfort now he was standing. "It's nice to meet you."

"I've been making discreet enquiries about what to do, but we haven't come up with a solution," Dot said. "We're hoping you might advise and get it somewhere safe."

"You're talking about the treasure?" he asked Dot, as his pulse increased. "It's here?"

"You should see it for yourself." Brandon stood. "Follow me."

Dot nodded and he followed Brandon into the laundry. The linoleum floor had been rolled back, exposing a door in the wooden floor and Brandon lifted it, revealing a cellar.

"Is this where you push me down the stairs and lock me in?" Oliver joked.

Brandon smiled. "No, but I will help you down because bruised ribs hurt like a bitch."

Oliver used the man's broad shoulder as a crutch as he hobbled down the stairs. The small room had shelves on the walls and a small table, but it was the centre of the room which caught his breath. An old wooden travel chest, and surrounding it, several backpacks. "Holy shit." He examined the chest. It showed no signs of having been underwater for any length of time. "Where was it?"

"In a cave near the gulf," Brandon said.

Oliver frowned. "When did you find it?"

"A week ago."

Surely someone had explored the cave before now.

"The storm surge uncovered it," Lara said.

He glanced back to find half of the family had come into the room behind them.

"The cave was buried under sand," Tess added.

That made more sense. He ran his fingers over the rough wood. "May I open it?"

Brandon nodded.

Oliver winced as the lid creaked, and Tess moved to support its weight as it was opened. The chest was about half full of gold doubloons, necklaces and other precious jewellery. He grinned, the excitement of it washing through him. It never grew old.

He reached in and pulled out a handful, examining the

jewellery.

"We had to move some of it into bags because we were worried the chest would break," Tess said. "But Georgie took photos for provenance."

He glanced at the backpacks by his feet. "There's more in there?"

She nodded.

"This is incredible." What with the history of the ship, the Netherlands, Australia and Indonesia would all be interested in the find. "Why have you kept it a secret?"

"Because we didn't want Stonefish to get their hands on it, and we didn't know who it belonged to," Brandon said.

"It belongs to the people," Oliver said.

Georgie stepped forward. "But is there a finder's fee?" She shrugged. "We could do with a little extra cash right now. Stonefish has been running us ragged."

Everyone looked at him, hope on their faces. Dot's was the only expressionless one.

He knew a lot of people in the industry. This had to be worth hundreds of millions of dollars. "I'll do what I can. The first step is to get it to Perth safely."

"Tell us where it needs to go," Dot said.

"I'll need to make a few phone calls." But the treasure was up there on the best he'd ever seen. He examined the workmanship of the gold holding a large emerald in place on a necklace. Such fine work.

"Can you make them now?" It was Lara who asked.

These things took time, but he could tell by the eagerness on their faces that they wanted answers. "Yeah. Can I have a minute?"

Darcy herded everyone but Dot upstairs.

"We'll have to work fast after you make the call," Dot said. "Stonefish know we have it, but they don't know where. They'll want to intercept it enroute."

He hesitated with his phone in his hand. "Maybe I

shouldn't call and we just take it back with us."

"Call. We need to get it moved."

Oliver called his contact at the museum, who was dumbfounded by the news, but quickly decided what to do. He hung up and said to Dot, "We can transport it with the cannon. That way no one knows it's on board."

She nodded, relief on her face, and then turned to head upstairs, tugging on her hair.

Something was bothering her.

Oliver pulled her close to him. "What's wrong?"

"Nothing."

He frowned. "We promised to communicate, Dot. Something is bothering you."

She hesitated and then sighed. "I saw how your face lit up when you saw the treasure. I can't keep you from that."

He'd thought they'd put this behind them, but he needed to remember Dot was far more fragile than she appeared. "I get the same feeling when you walk into the room," he said. "You're my most precious treasure."

She squirmed. "You're talking nonsense."

"No, I'm not. If I had to choose, I would choose you every time." He smiled. "But this level of treasure is exceedingly rare, so it is exciting." He squeezed her hand. "I love the research and the history just as much." They would have to work on building their trust again. "I love you, Dot. I've never stopped loving you, and I want to live my life with you."

Her hand shook in his and she exhaled a shaky breath. "I love you too, Oliver. It might take me a while to believe this won't come crashing down."

"I'll prove it to you every single day," he vowed. "We'll talk all the time. Make sure neither of us goes to bed uncertain or worried about the other's actions. We'll be the best damned communicators it will put everyone else to shame."

She chuckled and then nodded. "To communication."

He grinned. "To communication. And to us." And then he kissed her to seal his vow.

Thank you for reading!

Did you know you can get bonus material if you join my reader group? You can read the entirety of Lilian's journal plus bonus and deleted scenes from this series just by signing up.

www.claireboston.com/reader-group

Acknowledgements

First of all I want to thank you, dear Reader, for your patience. I know the last couple of books in this series have been a long time coming and I appreciate you hanging in there. Nhiari's story, which will be the final book in this series is coming in 2024 and hopefully won't take as long as this last one.

I also want to thank Ann Harth and Teena Raffa-Mulligan who edited this book and helped me make it much better than it was.

www.ingramcontent.com/pod-product-compliance
Lightning Source LLC
Chambersburg PA
CBHW051259210726
48287CB00002B/584